SHE INFURIATED HIM.

Befuddled him and inflamed him.

In order to get a handle on things, he had to get a handle on her. He had to convince Beth to admit to her feelings.

He needed time and space to accomplish that.

Thanks to Ben's directions, Levi carried her through the kitchen toward the back storage unit, where interruptions were less likely to occur.

The moment he reached the dark, private area, Levi paused. Time to give Beth a piece of his mind. Time to be firm, to insist that she stop denying the truth.

Time to set her straight.

But then he looked at her, and he forgot about his important intentions. He forgot everything but his need for this one particular woman.

God, she took him apart without even trying.

I'm Your Santa

LORI FOSTER
KAREN KELLEY
DIANNE CASTELL

B
BRAVA

KENSINGTON PUBLISHING CORP.
http://www.kensingtonbooks.com

BRAVA BOOKS are published by

Kensington Publishing Corp.
850 Third Avenue
New York, NY 10022

All Kensington Titles, Imprints, and Distributed Lines are
available at special quantity discounts for bulk purchases
for sales promotions, premiums, fund-raising, and educa-
tional or institutional use. Special book excerpts or cus-
tomized printings can also be created to fit specific needs.
For details, write or phone the office of the Kensington
special sales manager: Kensington Publishing Corp., 850
Third Avenue, New York, NY 10022, attn: Special Sales
Department, Phone: 1-800-221-2647.

Brava Books and the Brava logo Reg. U.S. Pat. & TM Off.

ISBN-13: 978-0-7582-2860-4
ISBN-10: 0-7582-2860-0

First trade paperback printing: October 2007
First mass market printing: October 2008

10 9 8 7 6 5 4 3 2 1

Printed in the United States of America

CONTENTS

THE CHRISTMAS PRESENT

by Lori Foster

1

IT'S A WONDERFUL LIFE

by Karen Kelley

113

HOME FOR CHRISTMAS

by Dianne Castell

217

The
Christmas
Present

Lori Foster

One

Why, oh why, couldn't this be a normal storm? Instead of soft, pretty snowflakes dotting her windshield, wet snow clumps froze as soon as they hit, rendering the wipers inadequate to keep the windshield clear. Even with the defroster on high, blasting hot air that threatened to choke her, the snow accumulated.

Refusing to stop and refusing to acknowledge the headlights behind her, Beth Monroe kept her hands tight on the wheel. Let him freeze to death. Let him follow her all the way to Gillespe, Kentucky.

She'd still ignore him.

She'd ignore everything that had happened between them, and everything she felt, everything he'd made her feel.

Oh God, she was so embarrassed. If only she could have a do-over, an opportunity to change the past, to correct mistakes and undo bad plans. That'd be the most perfect Christmas present ever.

A simple do-over.

But of course, there was no such thing, not even with the magic of Christmas. And there was nothing simple about the current mess of her life, or the complicated way that Levi Masterson made her feel.

Finally, after hours that seemed an eternity, her stepbrother's hotel came into view. Beth breathed a sigh of relief. Now if she could just park and get inside before Levi shanghaied her. Ben knew of her imminent arrival. She could count on him to send Levi packing.

Not that she wanted Levi hurt . . . or Ben for that matter.

Fool, fool, fool.

Tires sliding on the frozen parking lot, Beth maneuvered her Ford into an empty spot. After shutting off the engine, she grabbed her purse, a tote bag loaded with presents, and her overnight bag. Arms laden, she charged from the vehicle.

Three steps in, her feet slipped out from under her. The stuffed overnight bag threw her off balance and she went flying in the air to land flat on her back. Her bag spilled. Wind rushed from her lungs. Icy cold seeped into her spine and tush.

For only a moment, Beth lay there, aching from head to toe, stunned and bemused. Then she heard Levi's hasty approach.

"Beth, damn it—"

Determination got her back on her feet. She gathered her belongings with haste and then, slipping and sliding, wincing with each step, she shouted into the wind, *"Go away, Levi."*

Harsh with determination, he yelled back, "You know I won't."

Daring a quick glance over her shoulder, Beth saw him ten feet behind her. He hadn't even parked! His truck sat crossways in the middle of the lot to block hers in, idling, the exhaust sending plumes of heated air to mingle in the frozen wind.

Good God, he looked furious!

Beth lunged forward and reached the door of the diner attached to Ben's hotel. She yanked it open and sped into the warm interior. The tote bag of presents fell out of her hands, scattering small gifts across the floor. Her overnight bag dropped from her numb fingers.

Several people looked up—all of them family.

Oh hell.

Why couldn't there have been crowds of nonfilial faces? An unbiased crowd, that's what she sought. Instead she found Noah and Ben in close conversation at a table. Their wives, Grace and Sierra, sat at a booth wrapping gifts. And her father and stepmother paused in their efforts to festoon a large fir tree situated in the corner.

Upon seeing her, her father's face lit up. He started to greet her—and then Levi shoved through the door, radiating fury, crowding in behind Beth so that she jolted forward with a startled yelp to keep from touching him.

In a voice deep and resolute, vibrating with command, he ordered, "Not another step, Beth. I mean it."

She winced, and peeked open one eye to view her audience.

Not good.

Levi obviously had no idea of the challenge he'd just issued, or the uproar he'd cause by using that tone with her in front of her family.

And now it was too late.

She hadn't wanted this. She wanted only time to think, to hide from her mortifying and aberrant behavior, to . . . She didn't know what she wanted, damn it, and it wasn't fair that Levi refused to give her a chance to figure it out.

Muttering to herself, she dropped to her knees to gather the now damp and disheveled gifts one more time. As she did so, she said, "Hello, Dad. Hello . . . everyone else." She tried to sound jovial rather than frustrated and anxious and at the end of her rope.

She failed miserably.

With a protectiveness that still amazed Beth, her stepbrothers moved as one. Noah's expression didn't bode well, and Ben appeared equally ready to declare war. Even her calm, reasonable father stalked forward with blood in his eyes.

Plopping her belongings on a nearby booth, Beth held up both hands. "Wait!"

No one did. From one second to the next, Levi had her behind him . . . as if to *protect* her? From her *family*?

Unfortunately, even that simple touch from him, in no way affectionate or seductive, had Beth's tummy fluttering and her skin warming.

She quickly shrugged off her coat.

Levi took it from her, then asked, "Did you hurt yourself when you fell?"

"No. You can leave with a clear conscience. I'm fine." She reached for her coat.

He held it out of her reach. "I'm not going anywhere, so you can quit trying to get rid of me."

The men drew up short. Her father barked, "Who the hell are you?"

Levi turned to face their audience. Positive that she didn't want him to answer that himself, Beth yelled from behind him, "He's a friend." And she tried to ease backward away from him.

"A whole lot more than a friend," Levi corrected, and he stepped back to close the distance she'd just gained.

"Where's her fiancé?" Noah asked.

"Busy," Beth said.

"Gone," Levi answered in a bark. He reached back and caught Beth's wrist. His thumb moved over her skin, a gentle contrast to the iron in his tone. "For good."

Confused, Ben asked, "You mean dead?"

"Far as Beth is concerned, yes."

Oh, for crying out loud. Knowing she couldn't let this continue, Beth yanked her wrist free and, without quite touching any part of Levi's big, hard body, went on tiptoe to see beyond him.

The masculine expressions facing her didn't bode well.

She summoned a smile that felt sickly. "Hello, Dad. Brandon is fine, but we're not engaged any more."

Kent Monroe brought his brows down. "Since when?"

"Since she's with me now instead," Levi told them.

"No," Beth corrected sweetly, "I'm not."

Levi half turned to face her. "Wanna bet?"

His challenge got everyone moving again.

Oh God, she had to do something. "Dad," Beth begged, "I don't want him hurt."

Her father stopped in his tracks. Noah and Ben did not.

But her lovely sisters-in-law took control.

"Noah," Grace called from across the room. "You heard her."

Frowning, Noah paused about three feet from Levi. "I also heard him."

Sierra, a little more outgoing than Grace, raced up to Ben's side and thumped his shoulder. "Knock off the King Kong impersonation, Ben. You're embarrassing me."

"You'll survive." Keeping his eyes on Levi, Ben crossed his arms over his chest and waited.

For reasons that Beth couldn't begin to fathom, Levi stood there as if he'd take all three of them on at once. Idiot.

Determined to gain control, she chanced touching him long enough to give him a good pinch. "They're my *family*, Levi."

He nodded, but didn't relax.

Fed up, Beth moved around him. "I'm sorry for the dramatic entrance everyone. Levi is a friend—"

"Damn it, Beth, we left friendship behind days ago."

Beth let her eyes sink shut. She'd kill him. She'd never speak to him again. She'd—

His hand caught her shoulder and he turned her to face him. As if they stood alone, as if he had no concept of privacy or manners, Levi lowered his nose to almost touch hers.

In a voice that carried to every ear in the room, he ground out, "I've had enough, Beth. I mean it. We're both adults, both healthy, and finally we're both single. It's ridiculous for you to be embarrassed just because—"

"Don't!"

But her warning came too late, and Levi had already said too much. Silence reigned as everyone absorbed his meaning.

Then she felt it, the smiles, the amusement, the awful comprehension.

It took three breaths before Beth could speak.

Eyes narrowed, she nodded at Levi, turned to face her family, and announced, "I've changed my mind. Hurt him all you want."

And with that, she literally ran away.

Noah and Ben kept Levi from following.

In rapid succession, a dozen different emotions zinged through Levi's mind. Damn it, he'd loved her forever, he'd finally had her, and the reality far outshone the fantasy.

But she was ashamed—of him, and of what they'd done. It didn't matter that he'd given her a dozen mind-blowing orgasms. It didn't matter that she'd taken everything he'd offered and begged for more.

Some ridiculous prudish streak now had her denying her own feelings.

One way or another, he'd get her to accept him, and to trust him and her own basic nature. Because one way or another, he planned to have her—for the rest of his life.

But when Levi started to go after her, two large muscled bodies got in his way. Why hadn't Beth told him that her brothers were enormous? Well, at least one was enormous. Noah was a big brick wall of a guy. But Ben, no slouch, stood on a par with Levi.

Together, they looked pretty invincible.

Removing his coat, too, Levi told them, "This is none of your business," and he knew that somehow, if necessary, he'd walk right through them. He would not let Beth keep dodging him.

Noah grinned—which only made him look more imposing. "It's our business now."

Levi glanced beyond the hulks, but the more reasonable women were nowhere to be seen. Damn.

"Forget it," Ben told him, knowing the direction of his thoughts. "They went after Beth to find out what the hell you did to upset her so much."

"She's not upset," Levi argued. "She's embarrassed when she has no reason to be."

"Says you," Ben remarked right back. "She thinks differently."

"She's in denial," Levi explained. "She's uncertain, and she's surprised. That's all."

First, he'd strip Beth naked and get her in bed, and then he'd hash out the future with her. He'd found that the more he touched Beth, the more reasonable she became.

Noah's grin widened. "I wonder why she's embarrassed. I don't suppose you plan to tell us?"

"No."

"Doesn't matter," Noah said. "I already have an idea what's going on."

"Me, too," Ben said. "But given Beth's reaction, you must not have handled it right. If you had, she wouldn't have come back to us."

Levi stiffened. "I'll straighten out everything. I just need her to listen to me."

Another voice, thankfully less provoking, intruded. "Quit crowding him, boys. He doesn't look like he's about to back down, and regardless of what Beth said, I don't think she wants him mangled."

Levi didn't think so either, but it surprised him that her father might be an ally. "Thanks."

The older man nudged Noah out of the way. "Let's all take a seat."

Levi shook his head. "I need to go after her."

"Not just yet," he was told. "Ben, could we get some coffee, do you think?"

Ben grumbled, but agreed and took himself off. Noah stepped farther to the side, giving Levi room to move and the opportunity to address Beth's father.

Pulling himself together, Levi eyed the man before him. He had Beth's blond hair and piercing blue eyes, but where Beth was delicate in the most delicious ways, this man looked solid and hard.

On the best of days, Levi hated meeting dads—not that he'd often been serious enough about a female to warrant the need of parental approval. In fact, since meeting Beth, no other woman had held his attention long.

Now, under these conditions, it really sucked to await judgment by Beth's father. The man knew she'd been engaged to a doctor. By comparison, Levi had to be one hell of a letdown. Brandon could have set Beth up in style. Lots of luxury. Guaranteed security.

All Levi had to offer was fidelity, devotion, and a job that barely paid middle-class wages.

Seeing no help for it now, Levi stuck out a hand. "You're Beth's father."

Accepting Levi's hand in a strong, calloused grip, he said, "Kent Monroe."

"Levi Masterson. And as Beth said, I apologize for the theatrics."

"That's my girl. She got that dramatic streak from her mother." Kent gestured him toward a table. "How about you tell me what's going on without all the drama?"

Because Kent was being reasonable, Levi hated to disappoint him. But much of the story would be Beth's alone to tell. The second they were seated and Ben had returned with mugs and a coffeepot, the three men stared at Levi in expectation.

To appease them, Levi gave the shortened, censored version of the past week. "Brandon is out of the picture. I'm in, whether Beth admits it or not. I love her, and I'm pretty sure she cares the same about me." He shrugged. "Either way, I plan to marry her."

Everyone waited.

Levi poured himself a mug of coffee.

"That's it?" Noah asked.

"Afraid so."

"What happened to Brandon?" Ben asked.

"You should ask Beth."

In disbelief, Ben fell back in his seat. "You really think that's all you're going to tell us?"

Levi sipped his coffee. "Yeah."

Kent laughed. "Did you propose to her yet?"

"I've tried, but she hasn't exactly given me a chance when she's avoiding me like the plague."

"And?"

"I'm working on it." Levi set the mug down. "That's why I'm here."

Noah propped an elbow on the table. "So you followed her here to propose to her?"

"I followed her here because she's been trying

to hide from me. I have to get her to accept all the sudden changes before I can ask her to marry me."

"Yeah," Ben said, "she sounds real smitten."

"She is." Levi *had* to believe that. Beth wasn't a woman who would go wild with a man that she didn't love. "It's just that she'd gotten really comfortable with her plans for the future, and now those plans are gone. Beth's having a hard time accepting it all. That's why I can't let her out of my sight for long. She'll convince herself she doesn't care, or that we don't belong together if she gets a chance to think about all this too much."

"Think about all what?" Noah asked.

Wild sex. Unrestrained passion. Fantasies come true, and imaginations gone wild. Levi cleared his throat. "You'll have to ask—"

"Beth," Noah finished. "Got it."

"So," Kent said, sounding cordial and almost amused, "you're stalking my daughter?"

"Sort of." But he didn't want Kent getting the wrong impression. "If she'll just admit it, she wants me to."

Ben tapped his fingers on the tabletop. "Did you know she was coming home when you followed her?"

"Yeah, I figured that's where she was headed." Levi shrugged. "It's the holidays. She's emotional and confused. Being with family made sense." He eyed each of the men in turn. "Maybe you can help me."

It was Noah's turn to drop back in his seat. "Help you?"

"That's right." Levi leaned forward. "For starters, I'd appreciate it if you'd keep her from running off again."

"For starters?" Kent asked. "I gather there's more?"

"Yeah. I wouldn't mind being alone in a room with her for a while, too." And before any of them could start grumbling about that, Levi added, "To talk. To work through things."

"The changes?"

"That's right." It wasn't every day a woman found her fiancé cheating, broke an engagement, and realized she loved someone else anyway.

Kent nodded slowly. "You know, I believe you."

"Thank you. I give you my word that Beth has nothing to fear from me. I love her. I would never do anything to hurt her."

"That's good," Ben told him. "Because if you do anything—"

"Yeah, I've got it. You don't need to finish that thought."

"Good."

"If one of you would go park my truck, I'd really appreciate it. I left it idling in the lot, blocking Beth's car."

All three of them looked toward the diner door, but none of them made a move toward it.

Levi settled back in the booth and lifted his mug of coffee. "Or someone can steal the damn thing. I don't give a shit. I just want to talk to Beth without being interrupted and without her sneaking away."

The gazes all transferred to him.

Levi felt his shoulders go rigid. If they thought to stop him, they'd be sorely disappointed. "So where is she? I don't think it's a good idea for her to have this much time away from me."

Kent tapped his fingertips together. "You could be right."

Taking their clues from him, Ben and Noah made sounds of reluctant agreement.

"But I won't send you off to a room alone with her, unless Beth decides that's what she wants. I remember being young and in love."

Ben snorted. "You're old and in love and no better now than you probably were then."

Kent just smiled. "Ben, can you tell Levi of someplace he can talk to Beth without interruption? Someplace that's not too private, though?"

"Someplace," Noah interjected with a narrow-eyed look at Levi, "where we can hear her if she calls out."

Ben thought about it a moment. "Sure, I know just the place. *If* Beth presents herself. Because right now, I have no idea where the women are. Sierra knows every hiding place in this joint. If Beth doesn't want you to talk to her tonight, then you won't be talking to her."

"We'll talk," Levi assured him with confidence. "She won't trust me alone with the three of you for too long. I'll give her fifteen minutes, tops. Then she'll be out here again, giving me the perfect opportunity I need."

Her head in her hands and her shoulders slumped, Beth sat on a stool between her sisters-in-law with her stepmother pacing in front of her. So far, they'd tried to make her eat, encouraged her to drink, smothered her with hugs, and very impatiently waited for explanations.

She had to tell them something.

The truth seemed her only option.

Forcing herself to straighten, Beth faced her

family. "Brandon cheated on me with a female colleague of his."

"That bastard," was followed by a heated, "Miserable jerk," and finally, "Oh honey, I'm so sorry."

Beth nodded in acknowledgment of each sentiment. "He claimed it was a mistake, that it just happened. He said he was sorry and that he still loved me." She gulped back her humiliation. "He said he'd make it up to me in our marriage."

All three women made sounds of disgust and disbelief.

"All I really wanted," Beth confided, "was to get even, to maybe make him as miserable as he'd made me. I wanted him to know what he'd thrown away and to regret what he'd done."

Sierra asked, "So you ended the engagement?"

"Yes."

"I hope you threw the ring at him," Grace said.

"I did."

"And?" Brooke asked.

Drawing a deep breath, Beth whispered, "I gave him tit for tat by sleeping with his best friend."

Mouths dropped open in shock, only to snap shut in realization. Beth could almost hear the blinking of their wide eyes and feel the burn of their condemnation.

Brooke recovered first. She looked back at the closed kitchen door, and for some reason, she spoke in a whisper. "That young man out there?"

"Yes." Hiding her face in her hands again, Beth wailed, "That's him."

Grace cleared her throat. "I take it he wants a repeat performance?"

"But I don't." She lifted her shoulders. "Only now he won't go away."

No one had any suggestions.

"Do you really want him to go away?" Brooke finally asked.

"I . . . I think so." Beth gulped, and wondered where to start. "It had seemed like such a simple plan in the beginning." She looked at Sierra and Grace and almost laughed at their identical expressions of disbelief. "It did, really."

"What was the plan?"

Saying it aloud made it sound even dumber, but Beth forced herself to honesty. "Brandon had cheated, so I would cheat. It was just supposed to be sex, and it was just supposed to be one time."

Sierra scooted closer. "It was more than once?"

Boy, was it ever. Beth nodded miserably, and her voice dipped to a mere whisper. "I went to his place on a Friday after work. I figured I'd be there an hour and be back home before dinner so I could call Brandon and tell him what I did. He'd be heartbroken and full of regret, I'd be avenged, and that'd be that."

"How long were you there?" Grace wanted to know.

"The entire weekend." To Beth's amazement, no one looked shocked. They didn't even look surprised. They just . . . looked curious to hear more. "Actually," Beth added, so they'd be sure to understand, "we both missed work on Monday, too."

Grace scooted in closer. "You're saying that you lost track of time?"

"I lost track of *everything*. The plan. Propriety. I lost track of *me*." And that was the hardest part of all. "I don't know what happened. I was a . . . a . . ."

"A what?" Sierra asked.

"A deviant," Beth blurted. "A sex freak. A . . . I don't know. Inexhaustible, I guess."

Brooke cleared her throat. "And that concerns you?"

"Well, of course it does." How could Brooke look so cavalier over her confession?

Grace grinned. "Nothing wrong with a little deviation now and then, as long as you're both willing."

"Yeah," Sierra agreed. Then she leaned closer. "So what exactly did you do that was so freaky?"

Brooke said, "Now Sierra. I don't know that we should be discussing this."

"Oh, come on," Sierra said. "Everyone sees how you look at Kent. And everyone sees Kent, so they all know why you look at him like that. You're not fooling anyone."

Pretending affront, Brooke said, "Young lady, that's entirely . . ." her stern expression broke into a grin, ". . . accurate."

Sierra and Grace chuckled. "We know."

"And that's probably something else that we shouldn't talk about."

Leaning in close again, Grace whispered, "You should see how Brooke watches your dad when he's working on landscaping."

"Now stop," Brooke insisted, but everyone could see that she didn't mean it.

Suffering a different kind of uneasiness now, Beth looked at Brooke.

"All right, it's true," Brooke admitted. "Kent looks incredible when he gets all sweaty and he takes off his shirt and his muscles are bulging." She shivered. "He's such a hunk. I'm so glad I met him."

Beth blinked. Her father was a *hunk*?

"Noah is very inventive," Grace confided without a single ounce of discomfort. "I can always trust him to keep things interesting."

"Ben's a nut." Sierra looked at her mother-in-law. "Don't listen to this part, Brooke."

After rolling her eyes, Brooke put her hands over her ears and paced to the other side of the room.

Sierra smiled. "Since Brooke is Ben's mother, she doesn't really like to hear about how sexy he is. She just wants him to be happy."

"And he is," Grace noted.

"So am I. But when I first met him, I thought he was a complete perv. And that he made me into a perv, too. It was really unnerving. I wasn't me anymore."

Because that was exactly how she felt, Beth nodded. "What did you do?"

"Well, whatever else Ben might be, he's incredible. And considerate. And I love him more every day. So naturally, I just gave in and enjoyed it." She gave Beth a certain look. "Trust me, I've never regretted that decision."

Brooke looked back at them, lowered her hands, and asked, "All clear?"

"Yes." Sierra stood. "So Beth, if you had a good time, there's no reason to be so upset."

"But . . ." Beth didn't know what to think. "It's like I went into this fog and I didn't want anything to stop, ever." Desperate to make them understand, Beth turned to Brooke as she rejoined their little circle. "It was never like that with Brandon. I mean, it wasn't bad, but it wasn't . . ."

"Overwhelming?" Grace asked.

"Mind-blowing?" Sierra added.

"Stupendous?" Brooke offered.

"All that." Beth slumped in her seat.

"I'd say it's a good thing you didn't marry Brandon."

Sierra agreed with Grace. "For sure." She patted Beth's hand. "You did the right thing."

"I don't know." In for a penny, in for a pound, Beth decided. "For those few days, I was shameless—and I loved every second. But now that I'm myself again, my behavior seems horrifying."

"You were a virgin when you met Brandon, weren't you?"

There were times, Beth thought, when Grace proved very astute. "Yes."

"When I met Noah, I was, too. But I just thought it was all really exciting."

Sierra gave Beth a sympathetic look. "Did you think it was exciting with Brandon?"

Beth started to say yes, but she hesitated. "I don't know. Cementing our relationship was exciting. And the sex was pleasant—"

Grace made a face. *"Pleasant?"*

Agreeing with her, Sierra said, "Brandon must've been a putz."

Brooke sympathized. "I'm so sorry, honey. Before Levi, you probably didn't even realize that sex could and should be more."

Beth decided that the conversation had veered too far off course. "The problem is that now I can barely look at Levi, but he won't give me any space. To hear him talk, you'd think we were engaged or something."

"Ah." Brooke pulled up a chair. "How so?"

Relieved to finally have someone to talk to, Beth blurted, "He says he always wanted me."

Brooke's eyebrows shot up. "Really?"

"He claims that he never said anything because he and Brandon have been friends since grade school. He didn't want to interfere between us."

"Wow." Grace let out a long sigh. "He put your feelings before his own. That's so romantic."

"Levi sounds like a great guy," Sierra agreed.

It struck Beth that he did sort of sound terrific—in an infuriating, devastating kind of way.

Sierra tilted her head. "So I'm dying to know—how did Brandon take it when you told him about Levi? Did you get your revenge?"

"I never told him." Beth winced with that admission. "I *couldn't* tell him. Not because I care about Brandon still. I really don't. And isn't that weird? I mean, obviously I wouldn't marry a cheater, but shouldn't I still be a little brokenhearted or something?" She didn't give anyone a chance to reply. "I'm not. I'm too busy dealing with this new situation to barely give Brandon a thought. And what happened with Levi . . . well, it feels very private now. I don't want anyone to know, not even Brandon."

Brooke smiled and took her hand. "Are Levi and Brandon still friends?"

"I don't know." That was another worry keeping her awake at night. "Since I've been trying to avoid Levi, and I haven't answered Brandon's calls, I don't know what's happening between the two of them."

"So," Grace said, "Levi might have lost a longtime friend for you."

"Maybe." Guilt nudged at her. Had Levi been motivated by caring, and not just lust?

Sierra stood. "You know, I think you just need to face up to things."

"Things?"

"How you feel about Levi. You have to decide that first, and then you can consider everything else."

"I almost lost your father," Brooke said, "because I didn't want to own up to my feelings for him."

"Same here," Sierra admitted. "I fought the idea of falling for Ben."

Grace looked at them both and shrugged. "Not me. I wanted Noah, and that was that."

Brooke grinned. "Beth should take a lesson from you, then."

"It did work out in the most awesome ways," Grace told her. "I say if you want Levi, then go for it."

"But . . . what about Brandon?" What about her reputation and her life and her sanity?

Sierra snorted. "Forget Brandon. He had his chance and he blew it."

And the rest? How did she forget the person she'd always thought herself to be, and just accept this new overly-sensual woman who threw caution to the wind?

Brooke squeezed her hand. "You said you didn't want anyone to know about you and Levi."

"No, I don't." And that was part of the problem. She could just imagine the gossip when everyone found out she'd jumped between best friends.

After glancing at the other women, Brooke gave her an apologetic smile that Beth didn't quite understand. "But you just told us."

"That's because it was eating me up inside. And Levi did follow me here, so I had to explain somehow."

Sierra caught on to Brooke's meaning. "You know, Levi could feel as conflicted as you do. Maybe he didn't mean for the one time to turn into a weekend marathon, either."

Grace followed their insinuations. "Yeah, and he's sitting out there with Noah and Ben and Kent. And like you said, his appearance and behavior need to be explained somehow."

Brooke nodded. "The same way that you told us, he could be telling them—"

"Oh my God." Beth shot out of her seat. "He wouldn't." She looked at the other women in a desperate bid for reassurance. "Please tell me he wouldn't."

Brooke lifted her shoulders. "I'm sorry, honey, but your father loves you an awful lot. He'll want to know what has you upset. I'm not sure he'd let Levi get by without an explanation."

"And," Grace pointed out, "you did tell them to hurt him. He might not have a choice but to explain."

"*Oh. My. God.*" Beth spun around and raced from the kitchen. Surely, the men wouldn't hurt Levi. They had to know sarcasm when they heard it. They had to have some concepts of the working of the female mind. After all, her sisters-in-law and stepmother had just confessed to being very, very happy women.

With her heart in her throat, Beth plunged through the double dining doors, charged into the dining room—and slid to a frozen halt at the sight of the men in close, amicable conversation.

They were drinking coffee.

They were smiling.

Sierra, Grace, and Brooke almost plowed into Beth, and still she couldn't unglue her feet.

Had Levi told them everything? Had he blurted out about her awful, wanton behavior to her *family*?

Heat flooded into Beth's face so quickly, it made her lightheaded.

She'd pay the men to beat him up.

She'd beat him up herself.

She'd—

Levi looked up and saw her. "Finally." Walking away from the male conversation, he strode toward her. As if he'd had his hands in it multiple times, his brown hair looked disheveled. Determination glowed in his green eyes. And that sensual mouth of his was set in a firm line.

When he reached her, Beth prepared to blast him with her ire.

But because he didn't stop before her, he didn't give her a chance. No, he just caught her wrist and kept right on going, towing her along with him.

"Levi!" She tried digging in her heels. "What are you doing?"

Without pausing in his exodus, he glanced over his shoulder and said, "Come along, Beth. Your brothers and father are curious enough without us putting on another show."

If they were still curious, then did that mean . . . In a squeaky whisper, she asked, "You didn't tell them anything?"

He stopped, turned to stare down at her in what looked like anger, then leaned close so she'd hear his whisper. "Of course I didn't."

Beth glanced around, saw they had the undivided attention of one and all, but she didn't think anyone could hear them. "Well, how was I to know? You're always trying to talk to me about it."

"There's nothing that you and I can't talk about. But what's between us is just that—*between us*. It's private." His eyes narrowed. "You should know better than to think I'd do anything to deliberately embarrass you."

"I . . ." Beth closed her mouth and swallowed. Face up to things, Brooke had said. She nodded. "You're right. I should have realized that. I'm sorry."

His eyes darkened even more, as if he didn't quite know what to make of any giving on her end.

"So." Beth took another quick glance at their rapt audience, and smiled an apology to them. She'd put on more spectacles tonight than anyone should share in a lifetime. Hoping to make amends for doubting him, she asked Levi, "If you didn't tell my Dad the truth, what did you say to him?"

"Only that I'm going to marry you."

Only *what*? New heat radiated through her. The world tilted. On a thin breath, she gasped out, "You didn't."

"I did." He smiled. "Because I am."

"But . . ."

Done talking, Levi lifted her into his arms. "No buts." He put a soft, fast smooch on her mouth. "Now come along quietly so we don't incite a riot with what I plan to say and do to you."

Her body tightened. "Do to me?"

"That's right." He glanced down at her. "And it's all best handled in private. Don't you agree?"

It took no more than that simple, sensual suggestion from Levi to have Beth melting in a dozen delicious ways. She might want to forget what transpired between them, but her body was in no hurry to give up the memory.

She gulped, thought again of Brooke's advice, and finally found her voice. "Yes, I suppose so."

Two

With each step he took, Levi pondered what to say to Beth. She needed to understand that she'd disappointed him.

Infuriated him.

Befuddled him and inflamed him.

In order to get a handle on things, he had to get a handle on her. He had to convince Beth to admit to her feelings.

He needed time and space to accomplish that.

Thanks to Ben's directions, Levi carried her through the kitchen toward the back storage unit, where interruptions were less likely to occur.

The moment he reached the dark, private area, Levi paused. Time to give Beth a piece of his mind. Time to be firm, to insist that she stop denying the truth.

Time to set her straight.

But then he looked at her, and he forgot about his important intentions. He forgot everything but his need for this one particular woman.

God, she took him apart without even trying.

Among the shelves of pots and pans, canned goods and bags of foodstuff, Levi slowly lowered Beth to her feet.

He couldn't seem to do more than stare at her.

Worse, she stared back, all big dark eyes, damp lips, and barely banked desire. Denial might come from her mouth, but the truth was there in her expression.

When she let out a shuddering little breath, Levi lost the battle, the war . . . he lost his heart all over again.

Crushing her close, he freed all the restraints he'd imposed while she was his best friend's fiancée. He gave free reign to his need to consume her. Physically. Emotionally. Forever and always.

Moving his hands over her, absorbing the feel of her, he tucked her closer still and took her mouth. How could he have forgotten how perfectly she tasted? How delicious she smelled and how indescribable it felt to hold her?

Even after their long weekend together, he hadn't been sated. He'd never be sated.

Levi knew if he lived to be a hundred and ten, he'd still be madly in love with Beth Monroe.

The fates had done him in the moment he'd first met her. She smiled and his world lit up. She laughed and he felt like Zeus, mythical and powerful. She talked about marrying Brandon and the pain was more than anything he'd ever experienced in his twenty-nine years.

Helpless, that's what he'd been.

So helpless that it ate at him day and night.

Then, by being unfaithful, Brandon had proved

that he didn't really love Beth after all—and all bets were off.

When Beth came to him that night, hurt and angry, and looking to him for help, Levi threw caution to the wind and gave her all she requested, and all she didn't know to ask for.

He gave her everything he could, and prayed she'd recognize it for the deep unshakable love he offered, not just a sexual fling meant for retaliation.

But . . . she hadn't.

She'd been too shaken by her own free response, a response she gave every time he touched her.

A response she gave right now.

They thumped into the wall, and Levi recovered from his tortured memories, brought back to the here and now.

He had Beth.

She wanted him.

Until she grasped the enormity of their connection, he'd continue pursuing her.

Lured by the sensuality of the moment, Levi levered himself against her, and loved it. As busy as his hands might be, Beth's were more so. Small, cool palms coasted over his nape, into his hair, then down to his shoulders. Burning him through the layers of his flannel shirt and tee, her touch taunted him and spurred his lust.

Wanting her, right here and right now, Levi pressed his erection against her belly and then cradled her body as she shuddered in reaction, doing her best to crawl into him.

His mouth against hers, he whispered, "I need you, Beth."

Beyond any real verbal response, Beth moaned and clutched at him.

And that gave him pause, because Levi knew she was with him—and he knew that she'd hate herself for it later.

Damn it.

Why did his conscience have to snap to life now? Why couldn't he have stayed in the sensual fog a little bit longer?

But he knew why; he loved Beth and he wanted her happy, not more humiliated. Until she admitted that it was love they shared, her embarrassment would continue. He had to remember that. He had to keep the ultimate goal—Beth as his wife—at the forefront of his every intention.

Lifting his mouth from hers, Levi whispered, "Beth, wait."

Her mouth followed, seeking his again. She licked his bottom lip, pressed her breasts against him.

Holding her shoulders, Levi managed to put a small distance between them. "Honey, no, wait."

Big sleepy eyes opened, heavy with lust, dark with desire. "I don't understand how you always make me feel this way."

"I know." He put his right hand to the back of her head and urged it to his shoulder. "But that's why we're here. So I can explain it to you."

Both rigid and soft, anxious and needy, Beth willingly leaned into him, giving him the weight of her worry. His left hand on the center of her back registered each broken breath, just as his heart understood her confusion. He put his cheek to her crown and inhaled the scent of her silky blond hair.

Muscles prepared for her reaction, Levi said, "I want to marry you, Beth."

As he expected, she almost lurched away.

"Shhh. I know that's something of a shock. You thought for so long that we were just friends. But it doesn't change anything—I want to marry you."

Her silence felt like condemnation. Like the ultimate rejection. "There's something going on between us." Something called love, but Levi didn't want to spook her. "You go wild when I touch you."

"I know." Her whole body trembled. "That's why you can't touch me."

Her panic struck Levi like a low blow. "Wrong. It's why I *have* to touch you. It's the only time you're honest with me and with yourself."

"No." She shook her head.

"Now that we've been together, the feelings aren't going to go away. You may as well accept that."

"There's nothing to accept."

As if she hadn't spoken, Levi continued with his well-rehearsed speech. "You have to accept that Brandon doesn't love you." The last thing Levi wanted was to see her hurt, but denying the truth would only spare her for so long. "If he did, he wouldn't have cheated."

"I *know* that. I'm not an idiot."

Relief closed Levi's eyes.

"But this . . ." Flattening her hands over Levi's chest, Beth tried to shove away.

Irritation brought his eyes open again, and he kept her secure.

". . . has nothing to do with Brandon."

"Of course it does." Taking her shoulders in his hands, Levi stepped away so that he could see her face. "You're condemning yourself because Brandon fooled you. He had you believing that you were in love with him, and that he loved you, too. He convinced you that you'd share this picture-perfect life together."

"And that was all a sham."

"Because he misled you."

"It's easy to fool a fool, apparently."

Levi wanted to shake her, so instead he released her and turned his back. It took two deep breaths to steady himself and tamp down on his anger. "You are not a fool, Beth."

"Then I'm a tramp."

He whirled around and stared at her in furious disbelief. "What did you say?"

With one arm crossed over her middle, the other raised so she could rub her brow, Beth laughed without humor. "You said it yourself. I thought I was in love with Brandon. I slept with him, made plans with him. But even I have to admit I wasn't really in love with him, or I'd be more hurt by his betrayal."

So she wasn't hurt. Levi considered that a very good thing.

Her gaze lifted to his, and she looked so lost and so ashamed, that Levi almost couldn't bear it. "Instead, all I can think about is the situation with you."

"It's not a *situation*, damn it. It's a relationship."

"A friendly relationship, or so I thought. But now . . ." She ducked her head and groaned. "I've known you for two years, Levi. And not once did I ever think of sleeping with you."

"Liar."

She drew back in affront. "I beg your pardon?"

Stalking closer, Levi said, "You've thought about

it, honey. At least admit to that much." Whether she'd ever planned to act on it or not, they'd been too close for her natural sensuality not to take over. "You've seen me at my worst, and at my best. We've swam together, danced together, laughed and complained together."

"Always with Brandon there!"

"So?" As Levi advanced, Beth sidled away from the wall and backed up. Levi kept going—and so did she. "It didn't stop me from fantasizing about you."

Her eyes widened.

"A lot. I never would have sabotaged your relationship with Brandon by acting on my fantasies, but you can bet your sweet little ass that you factored into my dreams on a regular basis."

She shook her head, and continued backing away.

"It's human nature, Beth. Men find it impossible to block a sexy woman from their thoughts." His gaze dipped to her heaving breasts, proof of her agitation. "And vice versa."

"You think you're sexy?" she taunted, hoping to distract him.

Levi grinned. "I'm the opposite of Brandon. Rough instead of polished. Open where he's reserved. Daring when he's cautious."

Beth had nothing to say to that.

"Most importantly," he added, watching for her reaction, "I would never cheat on you. I would never shame you." He stared at her hard. "I would never do anything that I knew would hurt you."

She bit her lip.

"Do you understand me, Beth? *Never.*"

In a small voice, she said, "I believe you."

Those words thrilled Levi. At least she knew him well enough to trust in his honor. That had to count for something.

He waited until she looked up at him, then added, "And whether *you* think I'm sexy or not, you've thought about me."

Temper sparked in her eyes. "Where Brandon's modest, you're obviously vain." Done retreating, Beth took a stance and lifted her chin. "Add that one to the list, why don't you."

Levi laughed. God, he adored her. "If I am conceited, then honey, you made me that way the night you came to me."

She inhaled so fast, she nearly strangled herself.

Levi grinned at her. "Don't get me wrong, honey. I loved it. A lot."

In a display of belligerence, Beth crossed both arms under her breasts. "So now you're blaming me for your character flaws?"

He stepped close enough to touch her, and then paused. "Think about it, Beth. When shit fell apart with Brandon who did you go running to?"

Her mouth tightened, but she refused to reply.

Levi touched a thumb to his chest. "Me."

"I thought you were a friend."

"Uh huh." Levi nodded. "That's why the first plan to come to your mind was having sex with me, right?"

A rush of color stained her smooth cheeks. "I wanted to get even with Brandon."

Slowly, so he wouldn't send her packing, Levi reached out and smoothed her hair behind her ear, then cupped her jaw. He could feel that flush of embarrassment, so warm and honest and sweet. "Sure you did." And already knowing the answer, he asked, "So tell me, honey, what did old Brandon say when you told him?"

Her brows came down, her eyes closed and her mouth pinched in denial of the obvious truth.

Using both hands now to hold her face, Levi repeated, "Beth?"

"I didn't."

He tilted his head in deep satisfaction. "What's that?"

Braced by irritation, Beth slapped his hands away. "I didn't tell him, all right? I couldn't. After that weekend . . . after we . . ." She shook her head hard. "I didn't tell him."

Of course, she hadn't. "I haven't said anything to him, either."

On a low growl, she stormed away, but only to put a little space between them.

Staring at her stiff back, Levi said, "It doesn't feel right to use something that was so wonderful as revenge, does it?"

She whirled on him in a blaze of anger. "Wonderful? Is that what you think?" Three big strides brought her within touching distance of him again. She leaned in to him, her eyes bright with fury, and used one finger to poke at his chest. "It was carnal and extravagant and totally inappropriate."

"It was incredible. And hot. And *honest*," Levi countered.

"Honest?"

"That's right." He was hard again, damn it. "You were everything I'd ever imagined and more. No one else will ever measure up for me now, not with the memory of how it is with you."

Beth's expression went from rage to awareness in a heartbeat. "Levi, don't."

"I lost count of how many times you came."

She groaned, and covered her face.

"I loved every one of them though." He eased himself into her space, then eased her into his arms—where she belonged. "The small sounds you made, and how they became throaty, rough sounds right before you climaxed."

"Stop."

That single word sounded weak and uncertain, so Levi disregarded it. "I have scratches on my shoulders, a bite bruise on my thigh."

"Oh God." Her forehead dropped to his chest and her groan became a moan.

Levi stroked her back, tangled his hand in her hair and kissed her ear. "When I close my eyes at night, I can still taste you, Beth."

Her hands curled into small fists. Her breathing deepened.

"I can still feel you around me, squeezing me tight, and I can still smell you with each breath I take. It makes me hard every time." Using the edge of his hand, Levi tipped up her face. "I'm hard now."

Her lips parted and he kissed her, soft and easy, long and deep. Without conscious thought, his hand sought her breast, cuddling her through the layers of her clothes and still able to feel her tautened nipple. Using his thumb, he circled her, rubbed over the tip, and gently applied pressure.

"*Levi* . . ."

"Yeah," he murmured in approval, "that's what I like to hear, you saying my name, your voice rough with lust." He kissed her temple, her cheekbone—and all the while, he toyed with her breast.

Beth leaned into him, nearly panting, heat pouring off her.

Once again, her physical need helped her to forget her grievances, her embarrassment.

It ate Levi up to know she'd also been with Brandon, and only one fact made it easier to take.

Brandon had never really satisfied her.

The night Beth came to him had started out awkward enough. She'd angrily stammered out what she wanted. He'd been floored, excited, and relieved.

Hearing of Brandon's infidelity had thrilled him, and that made him feel like the biggest jerk alive.

But he didn't turn her down on her offer. No way.

Seducing an enraged woman wasn't easy, especially when she'd asked him to "just get on with it." But Levi gave it his all.

Beth had wanted sex.

He wanted lovemaking.

Beth wanted revenge.

He wanted an opportunity.

At first, she'd been stiff and distant, guided by her hurt feelings—until she succumbed to her first climax with sheer astonishment. Levi would never forget her blurted words after he'd left her replete and lax, her skin damp with sweat, her hair tangled, her skin rosy.

Levi, she'd whispered. *I had no idea.*

Her shock had left him so pleased and proud he wanted to shout. Then she'd reached for him with enthusiasm, and the next few days had been an orgy of exploration and, as Beth claimed, carnality.

For Levi, they'd also been days filled with love.

Everything he did to and with Beth had left her

wide-eyed with wonder and excitement. She reveled in each new experience and glowed with sexual satiation. There'd been no denials, only anticipation.

Just as there was now.

"Levi," she said again, and he knew what she wanted, what she needed.

"Let me help you, honey." He put one leg between hers, cupped her bottom, and snuggled her in close. She shivered as she dropped her head back in wanton acceptance.

Levi guided her, one hand helping her keep a rhythm against his thigh, the other dipping into her shirt so he could touch the bare skin of her breast, really get to her nipples and—

A shrill whistle pierced the thickening air of the storage area.

Levi straightened in shock. Well, shit.

Knowing they were about to be interrupted, he looked at Beth's face. She looked relaxed in the way of rising release. Panting breaths puffed from between her parted lips. Her unfocused gaze and heavy eyelids, her warming skin, proved she wouldn't have needed but a few minutes more.

What to do?

The whistle sounded again, and Beth blinked into reality. "Levi?"

Damn, damn, damn. "I'm sorry, honey." His hands remained on her, but still now. "We're about to have company."

Confusion gave way to horror, and in a flash, she jerked free. *"Ohmigod."*

"Easy, honey. It's just your brother. I think." Keeping Beth shielded by his body, Levi half turned. He saw no one. "Ben?"

"Sorry to interrupt, kids."

The voice came from near the door—out of sight, but audible. Levi wanted to clout him. "What is it?"

"We're all ready to head to bed, so unless you two want to sleep in your vehicles, I need to know if I should put your coats and bags in two rooms . . . or just one? I have vacancies, so they're on the house, but I wasn't sure of your plans."

Levi said, "One room," at the same time Beth snapped, "Two."

"That's clear enough," Ben remarked, and he sounded amused.

Levi quickly cupped Beth's face. "I'll promise not to touch you, if that's what you want."

"Ha!" she said loudly, and then slapped a hand over her mouth. In a lowered voice, she whispered, "You know what I want, and you keep using it against me."

That almost made Levi grin—because it was partially true, although there were times when he just plain lost control. "You have my word, Beth. Unless you beg me, I won't touch you. But please, we do need to talk. I'm staying the night whether you hear me out or not. Tomorrow your family will cluster around you again and it'll be impossible to get any privacy without making an issue of it. Is that what you want?"

Ben rattled a pan, the bastard.

"Give us a minute," Levi snarled.

Beth hesitated, but Levi could see her weakening.

"I'll stay ten feet away from you," he cajoled, "if that'll help."

All morose, Beth admitted, "It probably wouldn't."

"You see," Levi teased in a whisper, "that's why I'm getting conceited."

Finally, she relented. "Ben, we'll take one room, please. But with two beds."

Levi let out a long breath.

"You got it," Ben said around a laugh. "You can have the same suite you always use when you visit, Beth."

Levi raised a brow. "A suite?"

"Ben saves it for family."

Proving he'd been able to hear their every word, Ben said, "Actually, I give it to family to use because most of my guests are only interested in a one or two-night stay in an economy room, which makes the suite available more often than not. But don't expect anything fancy. Being a suite just means you get a couch, microwave, and tiny fridge."

"It'll do," Levi told him. "Thanks."

"I'll get your bags to your room, but you'll need to come to the front desk for your keys."

Beth twisted her hands together. "Would you mind getting the keys from Ben?"

Levi raised a brow. Did she plan to slip out on him? "Ben parked my truck, honey. He has your coat and your purse. And your father and brothers have agreed to let me know if you try running out on me again."

"Traitors."

"I convinced them that I wanted only the best for you."

She made a face. "Great. If only I knew what the best might be. And no, Levi, don't say it." She scowled at him in reproach. "You've shown enough conceit to last a month at least."

She ignored his laughter.

"I'll have you know that I wasn't planning to

sneak off anyway. I intend to be with my family for the holidays."

"So why the delay, then?"

"I want to talk to the women before we . . . retire."

That made Levi a little suspicious. "Talk to them about what?"

Beth looked frazzled and on the verge of losing her temper. "None of your damn business. Now go get the keys. I'll meet you at the room in a few minutes."

Rather than push his luck, Levi agreed. "Don't be too long, okay? After chasing you across the state, I'm a little on the skittish side. I'd hate to call out the National Guard if you're just sitting in the kitchen lamenting the fates with family."

"Ha-ha." Beth flipped a quick wave in his direction and went in search of reinforcements.

Feeling success on the rise, Levi watched her go with a smile. He'd have the night with her. Surely, that'd aid him in making headway.

He could hardly wait.

Three

When Beth entered the dining room, only her father and Noah were there, and Noah had already donned his coat, ready to leave. Undecided on what to do, she stalled. It wasn't that she really wanted more time with the women; she just needed more time to prepare herself for the night with Levi.

It was herself and her own lack of restraint that scared her.

As Noah went out the door to the parking lot, her father said, "Come on in, honey."

He hadn't even looked up to see her. It seemed no matter how old she got, her dad always stayed one step ahead.

"We've got a few minutes," he assured Beth. "Grace is in the car waiting for Noah, Sierra has already turned in, and Brooke is just saying goodbye to Ben. Come sit with me."

Dragging her feet, Beth did just that.

"So," Kent said, "you and Levi, huh?"

There'd be no point lying to him, but that didn't

mean she wanted to make confessions, either. "What exactly did Levi tell you?"

"That Brandon is out of the picture, that he's now in the picture, and that if you'll stand still long enough, he intends to marry you."

"Oh." Beth put her elbows on the top of the booth and propped up her chin. "I caught Brandon cheating, so he's definitely out of the picture."

"How do you feel about that?"

Beth smiled. Leave it to her dad to hold off on the sympathy until he knew where she stood on the matter. "It's a little confusing, but in a way, I'm relieved." She thought about that, and felt compelled to add, "Humiliated and majorly peeved, too."

"Peeved I understand. You have every right. But why are you relieved?"

That one was easy enough to explain. "I keep thinking how close I was to tying myself to him. But what if I'd married him, and then found out he was a cheater? Everything would be so much more complicated."

"True."

"Obviously we weren't meant to be together, and this forced the issue sooner rather than later, when our lives might have been more entangled."

"Divorce, joint property, kids?"

"Exactly." Beth shuddered at the thought of so many legal and emotional ties.

"So it's a good thing then?"

Beth snorted. "It would be, except I really am too humiliated for words." And Levi refused to let her deal with that, blast him.

"I don't see why," Kent said. "Brandon is the one

who shamed himself with his behavior. He's the one who cheated, not you."

Her father definitely didn't know about her wild weekend with Levi, or he wouldn't be able to say that. "I suppose."

"How did you find out? Did Levi tell you?"

"No. Levi didn't know any more about it than I did." If he had known, Beth knew in her heart that he'd have found a way to tell her—after he gave Brandon hell for being a jerk. "He was shocked when I told him." And even more shocked when she shared her plan for getting even.

"You're blushing, Beth. Want to tell me why?"

No, never. "It's a curse of my fair skin, Dad. You know that."

"If you say so." But Beth could tell he didn't believe her.

She quickly distracted him. "Brandon and I were invited to a party with some of his colleagues. I had to work that night, so I told him to go on without me."

"And he did?"

She shrugged. "It didn't make any sense for us both to miss it." A dull throb started behind her eyes. "But then I got off earlier than expected."

"Let me guess. You decided to drop in and surprise him."

"It seemed like a good idea at the time."

Getting a mental picture of the ensuing fiasco, Kent made a face. "Ouch."

"Yeah. Ouch is right." Beth trailed her finger along the edge of the booth tabletop. "There were so many people there, and at first, I couldn't find Brandon. People kept looking at me funny, especially when I asked if they knew where he was. I suppose that should have been my first clue."

Retelling the story brought back the burn of embarrassment. "Finally one woman told me to check the hot tub. That didn't make any sense. It's winter and freezing cold, and Brandon was never that interested in anything to do with water. Whenever we went to a lake or the river, Levi and I would swim and Brandon would sit on the shore and read."

Kent's interest sharpened. "You three hung out together a lot?"

"Well, yeah." Why did her father look so funny about that? "Levi and Brandon were best friends."

"Did Levi bring a date to these little excursions?"

"Maybe a couple of times, but not usually." Frowning a little, Beth asked, "Why?"

"Hmmm." Kent reached for his empty coffee cup, tipped it up to get the last sip, then said, "No reason. Go on with your story. What happened at the party?"

He definitely had a reason for asking, but the hour grew late and she didn't want to hold him up, so Beth finished her tale. "I went around to the back of the house in the direction the woman had pointed. There was an enclosed porch and a fancy hot tub, and sure enough, I found Brandon there."

Kent plunked the coffee cup back down. "With company, I take it."

"He was making out with a woman I'd met several times, but didn't know well."

"One of his colleagues?"

"Another doctor. They might have had their underwear on, but with the churning water, it was hard to tell. They sure weren't wearing much more than that." Beth flopped back in her seat. "I saw them, they saw me, and the woman screeched."

"Screeched?"

"Loudly." Beth snorted. "Then she started scrambling out of the tub. I don't know if she thought I'd cause a scene or attack her or what, but she was wrapped in a towel and running away before I could blink."

Her father coughed, probably to hide a laugh. "I reckon Brandon was surprised, all right."

Beth smirked, too. "No kidding. You should have seen his face."

"Comical?"

"Oh yeah. I've never seen him look like that because he's usually so self-assured. But then, I guess my face looked pretty ridiculous, too. And I had to go back through that whole room full of people so that I could leave. It was like walking the gauntlet. I could feel everyone watching me."

As the memory of it scoured through her, Beth squeezed her eyes shut.

"That was the worse part of it, the fact that everyone there saw me as this sad victim. Most of them were mutual friends."

"Were?"

"I don't think I could ever face any of them again."

"Then they must have been more his friends than yours." Kent put his muscled forearms on the table and gave her a direct look. "Just think about the fact that the other woman went through there first, wet and in a towel."

"Believe me, I've thought of it. It helps only a little."

Kent reached for her hand. "Want me to sic Noah and Ben on Brandon? You know they'd be happy to show him the error of his ways."

Beth shook her head at his teasing. Whenever possible, her father had always allowed her to fight her own battles. This time wouldn't be any different. "No. Brandon's not worth the trouble, especially during the holidays."

He nodded acceptance of that. "So where's Levi fit into this?"

Looking away at nothing in particular, Beth said, "I don't know yet."

Kent squeezed her hand. "I hope you'll give him a chance to help you figure out that one."

Beth didn't want her father to know she'd be spending the night with Levi, so she hedged a bit saying, "Levi and I will talk more when it's not so crazy."

"Tell me a little about Levi. Other than playing third wheel with you and Brandon, what does he do? What do you know about him?"

"I know . . . everything." As soon as Beth said it, she realized it was true. She knew Levi as well, and in some ways better, than she knew Brandon. "What do you want to know?"

"Start with what Levi does for a living."

Finally, a neutral subject that Beth could discuss with enthusiasm. "He's a physical education teacher at a middle school, and he coaches the soccer team."

"How about that?" Kent nodded in approval. "Teaching's a tough job. He has my respect."

Easier, happier memories filtered into Beth's discontent, helping her to relax. "You should see him with kids, Dad. He loves them, and they love him. He has this easy camaraderie that really reaches out to people of all ages."

"I must've missed the camaraderie when he chased you in the door."

Beth could tell by his wry smile that he only teased. "That really didn't make the best first impression, did it?"

Kent shrugged. "They say you can tell the character of a man by the way he interacts with kids and pets."

"He loves animals," Beth rushed to say in Levi's defense. "He doesn't have any of his own right now. He says it wouldn't be fair when he works so much. But if he ever settles down and gets married . . ." That thought petered off because, really, the person Levi mentioned marrying was her.

Her new discontent made Kent grin. "So you've seen him at work, huh?"

"Brandon and I used to go to the soccer matches. I enjoyed it more than Brandon did, so I volunteered to help Levi on field day. It was fun."

"I see." Kent rubbed his chin. "You always did like kids, too."

"They're great."

"Brandon doesn't like kids?"

"I guess he does. But he always had to work, so he couldn't help out with other stuff. You know how it is in the medical field."

"He sounds like a good man, honey."

"Brandon?"

Kent laughed. "I used to think so, but now I'd just say he's an ass." His voice softened. "I meant Levi."

"Oh. Yes, I guess he is." Beth didn't want to speculate on just how good Levi could be. Brooke saved her by walking in just then.

When Kent looked at his wife, something a little primitive gleamed in his eyes.

Beth saw it, and was amazed.

Own up to your feelings, the women had told her. It had sure worked out for Grace, Sierra, and Brooke.

Before Brooke reached them, Kent was on his feet. He greeted her with a gentle, short, but somehow intimate kiss that left Brooke flushed.

Clearing her throat, Beth pushed to her feet and said, "I'll let you two get out of here. It's getting late and I've kept you long enough."

Brooke leaned against Kent. "We were planning Christmas dinner when you arrived."

"It's at our house this year." Kent looped his arm around Brooke as if he'd been cuddling her all his life. "I know Christmas is a few days away, but we hope you can stay for an extended visit."

"I'd like that, thanks."

Nonchalant, Brooke said, "And Levi? Will he be staying, too?"

Beth had no idea. "He's on a break right now, but," she warned them, "even during the holidays and summer he has things for the school that he works on. Sometimes he takes additional classes, and he often works with the soccer team."

"Just let us know when you can," Kent told her.

"I will. Now go." Beth shooed them toward the door where their coats hung. "That snow's piling up, and the temperature is dropping more by the minute. I'd hate to see you get stuck in this storm."

"Beth," Brooke said, "you know if you want to talk to either us at any time, we're only a phone call away."

Her heart softened. It was so nice to see her father happily settled with such a wonderful woman. "Thank you. I'm fine, I promise."

"Either way," Kent said, "give me a call tomorrow, okay?"

"Will do."

Kent gave her a quick kiss on the cheek. "Try to get some rest tonight."

Alone in a room with Levi? Not likely. But Beth smiled in an attempt to look agreeable.

As soon as her father and Brooke left, Beth girded herself, locked her trembling hands together, and went to find her room with Levi.

With every step she took, her anxiety grew. Would Levi keep his word and his physical distance, or would he finish what he started in the kitchen.

It was a toss-up on which one Beth would prefer the most.

When the tentative knock sounded on the door, Levi practically leaped off the bed. He swung the door open and there stood Beth. She looked a little uneasy, and a little turned on.

Damn.

This had to be the worst idea he'd ever had. But he wanted her so much, all the time, that sound thinking no longer factored in for him.

Beth smiled, and then looked beyond him. "Ben brought everything here?"

Levi glanced behind him at the stack of her once-gaily wrapped gifts. "Yeah. I can help you repair those tomorrow if you want."

"Why?"

He turned back to her. "Because you dropped them on account of me. Running away from me."

Her smile slipped. "I wasn't running."

Looked like running to him, but he didn't want to antagonize her. "Okay." Levi soaked in the sight of her, then caught himself. "Sorry." He held the door wider. "Come on in."

She did. Cautiously.

"We've got two beds, like you requested." The suite came with a queen-sized bed, but Ben had also delivered a rollaway. "I'll use the crappy one."

Beth frowned at the lumpy, bent-in-the-middle cot. "You'd barely fit. I'll use it."

"No, I—"

"Don't be noble, Levi, okay? I really don't mind, and I really will fit better." She eyed him head to toe and back again. "You're what? Over six feet, right?"

That look put him back on his heels. In a low voice, he said, "Six-two."

"There, you see?" She nodded. "A good eight inches taller than me. And heavier."

Why this conversation made him hot, Levi didn't know. But maybe just the comparison of her small female frame to his larger, stronger body was enough to remind him how well they fit together. "By at least seventy pounds."

As if that proved her point beyond argument, Beth said, "So I'll use the rollaway and you can have the queen, and we'll both be comfortable."

Baloney. He'd be miserable all night and he knew it.

Beth waited for his agreement. "Okay?"

"Fine." Since they wouldn't be sharing one, he didn't want to argue about the beds. "Are you hungry? Ben was nice enough to bring us up some stuff from the kitchen. I put it in the little fridge."

"Ben is my hero. I'm starved." She headed for the kitchenette. "What do we have?"

"I'm not sure. It was all in containers." And he'd been too anxious to see her to worry about food. Levi followed her. "It smelled good."

"Well whatever it is, it's sure to be good. Ben's cook is the best." In short order, Beth emptied the fridge of the containers and opened them all on the miniscule counter. "Mmmm," she purred, peeking into the first container. "Chicken salad, my favorite." She also found croissants, pickles, fruit, and slabs of chocolate cake smothered in icing. "*Manna* from heaven."

Watching her made Levi hungry—just not for food. Beth wasn't a big woman by any stretch, but he'd never seen her fuss about her weight or struggle with a diet as most women seemed prone to do. "I have some paper plates here. Do we have anything to drink?"

"There's a cola machine around the corner." Assuming he'd go, she said, "I'll take a Coke."

"You'll owe me fifty cents."

Busy loading the croissants with the chicken salad, Beth laughed. "I'd rather owe you than cheat you out of it." She winked at him. "While you're gone, I'll put on coffee to drink with our cake."

Fifteen minutes later, Beth slumped back in her seat with a hearty sigh. "Delicious. I'm stuffed."

"You were right." Levi finished off his coffee. "Ben's cook is incredible."

"I'll tell Horace you said so."

Levi studied her relaxed pose. "It's nice seeing you like this for a change."

She immediately stiffened. "What do you mean?"

"Ever since last weekend, you've been so guarded

around me, it's like being with a stranger. I missed the old Beth."

After pushing out of her chair, she put her arms around her middle and paced across the small room. She kept her back to him. "I was trying to bring the old Beth back by pretending it hadn't happened, and there you go, bringing it up again."

Levi's temper went up a notch. "I won't let you pretend, so forget that."

"Right." Taking Levi by surprise, Beth spun around and blasted him. "You won't let me have any space. You won't let me deal with the changes." She punctuated each word with another stomp closer. "And now I'm not allowed to pretend, either? Well, newsflash, Masterson. You don't control me. I'll pretend all I want to!" She ended that challenge on a high note.

Levi, too, left his seat. In a metered pace, he finished closing the distance between them. "You've got one hell of an imagination, Beth. I know because I benefited from it for a whole weekend and a day."

She gasped.

"But even your imagination isn't good enough to pretend nothing has ever happened between us. It's there, and we both remember it."

"*You* . . ." She seethed, but apparently she couldn't think of anything to say. With visible effort, she gathered herself. One deep breath, then another.

Fascinated, Levi watched her. Her behavior even sparked a memory, one that amused him and left him a little more controlled, too.

He and Beth had a history; he could build on that.

Little by little, Beth's tensed muscles relaxed and she even smiled. Sarcastically. "I'm done talking to you, Levi."

Even her acerbic smiles looked beautiful to him. "Is that right?"

"Yes. I'm going to take my shower and go to bed." With that, she grabbed up her overnight case and stormed toward the bathroom. "I'd prefer it if you did the same."

"With you?"

She almost tripped. *"No."* Spine stiff, she took a few more breaths. "You may use the shower when I'm done."

"Thanks. I showered right before I found out that you'd skipped town. I'll just clean up our mess and go to bed." Maybe in bed he'd have power over his libido. Because right now, he could feel himself getting hard again.

Maybe it was the thought of Beth naked, under the water.

Maybe it was just being with her.

Whatever the case might be, he needed to be a calm, rational man with her, not a lust-craved maniac with a perpetual boner.

"Suit yourself," Beth said, right before she closed the bathroom door.

Right. If he did that, they'd both be on the bed, naked and entwined right now. Better that he go with a plan.

By the time Beth came out of the bathroom, Levi was in the bed, under the covers, and ready to tackle her stubbornness.

Other than the bathroom light slanting across the darkened floor, Beth couldn't see a thing. "Levi?"

"Careful, honey. Your bed is all ready for you. Do you need me to turn on a lamp?"

"No." Feeling like a prude, she'd put on her heavy flannel pajamas, the ones that were too big but comfy, the ones that hid every speck of skin and any curves she might possess. "I'm fine, thank you."

"Do you feel better now after your *long* shower."

Levi's emphasis couldn't be missed. But then, she *had* lingered in the shower for a good hour, thinking over everything the other women had said. Though they'd reassured her on many levels, it was still unsettling how Levi affected her so easily. It seemed that whenever she was alone with him, she wanted to rape him, harangue him, or flee him.

Why couldn't she just be herself?

For a little while there, after she'd first come into the room, the old familiar companionship returned. Talking with Levi had always been easy. Enjoyable. Somehow . . . comforting.

That insight was a little too profound, because it made Beth consider the possibility that she'd always had hidden feelings for him.

And the possibility that she'd been oblivious to *his* feelings.

"I'm fine," Beth finally told him. "The hot water felt so good after this nasty frigid weather that I just hung in there for a while. I hope you didn't really mind?"

"Course not."

Beth could hear him shifting on the bed. She cleared her throat. "I'm pretty tired tonight. Do you think we could just talk more in the morning?"

"Sure."

She found the edge of the little cot and eased down. "Thanks for clearing up our food mess."

"I stacked everything. Tomorrow morning the maid can grab it."

"That works." The new awkwardness was crushing. A little chilled now that she'd left the steam of the bathroom, Beth tucked under the covers. "Good night, Levi."

At first, she didn't think he would respond. Then he asked, "Remember that time you were upset and we talked for hours?"

By necessity, Levi had opened her cot at the end of the queen-sized bed. The dimensions of the room didn't allow for any other positioning, not if they hoped to be able to move around without bumping their shins.

Beth turned her head and stared toward Levi's voice in the darkness. "Yes."

"You were thinking of buying a new car because a few of Brandon's associates had teased you about driving an older model sedan with primer on the fender."

"My old faithful transportation. That car got me through college." She averted her gaze toward the ceiling. "Brandon agreed with them. He said as his fiancée, he wanted me to look classier."

The bed springs squeaked as Levi sat up. "I didn't know that."

A reluctant smile tugged at her lips. "You were already lecturing me for caring about what others thought, so I saw no reason to tell you that I cared what Brandon thought, too."

"As I remember it, you got mad at me for lecturing you." And then: "Brandon actually agreed with those idiots?"

Shadows shifted with the wind outside the window. Beth went back in time, to the first and, other than recent events, only conflict she'd ever had with Levi. "I wasn't really mad at you."

"No?"

"It's just that I knew you were right. What they thought didn't matter, not even a little. I was too old to give in to peer pressure or to start feeling inadequate about anything as superficial as the appearance of my car." She shifted onto her side. "And yes, Brandon agreed with them."

"You stayed for three and a half hours that night." Levi's voice was low and even, and she could hear the smile in his tone. "We ordered Chinese takeout and watched a back-to-back Jeopardy marathon."

Beth remembered every second of that night, but it surprised her that Levi recalled so much.

"I suppose if you weren't mad at me," Levi questioned aloud, "then you must have been mad at yourself?"

"Yup. For letting those judgmental snobs get to me."

Levi laughed.

"That was almost a year ago, wasn't it?" The winter storm stirred the air outside, sending sleet to peck gently against the window. The wind moaned and a chill pervaded the room.

But in the dark, talking with Levi, Beth felt warm and cozy and strangely at peace. "What made you think of it?"

"Earlier, when I made you mad. You acted the same way you did that night. You deliberately reined in your anger. It's amazing to see. And cute." Before she could get too riled over that, Levi said, "I'm sorry that I upset you."

He was such a macho guy, yet he didn't hesitate

to apologize when he felt the need. For Beth, that made him more macho than any other man she knew. "Thank you, but an apology isn't necessary. Once again, I'm more angry at myself than you."

"I wish you wouldn't be. There's no reason." He sat up again in the bed. "I never told Brandon about that night. Did you?"

"No. He wouldn't have understood."

Two heartbeats of silence passed before Levi asked softly, "Understood what?"

In the dark and quiet, alone and relaxed with Levi, it never crossed Beth's mind to give anything less than the truth. "That talking to you was easy."

The bed squeaked as Levi shifted around. He moved toward the foot of the bed—closer to her. Even without seeing him clearly, Beth knew he rested on his stomach with his fists beneath his chin.

"Ever wonder why, honey?"

His close proximity did crazy things to Beth's libido. "No."

He tsked. "Your nose is going to grow with all that fibbing."

Beth didn't confirm or deny that charge, but she did smile to herself.

With the casual comfort of long acquaintance, Levi rolled to his back. Their heads were close together, but their positioning felt more easy than intimate.

"I remember that time you got sick with a nasty chest cold. Your nose was bright red and you sneezed in the middle of every sentence."

Beth remembered it well, too. "Brandon had an extra long shift at the hospital, so you brought me soup."

"And a video."

"One of my favorites." Because she'd seen him in that position many times, Beth could almost picture Levi with his arms folded behind his head, biceps bulging, chest muscles defined. As a phys-ed teacher, he stayed active and in shape, and it showed. "Brandon always refused to see it with me."

"I know."

The way he said that twisted Beth's heart. "It surprised me that you liked it."

"Liked it?" Levi gave a short laugh. "I hated it. It sucked. It was too sappy and over the top emotional. Give me a good old-fashioned action flick any day."

"But you rented it!"

"Yeah." His tone softened and became every bit as sweet as the movie. "Because like the soup, I knew it was your favorite."

Beth held silent for several moments. Brandon hadn't known about her favorite soup, or her favorite video.

Was Levi that much more observant?

"You watched it with me," she accused.

"I watched you watching it," he corrected. "There's a difference."

When Levi turned back onto his stomach again, Beth could not only see the glow of his eyes in the darkness, she could actually feel his gaze touching on her.

"Back then," he whispered, "I guess I was into masochism, because being there with you, so close when you were so untouchable, was pretty torturous."

In the same whisper, Beth asked, "So why did you do it?"

"Because not being with you was worse."

Oh God. An invisible fist squeezed her heart, and Beth couldn't bear it. She came to her knees on the lumpy cot mattress. "Levi?"

He sat up to face her, only inches away. "I'm right here."

Beth laced her fingers together to keep from reaching for him. "Why do you want me?"

"You're smart."

That ultra-quick answer surprised a laugh out of Beth, and helped to put her need in check. "And brains turn you on?"

"Your brains do." He said that with a lot of gravity. "Especially when they're mixed with a great sense of humor, and sensitivity, and a big heart."

Beth inhaled his scent, somehow warmer now, more potent. "So it's not how I look?"

Sounding darker and deeper, he asked, "How do you look, Beth?"

"Female."

He fell silent for a moment. "Very female."

She sensed his restraint and it turned her on, making her feel powerful, seductive, and sexy.

In near confusion, he whispered, "I always thought I preferred dark women. Rich, dark hair, chocolate brown eyes. I always thought long legs were the sexiest. And big boobs."

"Gee, that's a surprise."

He paid no attention to her mocking interruption. "And lots of confidence."

"I'm confident."

"Maybe. Sometimes. But you're also petite and

fair skinned, and you have beautiful legs, but honey, they're not super long."

Quickly passing the point of no return, Beth sighed. "I guess I'm not really overly endowed in the chest department, either."

Somehow, even without the aid of light, his hands found her face. They were big and warm, and oh so gentle as they touched her. "You are perfect."

"I am?"

His thumbs brushed her cheekbones. "And very sexy."

Beth thought about that. "If you could change one thing about me, Levi, what would it be?"

"Your worries."

Her heart melted. So he wouldn't make her better endowed, sweeter, less headstrong?

"Levi," she chastised, because he hadn't taken any time to think about it, to consider all the possibilities. Still, his answer touched her. "I meant physically."

"Weren't you listening when I said you're perfect? You are. You're the most beautiful woman I've ever met."

Beth figured she could pass for pretty, but beautiful wasn't a word to describe her. She hesitated to speak her mind, but fair was fair—and fair was easier now, in the dark and in the quiet. "I think you look pretty perfect, too."

Levi said nothing.

"And . . . I have thought about you."

A sexual charge broke the stillness of the room, splintering it like static electricity. Then Levi's hands fell away from her. "I would love to hear more about what you thought, but I made a promise to you, and that means I need to go take a cold shower. Right now."

Thinking that he joked, Beth started to laugh, until she heard him leave the bed and she felt him move past her. "Levi!"

"Stay put, honey. I'll be back out in two minutes. Five if I decide I have to take care of business first, in order to keep my word."

Beth almost fell off the cot. She did stumble to her feet. *Take care of business?* Surely, Levi didn't mean what she thought he might mean.

Or did he? *"Levi."*

His only answer was the closing of the bathroom door. A light came from beneath the door, and then the lock clicked into place with a quiet snick.

Staring through the dark and mostly empty room toward the bathroom, Beth stood there utterly mute.

Seconds later, she heard the shower come on.

In disbelief and pounding disappointment, she crawled face down onto the cot and pulled the pillow down over her head.

She would have screamed in frustration, but she was so turned on she couldn't draw a single deep breath. Her sisters-in-law and stepmother were right. She had to face the facts that her feelings for Levi were physical, but they were more than that, too.

She wanted him, yes indeed.

But because she admired him and appreciated him, and had always respected him; talking with Levi only made the physical need more acute.

Brooke, Grace, and Sierra knew what she hadn't wanted to accept: Levi was the guy for her. For too many years she'd missed the obvious. She'd been so blind that she'd almost married the wrong man. Brandon's unfaithfulness had given her an opportunity to set things straight.

Now she had to decide what to do about it.

Four

Levi stood beneath the spray of the icy water and called himself ten times a fool. He couldn't touch her. He *couldn't.*

God, had he really made such an asinine promise?

Idiot.

Moron.

He pictured Beth on the cot, heard again her quiet confession, and knew he'd never survive his stupid promise without taking care of business first.

Letting his imagination go, he wrapped a hand around himself and slowly stroked. His teeth locked.

He saw Beth's eyes, dark with excitement. His muscles twitched.

He remembered the bite of her nails on his shoulders when he'd given her a third climax. Tension coiled inside him.

He felt again the way her teeth closed on his shoulder in an attempt to muffle her own shouts of pleasure. Close, so close.

He remembered when he took her from behind

doggy-style, how he'd touched her belly, and lower. He visualized the mix of pleasure and uncertainty when he'd put her legs over his shoulders and entered her so deeply that she couldn't have taken any more of him.

He recalled the taste of her when he'd knelt on the floor and opened her thighs wide . . .

With a low groan, icy water streaming over his body and visions of Beth spurring him on, Levi came. It wasn't the same. It sure as hell wasn't enough.

But for now, it'd have to do.

With the edge of tension removed, Levi slumped against the hard-tile wall and tried to even his breathing as the cold water washed away the evidence of his release.

What was Beth thinking?

Would she be as ashamed for his behavior now as she'd been of her own during their long weekend? Would she even be waiting for him when he returned?

That thought got him moving and he dried off in record time. Without bothering to dress, he switched off the light and jerked the door open. "Beth?"

Like nails on a chalkboard, she gritted, "What?"

Uh oh.

She didn't sound embarrassed. Nope, she sounded pissed.

Oddly enough, that relieved Levi. He'd take anger over her humiliation any day. "Just making sure you didn't skip out on me." He refrained from saying *again*.

"Where would I go, Levi? What would I say to Ben if I up and left?"

There was a punching sound as if she mauled her pillow, then she heaved an angry, frustrated sigh.

Poor baby. He doubted a cold shower would have the same effect on her. She was too new to satisfaction to take half measures.

"You know, Beth, you could say that you're so ir-resistible I couldn't take it anymore, but that I made you a promise I didn't want to break, so I had to excuse myself to—"

"Argh! It was a rhetorical question, you jerk. I do *not* want a blow-by-blow report of your . . . shower activities."

Levi stepped into his boxers. "No?" And just to tease her, he asked, "Are you sure?"

A pillow hit him square in the face.

Levi stumbled back into the wall, nearly falling. Good shot, especially in the dark. She impressed him, but he wouldn't tell her so. "Damn it, woman. Don't throw things at me."

Another pillow barely missed him, but knocked a lamp off the dresser. It crashed to the floor.

They both went silent.

"Now see what you made me do." Beth flipped on a light, turned to Levi, and froze.

Dressed only in black boxers, he straightened. "Sorry. I left the shower in a hurry when it oc-curred to me that you might flee."

She stared.

He nudged the fallen lamp with a bare toe. "It isn't broken, luckily."

She blinked, swallowed audibly.

Taking a relaxed stance, Levi let her look. "You've seen me before, Beth."

Without shifting her gaze to above his neck or below his knees, she said, "Shut up about that."

Exasperated, Levi put his hands on his hips. "I meant even before last weekend, actually. We've swam together so you've seen me in trunks plenty of times. And you've helped with practices, so you've seen me play shirts and skins in soccer. You've even seen me—"

"Yeah, yeah. But this is different."

Because now she knew what was under the boxers, and she knew how good they were together? Levi wanted to hear her say it. "Why?"

"Because now I know you . . . intimately."

"And that makes it different?"

She nodded.

"Beth?"

"Hmm?"

"Do you think you could look at my face?" At his leisure, Levi leaned against the wall. "I mean, I did just come, I won't deny that. But I'm not sure how helpful that'll be if you keep looking at me like you want to eat me alive."

Her gaze clashed into his. Her hands fisted. Lips stiff and voice low, she growled, "You are such a jerk, Masterson."

"Maybe on occasion. I'm human. But you want me anyway," he taunted. "Don't you?"

Her teeth sawed together. Her eyes sparked. Then . . . on a sigh, she said, "Yes."

That knocked the humor right out of him. Levi straightened. "I wish you'd have admitted that before I made my promise."

"Forget your promise."

If only he could. "You might feel differently in the morning, honey. You might be mad at yourself again, and you'll take it out on me."

She bit her lip. "What if I swear not to?"

Heart hammering, Levi lifted the lamp off the floor and plunked it back onto the dresser. As he gathered his thoughts, he approached Beth's narrow cot. Though he didn't like himself for trying it, her need right now could be a bargaining chip toward their future.

Anticipation burned through him. "What if you swear to me that tonight won't be the only night? What if you marry me and—"

She blanched.

Damn it. "I take it that appalled look on your face is a no?" Propping his hands on his hips, Levi shook his head. "You think I'm asking for too much, don't you?"

Pleading, Beth whispered, "It's too much for so soon, yes."

For her, maybe. But not for him. Levi knew how he felt, how he'd always felt. He'd never acted on his feelings because Beth was as off-limits as a woman could be.

Was.

Not anymore.

"Sorry," he muttered, unwilling to torture himself further tonight. "Let's just go to bed and forget about it." Ignoring her stunned and disappointed expression, he stepped past Beth, stretched out on the bed, and pulled the covers over his body.

Beth kept her back to him. "No."

Levi eyed her militant stance. Her disheveled hair tumbled down her back. Pajamas a size too large swallowed her petite body. And still he could see the rigid way she held herself. "What did you say?"

She turned and began marching toward his bed. "I said no."

She looked so resolute that Levi hurried to sit up. But she'd already reached him and before he could stop her, before he even realized her intent, she grabbed the covers and ripped them right off the bed.

Wow.

Forget the shower; Levi was hard in a nanosecond. His heartbeat thundered, but he said calmly enough, "Now Beth . . ."

Flattening both hands on his bare chest, she shoved him onto his back. "You started this, Levi, and you can damn well finish it, whether we have a lifetime together, a year together, or even just tomorrow together."

As Beth threw a leg over his waist to straddle him, Levi gave up. He was only human. And male. And madly in love.

He cupped her face. "At least give me tomorrow, Beth."

She bit his chin, his bottom lip. "Tomorrow," she agreed. And then her mouth was on his, her kiss grinding and brutal and devouring him. Her tongue slicked over his lips, and then past them to tangle with his.

When she switched to his throat, he said, "Beth," meaning to slow her down.

"No more talking," she commanded. She nipped his earlobe, his collarbone.

"But honey . . ." Levi fought to remember his promise. "Beth, my willpower is dwindling fast."

"Good."

But his love for Beth was too important to give up to a flash of sexual satisfaction. "I promised you that I wouldn't—"

"Wouldn't touch me unless I begged." She sat up on his abdomen, looked down at him, and said, "Please, Levi." She spread her fingers over his bare chest and purred, "I'm begging."

His control evaporated. "Come here."

Full of enthusiasm and need, Beth fell on him. Trying to slow her down, to dredge up a bit of much-needed finesse Levi gentled her with a deep kiss.

When she went soft and warm against him, he coasted his hands over her narrow back to her waist, where he encountered the baggy pajama bottoms. With no more than a tug, they slid easily to her knees. Hooking his toes in the material, Levi kicked them away from her body and then off the side of the bed.

Beth raised herself above him. Her eyes were glazed with need, her lips parted. One by one, Levi opened the buttons of her pajama top and parted the material, leaving her breasts exposed. He wasted no time lifting himself up for a leisurely tasting of each swollen nipple.

Beth dropped to her elbows with a groan. Her thighs tightened around him, her eyes closed.

Carefully, without releasing her nipple, Levi turned her to a more submissive position under him. Giving her all his weight, he pinned her down and took his time licking a puckered nipple. He loved the texture of her, the scent that clung to her body, the broken sound of her breathing as he went from licking to sucking gently, then not so gently.

Her hips lifted against him in a frantic rhythm.

"*Levi . . .*" she begged again.

Never would he tire of hearing her say his name, especially in such a pleading way. "Patience, honey." He went back to kissing her breasts.

She tangled her fingers in his hair and forced his gaze up to hers. "Now, please."

Doing his best to hide a smile, Levi nodded. "You've got it."

She tried to pull him up to her then, but Levi had an alternate plan. Kissing a lazy, damp path down her rib cage to her belly, he let her know his intent. She groaned again, this time in eagerness for what he would do.

Voice hoarse and rough, he murmured, "Let's get rid of these panties."

Beth lifted her hips to accommodate his request, and Levi skimmed the slinky scrap of material down her legs. On his elbows, he looked up the length of her.

So beautiful. And all his, whether she accepted that yet or not.

Except for the pink-flowered flannel shirt framing her shoulders, she was completely naked.

Levi wanted to tell her that he loved her, but she wasn't ready to hear that, not yet. Hell, he'd barely gotten her to commit to tomorrow, when what he really wanted was a lifetime. If he rushed things, he could scare her off. Again.

For now, for right this moment, Beth only needed the relief he could give her.

He laid a heavy hand on her belly. She kept her eyes closed, her bottom lip caught in her teeth. Her breasts shimmered with each anxious breath she took.

Tonight she admitted to wanting him again. That was more than he'd had yesterday.

He'd drown her in pleasure, and maybe tomorrow she'd acknowledge that what they shared was more than sexual, and more than temporary.

Then she'd ask for a repeat. Tonight, tomorrow, the day after, and the day after that . . . until finally she realized that their friendship had grown from a mutual belief in life and love, a bone-deep compatibility enhanced by sexual chemistry and a shared view of the future.

She'd understand that love made it so special between them, and then she'd agree to a lifetime with him.

Keeping his hand on her belly, Levi said, "Open your legs, Beth."

Her muscles twitched—and she complied. But not enough to suit him.

"A little more, honey. Bend your knees, don't be shy . . . that's it." And just to tease her, he added, "I want to taste you."

Her breath shuddered out. Her belly sucked in.

"You're going to come for me, Beth. And you're going to love it, just not as much as I will."

Her neck arched, and her body bowed as she lifted herself toward him. "I want you to come, too."

With his mouth touching her heated skin, he groaned. Yeah, he'd come. No doubt about that. She was so soft that Levi loved touching and kissing her. And she had a unique scent that affected him more than a potent drug. He got near Beth, and his head swam, his heart raced, and heat suffused him.

Even before he could make a move on her, he'd known she was the woman meant to be his mate, just by the primal reactions of his body.

There was so much pleasure in being near her that Levi could have spent the rest of the night just nibbling on various erogenous parts of her body and enjoying her response to each flick of his tongue or warm suckle.

On her inner thighs, he left hickeys that no one would see except him. But Beth would go through her day tomorrow knowing they were there, and remembering him.

Though it wasn't necessary, he held her legs open as he teased his tongue along her pelvic bones, dipped into her navel, and trailed downward.

Finally, when he knew she couldn't take much more, Levi glided his fingertips over her and found her damp and swollen. In a gentle back and forth motion, he insinuated two fingers into her, all the while watching her face and seeing how even that simple touch nearly put her over the edge. Between her expression and the feel of her slick, hot, and tight around his fingers, he nearly lost control.

"You're squeezing me, Beth. I like that." He pressed a little deeper, slow but firm, until she gasped. New moisture bathed him, and he bent to nuzzle his lips around his fingers, tasting her and exciting himself more.

Trying to find relief, Beth moved her hips against him. Her inner muscles rhythmically clasped and released him in a building torrent of sensation.

Levi inhaled the spicy, pungent scent of her arousal, licked his tongue over her, around her, and gently drew her throbbing clitoris into his mouth.

Her reaction was instant and explosive.

With a throaty groan she came, her entire body rigid, pulsing, suspended with pleasure. Once again, her nails stung his shoulders as she struggled to ground herself and keep him as close as he could be.

The rush of it almost had Levi spiraling away, too. He eased the pressure as her body slowly sank back to the mattress and only little aftershocks rocked her. He took one last lick over super-sensitive flesh, felt her flinch, and retreated. Her ragged breathing filled the air. The mattress shivered with her pounding heartbeat.

Levi didn't want to leave her, didn't want to give up the heady taste of her, but he forced himself to move up beside her.

To his surprise, she immediately turned into his arms, tucking her head under his chin as she squeezed him tight.

"Hey?" he murmured, still a little unsteady himself from her release. "You okay?"

In answer, she took a gentle bite of his pectoral muscle.

"Ouch." Okay, so a bite wasn't tears. Or regret. It was sort of . . . playful.

He felt her smile against his heated skin. "Thank you, Levi."

Confused, he considered her actions and her sentiment before cautiously replying. "You're welcome."

"Now it's your turn."

He squeezed his eyes shut. "I don't know if that's a good idea."

But Beth wasn't listening. Lazily, given her recent climax, she sat up beside him. "Off with the boxers."

Levi weighed his options, knew he wasn't strong enough to resist, and decided he'd better ensure protection first. "Give me just a second." Sitting up, he stretched his arm to the chair beside the bed and snagged his jeans. From his back pocket he withdrew several connected condom packets.

"How many did you bring?"

"I don't know. When I realized you'd left, I just grabbed some." He separated one packet and, after shucking off his shorts, opened it.

Beth said, "Let me."

Just the thought of that had him shaking. "Not this time. If you start handling me, I'll be a goner."

She trailed her fingertips along his naked thigh. "Really?"

In a rush, Levi rolled on the condom. "Sorry, babe, but I've wanted too much for too long to show much restraint. Maybe in a decade you'll be able to tease me some. But not yet. Definitely not tonight." And with that, he put Beth to her back again. On the ragged edge, he growled, "Now open up and let me in."

Wearing a big, sexy smile, Beth did just that.

As he sank into her, Levi closed his eyes. Being joined to Beth made him feel like an idiotic poet. It was profound. It exceeded anything he'd ever known or felt.

He pressed in harder, deeper. "I'm not going to last." He pulled out, and then, watching her, thrust in again.

Her smile disappeared on a gasp. "Okay." Wrapping her fingers around his biceps, she held onto him. "Anytime you're ready." Her legs twined around him until she locked her ankles at the small of his back.

Levi straightened his arms so he could watch her breasts, and began thrusting in a steady rhythm. With each glide and retreat, Beth got wetter, hotter, and she clenched tighter. He locked his teeth. *Not yet,* he told himself, but he knew it was useless.

His fingers knotted in the bed sheets. "Look at me, Beth."

She did, her eyes smoky and dazed. "Levi?" she whispered.

He drove into her, unable to reply.

"I'm going to come again, too."

That did it, especially with the way her voice caught on the last word, the way she moaned and tensed and twisted beneath him.

He took her mouth, devouring her, their groans mingling together, so much a part of her that he knew sex with any other woman would never compare.

Spent, Levi relaxed his weight down onto her. He felt Beth's mouth touch his sweaty shoulder, felt her legs slide away from him.

Damn it. He couldn't take much more of this without her acknowledging their future together. Levi rolled to the side of her, staring at the ceiling, so aware of Beth that he felt her in his heart. Cool air wafted over his sweat-damp skin, but not for long. Beth curled into him and sighed.

Levi waited.

"It keeps getting better and better."

He smiled, ready to point out how great it'd be in a few years. But Beth wasn't finished.

"I keep saying this, but . . . could we talk in the morning?" She gave him a halfhearted pat on his chest. "I'm fading fast. You've worn me out with the chase and the capture and the awesome way you just made me feel."

Because she sounded sincere, and she ended that statement on a deep yawn, Levi relented. "Sure. Go to sleep, honey. I'll be here when you wake up."

"I know." She snuggled closer. "Because I'm not letting you go."

Levi's heart nearly stopped, then went into a fury of pounding that might have bruised his ribs. *She wasn't letting him go?*

After several moments of stunned silence, he lifted his head to look at her. "Beth?"

Her deep, even breaths gave the only reply. Well, hell. How could she make a statement like that and then just nod off? Did she mean what she said? Was she delirious? Too tired to think straight?

Confusing him with someone else?

No, not that.

Levi slid his arm out from under her and left the bed. Beth didn't stir so much as an eyelash. Feeling disgruntled, he went into the bathroom to dispose of the condom. When he returned, she didn't awaken but she did immediately settle back against him.

He understood her reserve, he really did. To go from being engaged to one man to marrying another in a matter of days wasn't an easy change to accept. But it was right. They were right together. This was their big opportunity at happily ever after, and Levi wasn't about to let her miss it.

Staring at the shadowy ceiling, Levi realized that he hadn't bothered to turn off the light. He looked at the lamp, but it was too far away from him to reach without getting up again.

He'd never get to sleep, damn it.

Confusion kept his thoughts churning for

hours, but eventually the warmth and comfort of Beth's body wrapped close to his lulled him. He listened to her breathe while stroking his fingers over her supple waist and hip.

Finally, he drifted into a deep sleep.

He didn't stir once the rest of the night.

Grace hung up her sweater and then turned to the big bed she shared with her husband. She almost sighed. Noah was by far the most gorgeous man on the earth, and so wonderful that she often wanted to pinch herself to make sure it was all real.

Not that she ever doubted his love. Every day, in a dozen different ways, he made his feelings for her well known.

Grace enjoyed the sight of him a few moments more, then whispered, "Noah?"

Sprawled on the bed naked, Noah peeked open one eye. When he saw her in her undies, the other eye opened, too, and his gaze slid over her with heated appreciation. "Hmmm?"

Grace knew that look oh-so well—and she loved it. But wanting them to stay on track, she quickly pulled a nightshirt over her head before going to sit on the mattress beside him. "I'm curious about something."

His big warm hand settled heavily on her upper thigh, and he made a sound that showed she had his full attention.

As always.

To keep Noah's hand from roaming, Grace put hers over it. "What could Levi have done to Beth that she thought was so kinky?"

Startled, Noah gave up his perusal of her body and jerked his gaze up to her face. "What? Who says they did anything kinky?"

"Beth was embarrassed over what they'd done. She said she behaved like a sexual freak."

For a single moment, Noah looked horrified, then he gave a chagrined half laugh. "Hell, honey, I don't want to think about anything like that, much less talk about it. Beth's practically a sister. A baby sister." He shook his head. "Her sexual activities are definitely on my list of taboo subjects."

Grace wouldn't give up so easily. "Don't be ridiculous. She's only Ben's stepsister, and though neither of you show it nor acknowledge it, Ben's a half brother. That mean's Beth's not a blood relation to either of you, but she's even less of a real relative to you than she is to Ben."

Noah blinked at that long jumbled argument. "A brother is a brother and a sister is a sister. Doesn't matter how it comes about, it's still the same."

Grace frowned at him. "I could see if Ben was a little squeamish talking about Beth and Levi, but you—"

Noah shushed her with a groan. "Knowing Ben, he'd probably want details—so he'd have more reasons to demolish the guy. In case you didn't notice, Ben doesn't seem to like Levi much."

Grace waved that away. "Ben was just blustering, playing up that 'big brother' role. But we both know he wouldn't actually hurt Levi without good reason, and no reason exists, so it's not a problem."

"If you say so."

"I do." Grace bent to put a quick but interested

peck on Noah's chest. "So, what do you think the two of them did?"

"I have no idea."

Grace bit her bottom lip. "Do you think they've done anything we haven't done?"

He made a sound that was half laugh, and half groan. "How the hell should I know?"

Grace huffed. Sitting straighter and frowning at Noah, she said, "Okay, let me rephrase this then. Is there anything we haven't done?"

Noah started to laugh, caught her frown, and changed his expression to one of serious consideration.

"You know what?" He hooked his arms around Grace, tumbled her down over him, and said, "Instead of talking about this, why don't I just run a few possibilities past you?"

It wasn't quite what she'd had in mind, but Grace gave into that suggestion with enthusiasm. "Now that you mention it, I like that idea even better." She put her arms around him. "Let's."

As Ben stepped out of the bathroom in the suite of rooms he shared with Sierra, she said, "We need to go shopping tomorrow. Can you free up some time?"

Still damp and busy drying, Ben glanced toward his wife where she sat cross-legged on the bed, a gift catalog opened over her lap. To his enjoyment, she wore only a ribbed undershirt and his favorite pair of pink and black barely-there panties.

Ben had bought her the underwear, and a dozen other pairs in a variety of styles, fabrics, and colors.

When Sierra opened her Christmas presents this year, she'd have a dozen more.

He loved seeing her in sexy panties. They were such a contrast to her take-charge, tackle-any-job attitude and her sleek feminine muscles gained from hard work as a landscaper.

As he looked her over, his blood heated. "I can take the afternoon off. But what are we shopping for? I thought we'd finished our holiday gift buying." And he could definitely think of better ways to spend a free afternoon than shopping.

Without looking up, Sierra flipped the page. "We need something for Levi. The problem is that I don't know him that well. I guess I'll get something generic. You know, something all men enjoy."

"Like?" If Levi wasn't chasing Beth, Ben would suggest all types of things. But a man didn't make sexual jokes about a sister.

Sierra shook her head. "I don't know yet. I'm hoping to find some inspiration in this gift book."

After briskly drying his hair, Ben dropped the towel over the back of a chair and strode naked to the bed. "Maybe Levi won't be here that long and we won't have to worry about it. Christmas is still a few days away and Beth seems to want him long gone."

Although, Ben reminded himself, Beth had asked for one room.

But with two beds.

Very confusing. Except that damned Levi had seemed awfully sure of himself . . .

"She doesn't." Sierra continued with her perusal of holiday-inspired presents. "Want Levi gone, that is. She's in love with him."

Ben cocked a brow over that disclosure. "You really think so?"

"I know so." And then, distracted, "It's as obvious as it can be."

"I'll have to take your word for that." How was it that women always saw something different from what men saw?

"You are such a smart man." Sierra's mouth curved in a smile.

"Since Brandon's out of the picture, can't we just give his gift to Levi?"

Her smile lowered to a frown. "Of course not. All things considered, it wouldn't be right to give the man Beth will marry a gift that was meant for the man we thought she was going to marry."

Amused by that convoluted explanation, Ben stretched out beside her, took her catalog and dropped it on the nightstand.

It was Sierra's turn to raise a brow.

While looking at her breasts beneath the undershirt, Ben asked, "Am I supposed to understand what you just said?"

Sierra laid down on her side, facing him. "You could just trust me, I suppose."

"That I do, sweetheart." Leaning forward to kiss her, Ben growled, "I trust you to keep me in a fog of sexual satisfaction."

Sierra snorted. "You're so easy, that job's a piece of cake."

Dead serious, he said, "I'm easy for you, Sierra. No one else." Ben drew her down over him, and Sierra got to work.

* * *

Standing in front of her dressing-table mirror, wearing only a camisole and panties, Brooke removed her earrings and a delicate necklace.

As always, the sight of her charmed Kent. The way she moved, her posture, and the grace of her hands never failed to mesmerize him and turn him on.

Brooke caught his reflection in her mirror and smiled. "You look pensive, Kent. Are you thinking about Beth and that brazen new man of hers?"

Kent could have laughed, but he stifled his humor. "No." At that moment, with Brooke nearly ready for bed, the last thing on his mind was his daughter. "I think it'll work out just fine between the two of them."

After closing the jewelry box, Brooke turned to face him. "You do? Why?"

"Because Beth looks at that young man the way you always looked at me." The way Brooke *still* looked at him on occasion.

Laughing, Brooke reached up to take down her hair. "And how would that be?"

"With a little fear and a lot of fascination." As her silky hair tumbled free, Kent caught her around the hips and dragged her between his legs. "It's an incredible combination that gets to me every time."

"Fear?"

Nodding slowly, he let his hands slide down to cup her bottom. "Fear at being so fascinated."

Brooke laughed again. "I'd say it was more awe than fear. You are such a big, impressive man, and so blatantly sexual. I've never known anyone else like you."

Filling his palms with her lush, soft backside

made it almost impossible for Kent to follow the conversation. "So you're in awe of me, huh?"

"What woman wouldn't be?" Inciting him with her gentleness, Brooke stroked her hands over his bare shoulders to his biceps. "Look at you."

"I'd rather look at you." Kent kissed her throat. "God woman, you are so hot."

Brooke cupped his face so she could see him. "And you think Beth feels about Levi the way I've always felt about you?"

His muscles tensed and heated. "This is not a good time to talk about my daughter."

Trailing one finger down the center of his chest, Brooke played coy and asked, "Why ever not?"

Kent growled, "Because I have a jones, woman, that's why."

Her gaze dipped down his body and she smiled. "Well my, my, my. I see that you do."

As if that wasn't reason enough, Kent rubbed his nose into the fragrant place between her breasts, whispering roughly, "And because you smell good and taste even better."

Brooke's fingers tunneled into his hair, drawing him closer to her.

Taking that as a sign of her readiness, Kent drew her down to the bed and turned her beneath him. "And because I know Beth can take care of herself."

After a deep breath, Brooke forced her eyes open. "I know you're right. And should she need anything, she does have Ben and Sierra in the hotel with her. It's not like she's alone—"

Kent silenced Brooke with a kiss meant to put her mind on the task at hand. He loved it that she cared so much for his daughter, and vice versa, but there was a time and a place for everything, and right now it was time to love his wife silly.

The second Kent nudged Brooke's legs open so he could settle between them, she gave in to him with familiar enthusiasm.

"That's better," Kent whispered to her. "Much, much better."

Five

Watching Levi sleep proved an interesting pastime for Beth. He looked just as rugged and sexy in slumber as he did awake. Even a serious case of bed head that had his brown hair sticking up at odd angles didn't detract from his masculine impact.

Dark-beard shadow covered his jaw, and a low, even snore half mesmerized her.

Never had Beth been this fascinated watching Brandon sleep. In fact, Brandon had never really fascinated her in any way. Yet looking back, she realized that she'd always been intrigued by Levi, his connection with kids and his easy smiles, his sense of humor and his loyalty to friends.

She'd always liked being with him.

She'd always enjoyed talking to him.

Levi was a man's man, but ladies adored him, too. Only . . . he hadn't had a serious relationship with a woman in all the time she'd known him.

Maybe because of that, she'd never consciously

considered him beyond a sexual fantasy. He hadn't struck her as the marrying kind, not when he seldom saw the same woman more than three times. To Beth, he was the quintessential bachelor—and that, along with his friendship to Brandon, had made him completely off limits for anything other than a very private fantasy.

Yet here she was, by her own volition, in bed with him. And he wanted to marry her, had all but insisted on it.

Out of guilt because he'd enjoyed making love with her? Or maybe out of that profound sense of responsibility, because she had been his best friend's fiancée and they would have eventually married.

Did he offer to marry her because he thought that's what she wanted? Or because he wanted it?

Did he hope to continue making love with her, except without the guilt?

There were too many questions, and not enough answers for Beth to consider marriage. The only thing she knew for certain was that she had it bad.

Unlike her mistaken feelings for Brandon, this was the genuine article. Love with a capital "L." The real McCoy. Everlasting, overshadowing, "till death do us part" love.

Now that she felt it, she knew how shallow and superficial her feelings for Brandon had been. At first, she'd have given anything to do over her wild weekend with Levi. Now she cherished the time she'd had with him. She wanted to do it over, again and again.

But . . . did Levi feel the same?

Her sigh roused him, and he began to stir. Stretching out his limbs while scrunching up his face a lit-tle, Levi flexed all those macho muscles that never failed to make her giddy. His biceps bulged, his ab-domen drew into a tight, sexy six-pack, and a deep rumble came from his chest.

Leaning over him, Beth put a peck on his mouth and whispered, "Good morning, Levi."

He froze in a comical pose. His movements halted, his breath caught. Suddenly his eyes popped open. When he saw her face so close to his, bewilderment darkened his green gaze. Without moving anything but his eyes, he searched the position of her body over him, then the room, and then her face again.

Alert and wary, he murmured, "Good morning."

God, he even *sounded* wonderful to her now-enlightened ears. "You look incredibly sexy in the morning, Levi Masterson."

Keeping his gaze glued to hers, he asked, "I do?"

Beth nodded. "I've been awake for an hour."

His brows pinched in a frown. "You should have nudged me or something."

"No, it's all right." She glanced down his body, but that took her thoughts in a dangerous direction so she quickly took her attention back to his face. "I stayed busy watching you sleep."

A new awareness came over Levi. His gaze grew piercing. "Busy how?"

"Just thinking."

His eyes narrowed. "About?"

Beth hated the watchfulness that tightened his expression. She'd been so unfair to him that he didn't know if he should expect rejection or interest.

She drew a deep breath for courage. "Levi, from now on I want to be as honest with you as I can be."

Relaxing into his pillow, he said, "So you're admitting that you haven't been honest?"

"Not with myself and not with you." Rather than explain that she hadn't misled him on purpose, Beth said, "I'm sorry about that."

"You're forgiven."

Knowing he waited for an answer to his question, Beth gathered her nerve. "Since I woke up and found you asleep, I've been thinking about how nice it was to be this close to you without you pressuring me, or me molesting you."

The corners of his mouth quirked. "You can molest me any time you want, honey. I don't mind at all."

That reply proved a perfect example. "There, you see? Now you're awake, so the pressure starts again."

"It was just a joke, not a suggestion." He encouraged her to continue by saying, "Tell me what else you thought about."

"Everything." Daring and brave in light of her new attitude, Beth stroked a hand over his warm chest. She relished the feel of his crisp body hair, his strong muscles. And looking at his chest instead of into his eyes made it easier to say, "Mostly, I've thought about how foolish I've been."

Annoyance had Levi shoving upright. "Damn it, Beth—"

She threw herself over him, flattening him again. "I *have* been foolish." A finger over his mouth quieted his protests. "In lots of ways, but mostly for thinking myself in love with Brandon."

He bit her finger, and when she yanked it away, he caught her wrist and brought it back for an apologetic kiss that made her tingly.

"You *were* in love with him." Levi held her hand close. "Weren't you?"

She'd always thought so, but now that she could compare her feelings for Brandon with her feelings for Levi, she knew there was no comparison. "I was probably more in love with the idea of being in love with him. If that makes any sense."

Levi began kissing her fingertips one by one. "If you weren't in love with him, I'm glad, but yeah, it makes perfect sense. You're a mature, domestic, caring woman. You wanted to settle down."

"Gawd, I sound like a grandmother."

Taking her seriously, Levi said, "No, not grandmotherly at all. But you're not a partier, either, and you're not a woman who wants to spin her wheels on the dating scene. Like me, you value commitment and security."

"Yes." Beth wished that she'd realized sooner how much they had in common. "I'm trying to come to grips with some truths about myself." She looked at his mouth. "Another truth is that I enjoy you."

"Sexually?"

"Yes, definitely. But I enjoy your company, too."

"You always have."

Why did it sound as if he'd known that forever, when she was just figuring it out? "You're probably right."

Her easy admission had him staring hard at her again.

"Okay," Beth said, "so what are *you* thinking?"

"That I need up." Those words struck Levi funny, and he turned his head on a rough laugh. "Hell, what am I saying? I've been up since I opened my eyes and realized you were still here." He looked back at her. "In bed." His voice lowered. "With me."

"Of course I'm still here." Beth pretended affront. "I told you last night that we'd talk this morning."

"You also told me that you weren't letting me go. But you were half-asleep and I'd just given you an orgasm, so I wasn't sure how much stock to put into those words."

"You thought that maybe after everything we did last night, I'd freak out in the light of day and dodge you again?"

"That worry did keep me awake for a while."

They needed time to iron out all the misunderstandings and come to an agreement, one they could both deal with, Beth decided. "Well, we're here, and we're talking now."

Levi smiled. "And I'm thrilled, I really am. Except that before we get too involved, I'd like to hit the john, brush my teeth, shave—"

"Modesty?" Beth teased. "You want to greet me at your best?"

"You deserve the best."

He said that so seriously that she wanted to confess undying love. But before she did anything like that, she needed to figure out how Levi really felt, and why he wanted to marry her.

"I snuck into the bathroom without waking you." She brushed his mouth with hers in a feather-light kiss. "No morning breath for me."

His thumb skimmed her jaw. "No whiskers, either."

"I like your whiskers, Levi." What an understatement. She loved everything about him. "And your disheveled hair, and the warm, sleepy way you smell . . ." She put her nose to his neck and inhaled.

On a groan, Levi caught her upper arms, lifted

her up and away from him and put her on her back beside him. "Do me a favor, will you, honey? Hold all those tantalizing thoughts while I do a rush job here, okay?"

Beth nodded.

His gaze dipped to her legs, exposed beneath the hem of her pajama top. Thanks to the cold, she'd buttoned up to keep her chest warm, but she hadn't bothered with her bottoms at all.

Levi slowly inhaled before visibly girding himself and, wonderfully naked, he strolled into the bathroom.

Beth watched him until he was out of sight, then she squeezed her eyes shut and hugged herself. Now that she'd accepted her involvement with Levi, things were easier.

And exciting beyond belief.

When she heard the water come on, she jumped out of the bed and called the front desk to request a pot of coffee and a basket of Danishes. Being Ben's stepsister got her priority service, and she barely had time to drag a brush through her hair and pull on her pajama bottoms before the knock sounded on the door.

Looking refreshed and resolute, Levi stuck his head out of the bathroom.

Beth deliberately confused him by grinning. "Unless you want to be seen in your birthday suit, you better duck back into bed."

"Breakfast?"

"Coffee at least."

"You're an angel." And with that, he stepped into jeans and went to the door for her. After signing the charge and slipping a few singles to the bellhop, he turned back to Beth, tray in hand.

Beth patted the bottom of the bed. "Put it here, and we can get comfortable together."

His jaw worked, but he gave in with a shrug. "If you say so."

Beth went about pouring coffee for them both. "I suppose you're wondering about my change in attitude, huh?"

"A little, yeah."

His dry tone made her chuckle. As she handed his coffee to him, she tried to explain. "Well, you know I talked with Grace and Sierra and Brooke last night?"

"Yeah." He took the cup from her and sipped.

"We talked about . . . us. You and me."

"I figured." He took another sip.

"I told them how I felt like a marauding sex fiend with you."

Levi choked. He looked at her, then sputtered and choked again. Quickly, he set the steaming cup of coffee back on the tray and stood.

"Are you all right?" Jumping to her feet, Beth went to the other side of the bed and started to pat his back.

Still coughing, Levi shot to the side to dodge her. "I'm okay," he wheezed.

"Are you sure?" He didn't sound all right.

Holding out a hand, he kept her at bay while he sucked in a few strangled breaths. When normal color returned to his face, he looked at her, put his hands on his hips and opened his mouth.

Beth blinked at him.

He said nothing. His mouth closed. He frowned.

"Did I embarrass you by telling them about us?"

He shook his head, more in confusion than denial. "Sex fiend?"

Maybe she shouldn't have shared that with him. "You have to admit that I'm not really myself with you."

"You're *exactly* yourself."

"I hadn't been that way before."

"Because you hadn't been with me before."

He sounded pretty confident about that. "It's not what I'm used to. It's not how I thought things should be."

"It's how I hope things will always be between us." Shaking his head, Levi said, "Forget what you told your family. I don't want to think about that."

"Not my whole family," Beth corrected. "Just the women."

"Ha." He shook his head again. "They probably made beelines to tell the men. They probably shared stories. Hell, they'll all be grinning at me this morning, you watch and see."

"They wouldn't do that!"

"No, you're right. Ben will probably want to kill me for debauching his little sister."

Beth rolled her eyes. "I'm not really his little sister, just a stepsister, and I seriously doubt that Sierra said anything to him."

"She's his wife. If she doesn't tell him everything, then she should."

Beth scowled. "So you're saying that you think she should have told him?"

Levi held his head. "I think you should have talked to me about this instead of telling them."

Damn it, Beth hated feeling guilt, and Levi had made her feel more guilt in a week than she'd felt in her entire life. "I'm sorry."

"Don't be." He dropped his hands. "We're here talking about it, and that's a big improvement to me chasing you. However we got to this point, I'm grateful." He came back to his seat. "So, you feel like a sex fiend, huh?"

Now he was smiling! Beth cleared her throat. "My point, before you started strangling to death, is that none of the women were surprised."

"You know why? Because what we did was perfectly normal."

"I didn't tell them anything we did."

"No?" He relaxed a little. "Then what did you tell them?"

"That it was more than I'd ever done before, and that it—*you*—made me feel so much more."

Levi absorbed all that before smiling again. "And they told you that was a good thing, right?"

"They told me to own up to my feelings, which is what I'm trying to do." To keep Levi from interrupting further, Beth shoved a cherry Danish toward him. "Now, since we've just established that I enjoy you, and you haven't denied enjoying me, I think we should continue to . . . enjoy each other."

Levi knew if he took a single bite of the Danish, he'd start choking again. He set it aside on one of the small plates that had come with the tray.

So, did Beth want to commit to him? Or just sleep with him?

It was a first, but damn it, he felt used. Insulted. He wanted everything, not just sexual satisfaction.

After a long look at Beth, he went to his overnight bag and withdrew a small wrapped package. "Here."

Rather than take it, Beth stared at the ribbon. "What is it?"

"A Christmas gift." Levi took her hand and

pressed the package into it. "I know it's not Christmas yet, but close enough, so open it."

Excitement twinkled in her eyes. "Okay." Careful not to rip the shiny paper, Beth opened the present. "A CD? Oh, by my favorite artist! I was going to get this next month."

"I know. I heard you mention it. You'd already spent so much on Christmas shopping that something for yourself wasn't in the budget." He went back to his overnight bag and withdrew a larger gift. "Open this one, too."

"But—"

"Just open it, honey. Please."

Happy to oblige, Beth tore through the tissue paper. "The decorating book I mentioned."

He tossed the next present to her, and without argument, she opened it, and then laughed. "Socks?"

"Special socks to keep your feet warm."

"Because I'm always complaining of being cold?"

He nodded. "That's right." Digging deeper into his bag, he withdrew one more gift. "I wrapped this up after."

"After?"

He looked into her beautiful blue eyes and said, "After you were no longer Brandon's. After you were no longer off limits."

Her lips parted. "Levi . . ."

"After you became mine." He handed her a beautifully decorated, slender box.

For long moments, Beth just stared at the package. Finally, with infinite care, she opened the red-velvet ribbon, parted the silky paper, and lifted the lid.

"Oh Levi." In no more than an awed breath of

sound, Beth lifted out the delicate bracelet with a dangling pearl held inside a three dimensional heart-shaped pendant. "This is the exact bracelet that I fell in love with last summer."

Levi crossed his arms over his chest. "I know. We were downtown for a play that Brandon wanted to see, and you stared at it in the jewelry window."

Slowly, Beth brought her gaze from the bracelet up to Levi. "You noticed that?"

"I notice everything about you. I always have. I just didn't let you or Brandon notice me noticing you."

Beth hugged the bracelet to her chest and gave a tremulous smile. "I've always noticed a lot about you, too."

"I know." He crossed the floor to sit beside her on the bed. "Sometimes it worried me, because I didn't want to be the cause of problems with you and Brandon. I kept wondering when the two of you would marry, and I didn't know how the hell I was going to handle it."

"Now you don't have to handle it, because Brandon and I are over and you had nothing to do with it."

Levi took her hands. "You like your gifts?"

"Yes, very much. All of them, but especially the bracelet."

"While you were still engaged to Brandon, I didn't dare give it to you. CDs and books were platonic enough, but jewelry . . ."

"It was so long ago, I'm surprised you were able to get it."

"After seeing you admire it, I bought it the very next day." He shrugged. "You wanted it, so I didn't want anyone else to have it. I'm glad I can finally give it to you."

Beth grinned. "It's so beautiful. Thank you." She reached for him.

He said, "Marry me, Beth."

She went still.

"You admitted to wanting me."

Nervousness replaced her elation. "I do."

"You admitted to liking my company."

"I don't think there's anyone I'd rather spend time with."

"Then marry me. Right now. The sooner the better."

She wavered. Levi could see it in her eyes. She wanted to say yes, but fear of condemnation held her back.

Tentatively, she asked, "Don't you think it's a little too soon for that?"

"Not for me."

"But . . . what will I say to everyone? I was just engaged to Brandon, and then poof—I'm marrying you."

"I don't care what anyone else thinks."

"Well, what about Brandon? Do you care what he thinks? How will he react to you, his best friend, wanting to marry me?"

Levi was about to reply to that when their phone rang. They looked at each other, Beth shrugged, and Levi reached out his arm to snatch up the receiver. "Hello?"

Beth watched him as he listened to the message from the front desk. Knowing she wouldn't like this new turn, but that perhaps it was for the best, he held her gaze.

"Okay, thanks. Tell Ben we'll be right there." Levi hung up the phone. "You're worried about Brandon's reaction? Well, now's our chance to find out what he thinks."

Beth's face went pale. "What do you mean?"

"Brandon's in the lobby, waiting for us."

"Oh no."

"Oh yes. And once again, your whole family is there. Seems they all came over to have breakfast with you. Only now they know that Brandon cheated on you."

"Oh no."

"Better yet, the desk clerk says it looks like Brandon tied one on last night, and he hasn't sobered up yet."

Beth rubbed her forehead. "Dad's reasonable enough. He won't meddle in my business."

"No? Well what about Ben and Noah?"

Beth jumped up from the bed and made a mad dash toward her clothes. "Hurry, Levi. Get dressed."

He narrowed his eyes and watched as she threw off her pajama bottoms and stepped into her jeans. He waited, but she turned her back to him before shrugging off her top and yanking on a sweatshirt.

"Are you so worried about Brandon's welfare?"

While stomping her feet into shoes, Beth scowled at him. "Don't be an idiot. I have no romantic feelings for Brandon anymore. It insults me for you to even suggest otherwise. But that doesn't mean I want someone else trying to punish him."

"You're sure about that?"

Beth stopped dressing long enough to stomp over to Levi, bend down close and snarl into his face, "I know I've been a little wishy-washy here, but don't insult my pride, damn it. Brandon burned his bridges as far as I'm concerned."

"And what about me?"

"I want you." Beth grabbed his ears and kissed him hard. "Only you."

His tension eased. "Okay then." In less than a minute, he'd pulled on a sweatshirt and socks, and tied up his boots. He took Beth by the hand. "Come on."

Before they reached the lobby, Levi could hear Brandon's loud drunken voice. The idiot. He picked one hell of a time to start drinking.

Worse, every word out of his mouth was an insult to Levi.

Looking down at Beth, Levi said, "Given his attitude, I'd say Brandon already knows about us."

"But how?"

"You spent a weekend with me, Beth. Plenty of people could have seen your car there."

She made a face. "Great."

"Did you tell anyone you were coming here?"

"My neighbors, so they would get my mail."

"And they would have told Brandon if he asked. And he would have seen my truck out front." So the cat was out of the bag. "Stay out of sight, honey."

"Why?"

"Because neither of us wants Brandon to say something stupid to you. If he does, your family will maim him."

"Oh, right." Beth stayed around the corner as Levi went into the lobby.

"You miserable bastard!" Brandon staggered toward him. "You fiancée stealing ass. You pretended to be my friend."

Levi stepped in front of Brandon to keep his attention away from Beth. Normally well suited and groomed, Brandon looked like hell warmed over.

Levi felt sorry for him. After all, he'd just given up the very best thing in his life. "I am your friend, Brandon."

"Bullshit!" He almost fell over with that outburst. "You stabbed me in the back."

Levi glanced around and saw the fury gathering among Beth's relatives. "Why don't we take this someplace private?"

"After you just publicly took her from me? Why bother. Let's settle it right here, you traitor. You Benedict Arnold. You—"

"Just calm down, Brandon. Let me explain."

"Explain!" Being drunk didn't suit Brandon at all. "You're not good enough for her and you know it."

Levi stiffened. He could feel everyone looking at him.

"You're a gym teacher, for God's sake." Brandon stuck his nose in the air. "She was going to marry me, a doctor."

His anger sparked. "Until you cheated on her."

"One time! Just that one itty-bitty time." Brandon listed to the left, then caught himself. "It was only a little indiscretion. Marcia isn't anyone important. She didn't mean anything to me."

The females in attendance all grumbled over that.

Hoping to divert the topic, Levi said, "You didn't drive here drunk, did you?"

"Like you care?"

"Did you?"

Brandon hiccupped. "I came down here last night, but the desk clerk refused to tell me which room Beth was in. Then I saw your truck, and I remembered everyone saying that her car was at your place for the whole weekend." He stabbed at finger at Levi. "Then I started drinking."

Damned fool. "Because you thought that would somehow help?"

Brandon's face fell. "Tell me that you didn't touch her. Tell me, Levi."

Levi clenched his jaw, but said nothing.

Brandon howled. "Where is she? I need to talk to her."

"No. Not like this. Not while you're crocked."

"Beth still wants me, I know she does. She deserves a doctor. A man of money. An educated man." He curled his lip at Levi. "She deserves a man who can give her anything she wants."

She deserved love, but Brandon didn't understand that. "She's mine now, Brandon. Accept it."

Screeching like a wet cat and looking just as pathetic, Brandon took a half-hearted swing at Levi's head.

Levi dodged him, and then had to catch him so Brandon didn't land on his face.

Brandon shoved him away, or more to the point, he shoved himself away and into a wall. "What do you mean, she's yours?"

Levi stood over him and gave him the truth. "I'm going to marry her."

Brandon's mouth fell open. "But . . . she loves me!"

"No, she doesn't."

"You're lying. She won't marry you. You barely make a middle-class income. You live in a cracker box, not a real house, not the type of house I was going to buy for her."

"*Shut up.*"

Everyone turned to look at Beth.

Her hands were fisted at her sides and she looked furious.

"Levi has a beautiful house, and a very important job, and he's a good man. An honorable man."

Levi felt the stares intensifying. True, he couldn't afford any of the luxuries that Brandon took for granted, but he knew those things weren't important to Beth.

He knew Beth better than Brandon knew her.

"It's all right, Beth."

"No," she said, "it is not."

Brandon's eyes narrowed with mean intent. "Did you go to bed with him, Beth?" His voice rose to a high pitch. "Did you?"

Levi said, "That's enough, Brandon."

"You did!" Incensed, he took two drunken, wobbly steps toward Beth. "Why you little—"

Levi pulled him back before he got close to her, but Ben and Noah, having seen enough, started forward.

In the awkward position of defending Brandon now, Levi said, "Come on, guys. He's had a hell of a blow."

Noah stared at Brandon. "He's a loud-mouthed idiot and he's causing a scene."

"And he's insulting Beth," Ben added. "Reason enough to toss his ass back outside. He can sober up in the snow."

Just what Levi didn't need: angry relatives. He glanced at Kent, but Beth's father looked ready to take Brandon apart himself. Shit. He could think of better ways to spend this morning.

To Noah and Ben, Levi said, "Back off, I've got it covered." His take-charge tone stalled everyone. "Look, Brandon messed up and he knows it. He lost Beth, and now she's with me. He doesn't usually drink, but you can see that he's so hammered, he doesn't even know what he's saying."

"I know the truth," Brandon slurred while struggling to stay on his feet. "And the truth is that Beth wanted to hurt me, so she crawled into bed with my *supposed* best friend."

On the surface, that was damn close to the mark. Levi leveled a warning look on him. "Shut up, Brandon."

"All this time," Brandon continued, too drunk to show common sense, "she's been pretending to be a goody-two-shoes but she's really no more than a—"

Levi slapped him. Hard.

Brandon's head snapped back, and as if in slow motion, he started to crumble.

Cursing to himself, Levi caught him by the shirt collar to keep him upright. "Drunk or not, Brandon, you won't insult her."

Practically on his knees, Brandon blinked at Levi. "You slapped me."

"Be glad I didn't break your damn nose."

Shrugging free of him, Brandon dropped to sit on his ass. "But you *slapped* me. Like a bitch."

Levi glanced at Beth, saw her reddened face and narrowed eyes, and wanted to choke Brandon for upsetting her. "Until you get over it, I'm sticking you in a room and by God, Brandon, you'll stay there until you're sober enough to make your apologies."

No one got in Levi's way as he more or less hauled Brandon with him to the front desk where a clerk quickly assigned him a room. By the time Levi actually got Brandon into the room, Brandon was dead on his feet. Levi let him fall onto the bed, and Brandon didn't move.

Levi pulled out his cell phone and dialed Beth. She answered on the first ring.

"Levi?"

"Yeah, it's me. You okay?"

"I'm fine. How's Brandon?"

Levi worked his jaw. "Passed out on the bed."

"Good. I hope he wakes up with a killer headache. He deserves it for being such a jerk."

"Look, honey, I want to talk to you. I want to be with you. But I don't dare leave him. If I do, he might end up right back in the thick of things—"

"No, I understand." There was a slight hesitation, and then Beth said, "Thank you, Levi."

"For what?"

"For being you."

She didn't elaborate on that, so Levi asked, "What do you have planned today?"

"Christmas shopping. I have to catch up to you."

He grinned. "Be careful. Think about my proposal."

"Levi."

"I'll see you later on." He hung up before she could say anything more, then looked again at Brandon. It didn't look like he'd be stirring any time soon, so Levi turned on the television.

It was going to be a long, miserable day.

* * *

He fell asleep.

Levi couldn't believe it when he opened his eyes and found the room empty. A glance at the clock showed it was time for dinner.

Damn, damn, damn.

He'd lost sleep the last few days, but that wasn't a good excuse. If Brandon had found Beth and upset her again . . .

Or worse, what if she forgave him? What if she reconsidered her position?

In record time, Levi was out of the room and heading for the diner. He walked in on a crowd of guests and family alike. Servers bustled back and forth. The clink of forks on plates mixed with the drone of multiple conversations. A quick glance around the congested room helped Levi to locate Beth at a far table with her family.

Brandon stood before them.

As Levi cut through the throng toward them, he saw Brandon gesturing, and Beth nodding.

Fury boiled up.

When he was within a few feet of them, he heard Brandon say, "I got spooked every time I thought of settling down forever. I mean . . . forever is a hell of a long time, and I'd spent my whole life working toward a goal. There wasn't time for fun, and finally when there was, everyone expected me to settle into married life."

Levi pulled up short behind him. So far, no one had noticed him. They were all too busy giving Brandon the floor. Somehow, without waking Levi, Brandon had washed and dressed and he looked more like his old stylish self now.

He looked like a very respectable doctor, like Beth's old fiancé.

Beth said, "Go on, Brandon."

"I know that what I did to you is unforgivable."

"Unforgettable, certainly," Beth said. "We can't go back, Brandon."

Stoic and proud, he nodded. "I understand."

"Is that all you have to say?"

"No." He cleared his throat. "No, of course not. I need to apologize for my display earlier, too. I've never before overindulged. It's unfortunate that I did this time."

"Very unfortunate," Kent said.

"From what I remember, which granted, isn't much, I was a total ass."

Ben and Noah nodded—until their wives elbowed them.

Brandon ran a hand through his hair, and then he straightened his shoulders and looked only at Beth.

"I'd like to say, with what little dignity I can muster, that I'm the one who was never good enough for you. In the long run, I'll make more money than Levi, but I don't have half his character, honor, or fortitude. In every way that counts, he's a much better man than me."

Shocked at hearing such a statement, especially when he'd expected Brandon to be schmoozing his way back into Beth's good graces, Levi snorted. "That's bullshit."

Brandon jerked around to face him. Beth and her family looked at him.

Shoving his hands into his pockets, Brandon said, "No, it's true, Levi. You've propped me up so damn many times I've lost count. But you've never needed propping. Not once."

"Levi is a rock," Beth said with a smile, and Brandon nodded.

"You've had your difficulties, Levi, but you always work through them." He pulled his hands from his pockets and held them out in a conciliatory way. "Not to get sappy, but I admire and respect you more than any man I know. If I have to lose Beth—"

Levi took a step forward. "You have to."

Noah and Ben chuckled at that.

"—then I'm glad I'm losing her to you. The one thing I remember saying that was true, is that she deserves the best." Brandon nodded. "That would be you."

Ben cursed, and when everyone looked at him, he shook his head. "I really wanted to hate the guy, you know? But I think his reasoning is starting to make sense to me."

Both Brandon and Levi grinned.

Turning back to Beth, Brandon said, "I think I knew all along that we weren't really meant to be. But you're a special woman, and even if I wasn't the right man, I hated to lose you."

"Too late," Levi said.

Brandon smiled, and turned back to Levi. "I concede the loss. And if you'll have me, that is, if Beth doesn't mind, I'd still like to be your best friend."

When Levi looked at Beth, she nodded.

He held out a hand to Brandon. "Still friends."

Brandon accepted the handshake with huge relief. "Not to push my luck, but I'd be honored to be the best man."

Levi grinned. "Your friends won't have a clue what to think."

"Yeah," Brandon agreed, a little sad, a little amused, and happy for them. "But who cares?"

Beth said, "Now wait a minute."

Levi cut her off, saying to one and all, "She's still resisting the idea of marrying me. But I love her enough that I won't give up."

Beth's mouth fell open. "What did you say?"

Levi cocked a brow. "I'm not giving up."

"No," she gasped out, "the other part. About loving me."

He shrugged. "I love you. But you already knew that."

She shook her head. "No. I knew you wanted to marry me. But I wasn't sure why—"

Rolling his eyes, Levi said, "Maybe it's time for us to have that long talk." He took Beth's hand and pulled her from her seat. To her family, he said, "Excuse us."

As Levi turned them away, Brandon dropped into her seat. Levi heard him say, "I know I don't deserve it, but I would sure love a cup of coffee."

Grinning, Levi tugged Beth through the mob of diners, out of the dining room, and down the hallway until he reached the privacy of their room.

Beth pulled back. "What are you doing?"

After unlocking the door, Levi urged her inside. "I'm going to convince you how much I love you."

Beth closed the door herself, and then licked her lips. Levi saw the start of a smile.

"How much?" she asked.

He cupped her face and held her still. "More than anything else in the whole world."

"Okay." She gave in to her smile. "Since when?"

"Since forever. Since I first met you."

"So even though we only got together because I offered myself to you—"

Levi shook his head in disbelief. "Think about it. Would I have run the risk of ruining a fifteen-year friendship just for a piece of ass?"

She started to chuckle. "Um—"

"And remember," Levi said, "at the time, I didn't even know what a hot piece you'd be."

"Levi!"

He laughed, too, knowing by the glow in her face and the love in her eyes that he'd won. "I did know, however, that you were smart and sweet and kind and caring and dependable and loyal—"

"Levi?"

"Yes?"

"I love you, too."

Finally, she admitted it. "I know."

Beth laughed. "And I'll marry you."

He slumped against her. " 'Bout damn time, woman."

Beth threw her arms around him. "I guess I get my do-over after all."

"Your do-over?"

"A chance to change the things I did wrong." She kissed him. "At first I wanted a chance to do over that weekend with you."

Levi frowned at her.

"But now I know that I get to do over a real mistake."

He crowded her back against the door. "Your engagement to the wrong man?"

"Yes.

He cupped her chin and turned her face up to his. "And marriage to the right man?"

She nodded. "Thank you, Levi, for the very best Christmas present ever."

It's a
Wonderful
Life

Karen Kelley

One

Jeremy Hunter yanked his pillow over his head, but the incessant ringing didn't stop. God, every buzz was like someone zapping his brain with an electrical current.

Damn, what did he drink last night?

He vaguely remembered a party, alcohol—lots of alcohol—a taxi ride home, and some chick name Cecily. Correction, not a chick. Cecily had been all woman, all curves, and all consuming.

That is, if the alcohol he'd drunk hadn't fogged his brain.

The ringing stopped. Good.

The pounding began.

Followed by a soft moan. "I think someone's at your door," a feminine voice softly slurred beside him.

He tossed the pillow off the bed and rose on one elbow. Dark blonde hair obscured most of her face except for full pouty lips. His gaze moved lower. Her other attributes were very nice, too . . . until she pulled the cover up, pushed the hair out of her eyes, and met his gaze.

"Cecily?"

"Andrea." She yawned. "Would you mind letting the person at the door inside? I've got a terrible headache."

He frowned as he dragged himself out of bed, wondering what had become of Cecily.

The pounding grew louder.

The clothes he'd worn last night weren't in sight. Nothing. Not even one sock on the floor. First Cecily and now his clothes. It was a conspiracy. He finally grabbed a towel off the back of a chair, slung it around his hips, and knotted it.

As he walked through the living room of his apartment, he glanced at the clock on the wall. Ten. Who the hell hammered on his door at this time of the morning? They'd better have a damn good reason.

He jerked the door open. "Yeah?"

Monty, his agent, stood on the other side of the threshold. Short, bald, and unassuming Monty. Most people in the business knew not to underestimate him. The ones who did soon learned their mistake. Right now, he didn't look happy. What was new?

"Is this how you usually open the door? Practically naked."

"No, I thought I would grab a towel and show you a little respect. Respect—you do know the meaning of the word? It's a hell of a lot more than you're giving me. You know I don't get up before noon."

"I brought you the morning tabloid. I thought you might enjoy reading it since you're the cover story—again."

"Coffee first." He turned and walked toward the kitchen.

"I'll fix the coffee, you get dressed."

He nodded and made his way back to his room. He needed time to get his head on straight, anyway. It must be bad for Monty to come over first thing. Damn, what had he done now? Or should he ask himself what *hadn't* he done?

He was so sick of his life being an open book. Didn't reporters have anything better to do than hound his every move? Apparently not.

He grabbed a pair of jeans, slipped his feet into loafers and washed his face before pulling on a shirt. The coffee was ready when he returned to the galley kitchen, the rich aroma wafting up to him. He poured a cup. Monty followed him to the living room without saying a word.

There was a lump on his couch. A sheet covered lump. He nudged it. One corner of the sheet moved. Red hair and a face appeared.

"Cecily?"

Even her smile looked hungover. "You were great last night." She belched and pulled the sheet back over her head.

At least he was great. He looked up and caught Monty's look of disapproval, then headed for the patio. He hoped there wasn't another female sleeping it off on one of the lounge chairs.

Monty hadn't said another word.

Not good.

He slid the glass door open and stepped outside into the California sun and the sharp December bite in the air. Good, maybe it would help clear his mind.

He pulled out a chair at the table and sat. Monty

took the one opposite him, tossing the tabloid on the table. He glanced at it without picking it up. A dark grainy picture of himself . . . and Cecily, stared back.

"They caught my bad side again," he said.

"They're thinking of using DiCaprio for the lead."

His jaw twitched. He slowly raised his cup and took a drink. "I thought it was a done deal."

"Not after last night. The studio exec called me this morning. The big guy is royally pissed. He wants a cleaner image to play the lead. Damn it, Jeremy, this is supposed to be a Christmas picture. He wants it to have meaning."

"And?" He could feel the blood coursing through his veins, the pounding of his heart. Everything around him seemed to move in slow motion. Outwardly, he knew nothing showed. The benefits of being one of the highest paid actors in the business.

"How the hell do you think you can pull off the part of a traveling preacher if you're out whoring and drinking all night?" he countered.

"Because I'm damn good at what I do."

Monty shook his head. "Not this time. And if you haven't noticed, your ratings are dropping. You shot up quick enough, but now you're spiraling downward like a bottle rocket on the fourth of July, and it's only a matter of time before your light fizzles." He shook his head. "You haven't even researched this part. You're a playboy. You'll never pull it off." His laugh was bitter.

Jeremy abruptly stood, his chair scraping along the tiles. He walked to the edge of the balcony, lost in his thoughts. What did they expect when the only roles he got were fluff? He was only acting the part.

He gripped the rail until his knuckles turned white. They said he was the wild child of the cinema but they had created him.

And he'd let them.

He closed his eyes, breathing in the pure salt air. When he opened them, he stared at the magnificence before him. There was something powerful about the waves as they crashed against the rocks, white spray shooting upward.

There was a time in his life when he would've sold his soul to the devil for all this. Maybe that's what had happened. The devil was calling in his marker.

This was the role of a lifetime. He'd known it as soon as he'd read the script. It had raw substance, something he could sink his teeth into, unlike the parts he'd played up until now.

He wanted it and he was willing to go to any length to get it. "What do I have to do?"

"I'm not sure you can do anything."

Jeremy turned. "Then why am I paying you?"

Monty hesitated. "There is one thing the executive said would save your ass, but you're not going to like it."

"I'll do it."

"Even if it means going incognito?" He waved his arm, encompassing his surroundings. "Leaving all this and living the part. Changing your looks. Becoming the character, becoming Trey Jones."

"That's crazy. How the hell can I pretend to be a preacher? And the press will find out."

"We'll put out a release that you've gone to the south of France to study for your upcoming part."

"People won't buy that I'm a traveling preacher."

"How can you sell it on the screen if you can't

fool a few people in the public?" He shrugged. "I wouldn't blame you if you turned it down. Pretending to be a traveling man of the gospel would be a stretch. A long one. You asked, I told you, and that's why you pay me."

Monty looked pointedly toward the patio doors, toward where Cecily was sleeping on the other side. Jeremy crammed his hands into the pockets of his jeans. His gaze fell to the terra-cotta tiles, the brown-grout lines.

"They did offer you the role of the brother," Monty mentioned.

His head jerked up. "Supporting actor? I don't think so." Monty was good at pushing all the right buttons. "When do I leave?"

Bailey tossed back the rest of her drink. This was the fix she needed.

"Want a refill?" Kathy asked.

She had to think about it. She was already at her limit.

"I'll make it a triple," Kathy added temptingly.

"You're killing me. Besides, I really need to get home." Bailey couldn't help eyeing the tubs of ice cream, though. No, one double chocolate raspberry swirl malt was all the indulgent calories she needed this week—shoot, this month.

As if that was going to happen. Her mother had already started her Christmas baking. Pure torture. But the malt had been sooo good and she'd really needed a chocolate fix.

Being a fourth-grade teacher was not easy sometimes. Why hadn't she chosen something less taxing?

Like brain surgeon, astronaut, tightrope walker, sky-diver . . .

But school was out for the next two weeks! She loved Christmas vacation.

The roar of a motorcycle caught her attention, drawing her back to the present. She swiveled her stool toward the door as the man on the cycle pulled under the awning of the burger shop.

"Someone passing through," Kathy mumbled. "I don't know anyone in Two Creeks with a cycle be-sides my brother."

"Not just any cycle. That's a Harley." A big black Harley. She sighed. There was just something about a motorcycle that made her want to straddle the leather seat and feel all that power nestled be-tween her legs.

When she'd only mentioned that she'd like to have a motorcycle, her brother almost had a coro-nary. Her sister-in-law had liked the idea. But Wade had raised such a fuss that she'd given in and bought a cute little sports car instead. Man, could it corner. Not that she'd tell her brother.

But this bike was sweet. The guy getting off it wasn't bad either. She couldn't see his face very well because of the dark sunglasses and helmet he wore. But the black-leather pants and jacket were sinfully sexy. The bad girl inside her emerged thinking all kinds of naughty thoughts.

Man, she really must be bored. It was just like she'd told the people of Two Creeks at the last com-munity meeting; they needed to bring in new busi-ness and more people or the town was going to die.

Point in fact, she was lusting over the stranger and he was probably ugly as sin . . .

He removed his helmet and placed it on the back of his bike, then combed his fingers through thick black hair. When he turned around, she got the full effect of him. At least six foot two inches of pure male testosterone at it's finest.

Her breath caught in her throat. Everything about him was dark: his tan, the stubble of beard . . . his eyes. He was hell on wheels and Bailey knew she'd burn for the kind of thoughts she was having. Oh, baby, she could already feel the heat.

"Nice package," Kathy choked out.

"You're engaged."

"Am I? To who?"

"It's whom and his name is Chad, remember him?"

She sighed. "Vaguely."

They looked at each other and chuckled.

"Looks like the eye candy is hungry. I'd love to be his next meal. Maybe I have enough time to scribble my name on the menu. TODAY'S SPECIAL: KATHY . . . NO CHARGE"

"Shh," she whispered. "Just act natural."

"Then you think throwing myself at his feet would be a little too much?"

Bailey smothered a laugh. "Be good, and get me a soda—diet."

"I thought you had to get home?"

She stuck her tongue out but quickly straightened in her seat as the bell jingled over the door. She didn't look toward it. She didn't have to. Bailey felt him. Her body tingled with awareness. It was a sin for a man to look that damn sexy.

Out of the corner of her eye, she saw him slide onto a stool. There were only two between them.

"What's good?" he asked, words raspy, rough.

She quickly took a drink of the soda Kathy handed her, hoping the cold drink would cool her down. Didn't work, darn it.

Kathy leaned against the counter. "I make a mean burger—best in town."

Bailey swiveled slightly in her seat and studied him, then frowned. He looked familiar. Why did he look familiar? Had she dreamed about him? Maybe he was her soul mate.

If she believed in that sort of thing—and she didn't. But still . . .

"You remind me of someone . . ." Her brow furrowed.

He looked right at her and she almost had an orgasm. His intense gaze stripped her clothes away as it meandered over her body. Her nipples tightened. Oh, man, he started an ache deep inside her. She needed a fire extinguisher!

"Jeremy Hunter?" he supplied. "I hear that a lot."

"Huh?"

He grinned, as if he knew exactly the effect he had on her. "People tell me I look like Jeremy Hunter, the actor."

She mentally shook her head to clear it, not sure exactly what had passed between them. Yeah right, she knew exactly what had happened. Testosterone had crashed into estrogen and there'd been a sexual explosion.

She drew in a deep breath. "Except he has blue eyes and brown hair." She studied him—which wasn't hard at all. "And you have a thin scar down the side of your face."

"And the fact I'm not an actor," he said.

She really liked the sound of his voice. Listening

to him talk was better than drinking a triple chocolate raspberry swirl.

"You could be." Kathy blushed. "I mean, you look like one."

"Except I'm not."

"So what do you do?" Bailey knew she was crossing the line from friendly to nosy but she couldn't help herself. She was curious. Male stripper? Yum, she could envision him slowly peeling off his clothes and . . .

"I'm a preacher."

Bailey had the straw in her mouth but rather than sucking, she blew in it. Her drink became Old Faithful as it bubbled over the top.

She quickly set it on the counter and looked at the biker. "You've got to be freakin' kidding me."

She'd been lusting after a preacher! Oh God, she was going to hell for sure.

She grimaced. Had she just said freakin'? This was so not her day.

Two

Jeremy looked at the woman sitting next to him. He'd been watching her since he'd walked inside the burger joint. He definitely liked what he saw: straight blonde hair that brushed her shoulders and tight-fitting jeans—a deadly combination in any man's book and he was no exception. He briefly wondered how long it would take him to get her undressed and into his bed.

His sigh of regret was long and deep.

A damn shame that wouldn't happen. He was playing a part. He was Trey Jones, preacher, and he had all the papers to prove it. Monty had made sure of that. The playboy was dead and buried—at least for a while.

Damn, this was going to be harder than he'd imagined. Good thing he only planned to stay long enough to grab a bite to eat. Temptation would be a distant memory by this afternoon.

But he couldn't help smiling. He didn't think she'd expected him to say he was a preacher.

"You okay?" he asked when she took another drink and choked. "Do you need saving?" He swiveled his stool around until he faced her, his gaze drifting over her. She filled out her clothes very nicely.

"I'm fine," she managed to answer after she caught her breath. "But yeah, after the thoughts I was having I probably do need saving," she mumbled.

No more than the ones I was having, he thought to himself, but kept a look of innocence plastered on his face.

The waitress quickly mopped up the spilled drink with a towel. "I'll get that burger started, Father . . ." She frowned. "Pastor . . . uh . . ."

"Trey is fine." The waitress was cute with auburn curls bouncing all over her head as if she'd stuck her finger in a light socket or something.

She sighed with relief. "Good. Father just kind of sticks to the roof of my mouth."

He chuckled. "Yeah, people don't really expect me to tell them I'm a man of God."

"You're not Catholic, are you?" the waitress asked.

He shook his head. "Why?"

"It would be a sin if you didn't procreate." She shook her head and walked toward the back.

"That's Kathy," the blonde quickly spoke up as if she could cover what the waitress had said.

He turned his attention back to her and watched as she blushed. How long had it been since he'd seen a woman embarrassed?

No, the women he knew played hard and fast. They were out for a good time, maybe a little publicity if they were trying to claw their way to the top of the movie industry, which was fine with him. He didn't have any desire for long-term relationships.

But she was cute and sexy and looked hot in a pair of tight hip-hugging jeans and a little blue T-shirt that clung to her curves. His gaze rose to meet hers. "You know my name, what's yours?"

"Bailey . . . Bailey Tanner."

"And what does Bailey Tanner do?"

"I'm a fourth grade school teacher."

Ouch.

It was worse than he'd thought. Sweet *and* pure. She was off limits, but damned if he didn't want to test the waters. There was just something about her that made him want to linger.

Another reason to get out of town as fast as he could. She lived in little Two Creeks, Texas, where they probably still believed in right and wrong. He didn't play by the rules. Hell, he didn't even know what the rules were and for that matter, didn't really care.

"Here you go." Kathy set the burger down in front of him. "What do want to drink?"

"Cola is fine."

She nodded and got his drink.

He bit into the burger. She was right. Best burger he'd ever eaten. He'd almost finished before looking up. "It's dam . . ." He coughed. ". . . darn good."

Kathy smiled. "That's because we raise our own beef."

He looked at his burger. He was eating Bossy. Yeah, now he felt a hell of a lot better.

He washed down what he'd eaten and stood, fishing some bills out of his pocket. "You ladies have a nice day." He nodded, then headed for the door.

Monty said he couldn't pull it off but everywhere he'd gone, people had believed he was a preacher. He was ready to get back home. A week on the road was enough research for anyone.

But as he stepped out the door, he had to take one last look at Bailey Tanner. Another time, another place, and he would've shown her what being a woman was all about.

She winked.

Not a quick good-bye wink. No, her wink was slow and sexy. Definitely an invitation wink. A burst of heat rushed through him. If a wink could do that much damage then what . . .

He missed the last step, grabbed for the door but he'd already let go. His foot twisted as he tried to stop his fall. The tendons and ligaments stretched, there was a pop and burning pain shot up his leg. He hit the ground with a hard thud.

God was punishing him. Maybe this was one role he wasn't meant to play.

Bailey ran out the door. "Are you okay?" she asked as she knelt beside him.

"My foot. I think it might be broken.

"I called an ambulance," Kathy said as she ran out the door a few seconds later. "Are you okay?"

"He might have broken his foot," Bailey nibbled her bottom lip.

"I'll get an ice pack," Kathy said and ran back inside.

Sirens blared in the background.

This wasn't happening. How was he going to get home? He closed his eyes. Oh, yeah, he was definitely paying for his sins.

"Did you hit your head?" Bailey asked.

"Did you wink at me?" he countered.

"Uh . . . no. I had something in my eye."

She was lying. Wasn't she? He wasn't positive. The only thing he knew for sure was the fact she was beautiful, and his foot hurt like a son of a bitch.

But she was certainly sweet temptation.

A spark of conscience flared inside him. Bailey was off limits. She probably believed in the little house with a picket fence, a couple of cute kids, and a husband with a regular job who actually came home at night. But it was nice that she seemed to care.

He mentally shook his head to clear it. She was probably afraid he'd sue her because she'd winked and caused him to miss his step. Yeah, she was lying. Bailey had winked. She looked too guilty.

Crap, he hadn't planned on this snag. How the hell was he going to shift the gears on his motorcycle with a bum foot?

Just looking at Trey as he lay on an emergency-room cot was enough of a guilt trip for Bailey. If a hole opened up, she'd crawl into it, and never look back. She'd lied. She really hated lying.

She drew in a deep breath. "I'm sorry I . . . uh . . . winked at you," she apologized. Had she ever been more mortified? Probably, but this time was different. Her actions had caused someone to get hurt.

"So you didn't have something in your eye?"

She shook her head.

Janet, the ER nurse, had already taken his vitals and left the room. Thank goodness, they were all normal or she would've felt horrible. Not that she thought she could feel any worse than she did right now.

"I should've been paying more attention," he said.

Oh, no, he was being nice and taking some of the guilt. She'd been wrong. She could feel worse.

"It's Saturday," a loud voice boomed.

Bailey bit her lip. The doctor was here.

"Everyone knows that's the day I go fishing," Dr. Canton's voice bellowed at the nurses' station. "We need more doctors. Maybe then I could get a blasted day off."

"Please tell me that's not the doctor who'll be seeing me."

She smiled, relaxing for the first time since Trey's accident. "His bark is much worse than his bite."

"That makes me feel loads better." His mouth turned down into a very attractive frown.

"He really is good."

She turned toward the door as Dr. Canton came in. The old doctor stopped in the doorway, removed his glasses and held them up to the light. He pulled a white handkerchief out of his back pocket and cleaned the lenses as he walked the rest of the way into the room.

He stuck his handkerchief back in his pocket and his glasses back onto his face and stood there looking at Trey. "Well, you gonna tell me what's wrong or do you want to play twenty questions?"

Bailey bit back a laugh, clamping her lips together.

Trey frowned. "Since you're the doctor, I thought you would tell me."

"I'm a doctor, not God."

"I fell. I think my foot's broken."

"You're a doctor?" Dr. Canton asked.

"No."

"Then how the hell do you know it's broken?"

This wasn't going at all well. "He's a preacher, Dr. Canton."

He looked at Trey over the top of his glasses. "You don't look like a preacher. Never saw one wearing leather pants, leastways."

The doctor's gaze turned on her. She almost started fidgeting but held her stance.

"You know him?"

"I was there when he fell."

"Janet," he yelled.

"I can hear you, you don't have to holler," she said as she came to the door.

"We need an x-ray."

"I've already called and the tech's on her way in."

He nodded. Janet left.

"Good nurse but kind of sassy."

"I heard that."

A grin started to form but Dr. Canton quickly quelled it before it got out of control and became a full-fledged smile.

Over the next hour and a half they x-rayed Trey's foot, then wrapped it and measured him for a pair of crutches. Bailey thanked her lucky stars it was only a bad sprain. At least she didn't have to live with the guilt that she'd caused him to break his foot.

"You traveling by yourself?" Doc asked.

"He has a motorcycle," Bailey quickly told him.

"His ankle's sprained, not his tongue." He looked at Trey. "You won't be riding it for a while. You got a place to stay for about a week or so?"

"He can stay with me." When both men looked at her, she felt the heat climb up her face. How did she manage to find herself in these situations?

"In the guesthouse," she clarified, then looked at Trey. "It's not much. Just one room and a small bathroom. It's behind my house but you're welcome to stay until your foot is better."

"Thanks," Trey told her, looking surprised she'd even offer.

It was the least she could do to make up for the fact she'd caused his accident. Besides, he was a preacher. What could possibly happen?

Three

He could remember the phony name. Hell, he even thought of himself as Trey, but as he looked around the one room guesthouse, then at Bailey . . . well, it was difficult remembering he was Trey the preacher.

"Is there anything you need?" she asked after lighting the gas heater.

"Yeah, a drink."

"I beg your pardon?"

"Of water," he lied, then reached up and rubbed his throat with a grimace. "Throat's parched. I guess from the pain pill the doctor gave me."

No, this wasn't as easy as when he told someone he was a preacher then roared out of town on his bike. Now he had to actually act the part.

Okay, how hard could it be? This is what he got paid to do.

Bailey went to the cabinet and reached up. When she stretched, her shirt rode up in the back a few inches showing pale, smooth skin. She filled the glass half-full and brought it to him. There was just a little bit of natural sway in her hips.

Maybe not so easy.

"Here you go," she said as she handed him the glass.

He dutifully took a drink. Vodka, it wasn't. Hell, he'd bet it wasn't even filtered.

"I can't believe I'm letting you stand around leaning on a pair of crutches," she said. "There are clean sheets in the closet. I'm just sorry the place is so small."

He inhaled the clean fragrance of soap and herbal shampoo as she wiggled around him. He wasn't at all sorry. "Beggars can't be choosers."

She grabbed sheets and began to make the bed. All that twisting and turning . . . damn, talk about dying a slow death. He was beginning to think this part just wasn't worth it. She bent at the waist, her sweet ass sticking up in the air and twisting left then right as she tucked in the corners.

"That should do it," she said as she pulled back the sheet, then straightened and glanced his way.

She bit her bottom lip, looking anxious. He didn't know what her problem was but he knew his. The only thing on his mind was pulling her into his arms and kissing her luscious lips. How much torture could one man be expected to take?

"You don't look at all well." She shook her head. "You're pale and sweaty. You'd better lie down. Heaven help us if you pass out." Her teeth tugged at her lip again. "That wasn't like . . . irreverent or anything was it? I didn't mean anything when I said heaven help us. It was just . . ."

He touched her arm, wanting to reassure her, but got lost in the warmth and softness of her skin.

What it would be like to kiss her. He didn't think she'd resist. He could see the need in her eyes.

Most of his roles on screen had been acting the part of the playboy. He had all the moves down pat. He knew what to say, what to do so a woman was all too willing to crawl between his sheets.

But that wasn't the part he was playing now.

He drew in a deep breath and let go of her arm as he crossed the small space, propped the crutches against the wall and sat on the side of the bed.

"God knows exactly what you meant . . . my child."

"Oh . . . uh . . . good. I'll let you rest while I take care of a few things at the house." She left the guesthouse in a hurry.

He stretched out on the bed. Ending with "my child" had been a good touch. It sounded very godly. He grinned until he turned and bumped his injured foot.

"Crap! Shit! Damn . . ." He quickly glanced out the window beside the bed, breathing a sigh of relief. Bailey was just closing the backdoor. Okay, so he needed to work a little more on this character.

He reached into his pocket for his cell phone and speed dialed Monty. His agent picked up on the second ring.

"I thought you were going to check in yesterday?"

"Hello to you, too. Don't tell me you care."

"Of course I care. I get fifteen percent of everything you make."

Trey grinned. He knew better. Monty had been with him almost from the beginning, encouraging him, chewing his butt when he screwed up, picking him up when he fell, being more of a father than his own had ever been. Yeah, he knew better.

"You coming in tonight?"

"Not exactly. I've had an accident . . ."

"Son of a bitch! I told you that motorcycle was a bad idea . . ."

"It wasn't that kind of an accident. I missed a step and twisted my ankle. I'm in Two Creeks, Texas."

"Do you want me to send a limo? I'm sure there's a company in the closest big town. They could probably have you at an airport in a few hours."

He looked toward Bailey's house and could see her moving around inside. Something bothered him but he couldn't put his finger on it. He wanted to find out what it was.

"No, I think I'm going to stay here a few days. It'll give me a chance to see if I can handle the role of preacher for longer than a few hours."

"What's the name of the hotel?"

He paused. "I'm staying in a guesthouse."

"Female?"

He frowned. His agent should give him a little credit. "It's not like that."

Monty chuckled. "If you can pull this off without taking her to bed then you'll be able to play the part, but I'm not going to place any bets."

"I'll do it. I've never let a woman get in the way when it comes to my acting and I'm not about to start. This is business."

"Call me if you change your mind and want me to send a car."

"Yeah." He closed his phone and laid it on the bedside table. Monty had no confidence in him. On this, he was wrong. There was nothing in life that he wanted more than this role.

He closed his eyes as the pain pill the doctor had given him, and days of getting less sleep than he was used to, began to take their toll. He was so friggin' tired, but as sleep began to envelop him in her embrace it was another's arms going around him that filled his mind.

Bailey grabbed the ringing phone. "Yes," she said breathlessly.

"What's going on? I heard you brought some man home with you. Is he there now? Why do you sound out of breath?" Wade asked.

Her brother. She should've known. She shook her head and took a deep breath. "Nothing. I did. No. Because I couldn't find the phone."

"Huh?"

She chuckled. Bailey loved her brother but he really had to remember she was a grown woman. He also believed the cliché that a fourth grade school teacher couldn't possibly have any sexual drive let alone a fantasy or two.

Just mentioning her name and sex in the same sentence always gave him the shakes. She sighed. If he only knew, but she didn't want to cause him to have a heart attack so she kept silent.

"Did you or didn't you?"

"What? Bring a man home? Yes, I did."

"What the hell were you thinking?"

"He's a preacher."

Silence.

"Catholic?"

"No."

"Then it's not okay. Kick him out."

"I will not."

"Do Mom and Dad know?"

"Is that a threat?" Her frown deepened. "I'll have you know Mom and Dad trust me, which is a hell of a lot more than you do. I'm over twenty-one in case you haven't noticed, and if I wanted to sleep with someone, I would." She drew in a deep breath. "And what makes you so pure as the driven snow? Don't even try to tell me you didn't sleep with Fallon before you were married. The twins' birthdays don't lie."

"That's different . . ."

"Are you badgering your little sister again?" Fallon's voice could be heard in the background.

"She has a man staying at her house," Wade said.

"The guesthouse," Bailey clarified.

"Give me the phone," Fallon said. "Hey, Bailey, you finally gettin' a little action?"

Bailey could hear Wade choking.

"Go check on the girls," Fallon told him. "All clear," she said into the phone after a few seconds. "Can you even imagine what he'll be like when the girls reach their teens?"

Bailey laughed. "No."

She really liked her sister-in-law. She was an undercover CIA operative until Wade stole her heart. They'd needed each other.

"Give me the scoop on this guy."

Bailey quickly filled in the details, even the part about her winking and causing the accident.

"Is he cute?" Fallon asked.

"Cute doesn't even begin to describe him." She squeezed her arms around her middle. Boy did it not describe him! "He looks like Jeremy Hunter except for the color of his eyes and his hair is darker. Oh, and he has a scar down the side of his face but it only makes him look dangerous. *And* he rode up on a bad ass Harley and he was wearing black leather. How damned sexy is that?" Her pulse sped up remembering his arrival at the burger place.

"What does he think about you?"

She sighed. "Probably nothing. He's a preacher. It really should be a sin that a man of God could cause such impure thoughts."

"Is he breathing?"

Her brow creased, wondering exactly what Fallon was getting at. "God, I hope so since he's in my guesthouse."

"He's a man, he's breathing, then believe me, he's had a few thoughts about you."

She looked toward the guesthouse. *Had* he thought about her? Interesting. But the man was still a preacher. He wouldn't . . . did preachers really think about . . . of course they would, but Trey probably didn't think about hot sweaty down and dirty sex like she'd been thinking about hot sweaty down and dirty sex since she first laid eyes on him. His thoughts were probably pure. Chaste kisses, sex after marriage, lights off and all that. She sighed. What a waste.

"Wade is yelling," Fallon said, breaking into her thoughts. "I'd better check to make sure the girls are okay. Talk to you later. Oh, and don't forget practice tomorrow. Bring your preacher. It is a Christmas play, after all. He can make sure we get it right. Lord knows I'm not much on accuracy and all that. Gotta run."

"Bye." But Fallon had already hung up. Bailey replaced the phone but didn't move as she stared out the window. Her body tingled just thinking about Trey and what it would feel like to have him pull her close. She was so bad for even thinking like that.

She just had to keep repeating to herself that the man probably never thought about sex. A man of God would be more interested in bible stuff. Oh, but if he wasn't a preacher . . .

Chicken soup. That's what she should think about. Her mother's cure all. Not that she thought it would heal his ankle, but taking him a bowl of soup and a sandwich would be a good excuse to see him again.

Besides, she needed to get his keys so Kathy's brother could bring Trey's Harley over and park it at the house. She didn't like the thought of leaving it at the burger shop all night.

Maybe it would give her a chance to discover just how far a preacher would go.

She closed her eyes and thought about Trey pulling her into his arms, holding her close, his lips pressed against hers. She could feel the heat of his body, his hands caressing her.

No, no, no. She couldn't seduce the preacher. It was almost Christmas and she needed to be good. Though, seducing him might just be worth giving up a few presents.

Four

Trey opened his eyes and yawned. He must've dozed. There was a tapping on the door. Ah, that's what woke him. He blinked several times as he tried to clear the fog from his brain.

What was he doing in a strange bed? He moved and bumped his foot, gritting his teeth when pain shot up his leg. His memory immediately returned. Oh, yeah, he was a preacher and he'd sprained his ankle.

Ahh, but the dream he'd been having was anything but spiritual. He glanced down. And it showed. He dragged the blanket over his nakedness, bunching it up so that nothing of importance showed, then grabbed his T-shirt and pulled it over his head before calling out, "Come in."

The door opened and Bailey came inside, balancing a tray that contained a bowl of what looked like broth with floaties, a glass of milk—milk? ugh—and crackers. She carefully set everything down on a small table, then smiled at him.

Ah, that smile. Fresh, innocent . . .

"I thought you might be getting hungry."

He snapped back to the present. Dinner? It hadn't been that long since lunch. He glanced at the clock on the wall. He'd been asleep four hours. Wow, that was some pain pill. His stomach growled to let him know exactly how long it'd been since the burger.

"I guess I slept for a while," he said.

"That's okay. You needed to rest." She went to the closet and brought out a TV tray, setting it up beside the bed, then moved the tray over. "It's not much. Chicken soup and crackers. I was going to make you a sandwich but I didn't have any bread."

He didn't even want to think about Bailey and getting bred. He had to keep telling himself she was a fourth grade school teacher. Fourth grade school teachers didn't think about sex. At least, he was pretty sure they didn't.

He glanced at the bowl of yellow liquid. Noodles, those were the floaties. Five-star restaurant it wasn't, but he didn't tell her that. "It looks good." He swallowed past the lump in his throat. Chicken soup? A nice juicy steak sounded a lot better.

She waited.

Okay, he'd take a few bites. He tugged the cover around him and moved slowly until he was sitting on the side of the bed. He reached for the spoon but at the last second remembered the part he was playing and closed his eyes.

"Thank you Lord for this meal I'm about to eat, and bless the wonderful woman who prepared it."

He peeked and saw that Bailey had her eyes closed, head lowered, and her hands clasped respectively in front of her. Playing a preacher was a piece of cake.

"Amen."

"Amen," she murmured. Her eyes widened. "Oh, I almost forgot. Kathy's brother will bring your Harley to the house if you don't mind him driving it. He's very responsible and has a motorcycle of his own—although it's not a Harley."

His Harley! He loved his bike. No one drove it. He wasn't about to let some country hick . . .

She waited patiently.

He drew in a deep breath. "How very kind. I'll say a prayer for her brother."

She smiled. "I'll just need your keys."

"They're in my pants pocket."

"Oh, you don't have your pants on? Of course you don't." Her laugh was more like a choking cough. "I don't know what I could've been thinking. I mean, you'd want to be as comfortable as possible."

Flustered, she was something else. Innocent, sweet . . . crap, she was probably still a virgin and he'd embarrassed the hell out of her.

"I tossed them on the end of the bed. They must've fallen to the floor."

She nodded and went to retrieve them. Once she had them, she reached inside the pocket and brought out the keys . . . and a condom.

Damn!

Her mouth dropped open. She looked at the condom, then at him, then back at the condom. When she looked at him again, her eyes had narrowed.

Think! He wasn't ready to blow this role. He drew in a deep breath.

"The poor," he said. The poor? Crap, that was about the lamest thing he could've said.

"The poor?" Her expression changed from suspicion to confusion.

"I go to many places in my travels. Very underprivileged areas. I try to tell them about safe . . . sex."

Her face fairly glowed. "That's so wonderful." She replaced the condom and kept the keys. "I'll just get these over to Kathy's brother. Is there anything you need?"

"Only my Bible. I feel lost without it." He devoutly lowered his gaze.

"Of course."

She scooted out of the guesthouse. He watched through the small window as she hurried back to her house. That had been close. Had she really bought his story about giving condoms to the poor? He smiled. Pure as the driven snow.

Ah, hell, she *was* a virgin. Fourth-grade teacher, small-hick town. It all added up. The thought should've had him running as far away as he could but for some strange reason, it didn't.

He frowned. Then again, what was she? Twenty-eight or nine? Nah, no way could she be a virgin. Could she? Even if she wasn't, he'd swear she hadn't been with that many men.

He thought about how innocent and sweet she looked—and sexy. Definitely hot. He ran a hand through his hair. The doctor said at least a week or so before he'd be able to shift gears with his foot. Could he really stay celibate that long? That would be a first in many, many years.

He drew in a deep breath. Yeah, he could, because if he could fool her, then he could play the role of a preacher.

* * *

The evening air did nothing to cool Bailey's body heat as she hurried across the backyard to her house. She'd almost lost it when Trey said his pants must've fallen off the end of the bed. Her heart pounded just thinking about him practically naked beneath the covers. Boy, had it pounded.

She envisioned him tossing back the covers, inviting her into his bed . . .

Bad thoughts! Bad!

But, oh so delicious.

She went inside the house and grabbed her purse. Once she was in the car, she hit the button that lowered the window as she drove to the shop that Kathy's brother owned. Cold air swept inside sending a chilly shiver down her spine. It might've cooled her body but not her mind.

Damn, she was lusting after a preacher. She was going to hell for sure. At the very least, Santa would be putting coal in her stocking this year.

She turned the corner and pulled into the driveway. Albert must've been watching for her because he hurried out and climbed into the car.

"Hi, kiddo. It's getting colder out there."

Some of her anxiety was swept away by his comment. He was exactly two years and twenty-eight days *younger*, but he still treated her like a favored little sister.

"Hi. Thanks for doing this," she said.

He looked at her as if she'd just lost her mind. "You're joking right? I mean, this *is* a Harley we're talking about."

She grinned as she headed for the burger joint. "Yeah, I know. I'd have loved to take it home but if Wade found out all hell would've broken loose."

"That, and the fact you've never driven a motorcycle."

She was silent. Lying didn't sit well with her.

"When?" he asked with more than a little speculation.

"College," she finally said, breaking her silence. "A boyfriend. It wasn't a Harley but it was a pretty cool bike." She shrugged. "Only 250cc but it was enough power to give me a buzz. Unfortunately, the boyfriend didn't. We broke up, and Mathew and the motorcycle went their own way." It'd been nice while it lasted—the bike, not the boyfriend.

"If I'd known that's all it would take to get a date I would've let you ride my bike a long time ago." He frowned. "Course, then I'd have to put up with . . ." He lowered his voice. "*The Wrath of Wade.*"

She chuckled at his dramatics.

"Nah, you're sexy and all, but not worth facing your brother. I have something against dying young, and I'm afraid Wade might just kill me."

She sighed when the truth of what he said hit her. "Unfortunately, that's been the problem all my life. Everyone is afraid of my brother."

"He *is* the sheriff."

"So?"

"Does he know you have a guy living with you?"

She rolled her eyes. "He's not living with me. He's staying in my guesthouse. Besides, I'm sure Wade will check him out."

She pulled to a stop in front of the burger shop and let Albert out.

"I'll meet you at my house."

She made a U-turn and headed home. Just the thought of seeing Trey again sent goose bumps over her. That is, until she turned the corner that led to her house and saw the squad car parked in front.

"Great." She pulled in the driveway. As she got out of her car, Wade was leaving the guesthouse. "Excuse me? What exactly were you doing?"

"Making sure my baby sister is safe."

"And?"

"He checked out. He seems okay."

"And?"

"I warned him if he hurt you in any way that I'd hunt him down and he'd wish he'd never heard the name Tanner."

She really loved her brother—most of the time. "If you ever want me to get married then you have to stop threatening the men in my life."

"Is he in your life?" He raised an eyebrow, studying her.

"No, and I'm not a prisoner. You're not allowed to give me the third degree."

"Yeah, I am, because I'm your brother. Besides, I saw his bum foot. You could outrun him."

She ignored her brother's comments as Albert roared up on the Harley, pulling beside Bailey's car.

"Sweet." Albert turned off the engine and climbed off, stroking one hand down the body of the bike.

Wade stepped closer, nodding his head. "She's beautiful."

"If you like motorcycles so much, then why didn't you let me get one?"

"Women don't belong on a cycle," Wade explained, his gaze still on the bike. "Too dangerous."

"Yeah, well don't tell Cody that." Cody was married to Wade's best friend, Josh. Cody had an old Harley she'd actually helped restore. She was also a bounty hunter. No, Bailey had a feeling brother dear wouldn't say a word to Cody. She might just kick his butt.

"Cody is different," he finally said.

"I refuse to argue the point." She walked over and reached inside one of the saddlebags, didn't find what she was looking for so dug around in the other one until she felt the Bible and pulled it out. She grabbed the suitcase strapped to the back. "Trey asked for his Bible. You should've trusted *my* instincts. I know a fraud when I meet one."

"Come on, Albert. I'll give you a ride home." Wade looked at Bailey, then walked over and dropped a kiss on top of her head. She was five seven but he still towered over her. "I don't care that this guy checked out. If you need me, I can be here in less than five."

It was something that he didn't boot Trey out on his butt. Wade was loosening his hold. She could probably thank Fallon for that. Wade had mellowed since he'd married.

"You're on speed dial. No worries." She gave him a quick hug and stepped back.

She clutched the worn Bible as she watched them drive away in the patrol car. A slow smile curved her lips. Her brother was sweet—when he wasn't being an ass, that is.

She turned and sauntered toward the guest-house. When she reached it, she tapped softly on the door.

"Come in."

Her pulse sped up as she opened the door and stepped inside, setting his suitcase just inside the door. You'd think she'd never been around a man before. But when she looked at him, she knew she'd never been around a man who made her feel like Trey made her feel.

"Aw, you brought my Bible. Thanks."

Bible? Bible! She was squashing it against her chest. She quickly handed it to him.

He stroked it lovingly. "We've been together for a long time," he said softly.

She pulled a chair close and sat. "What's your favorite verse?"

He looked startled. "Why, all of them," he finally said.

Of course. What a dumb question. He was a preacher. He wouldn't have just one favorite. "How long have you been a preacher?" she asked.

He hesitated. "I think some people are born to walk with God," he said reverently.

"And your parents? I bet they're very proud of you."

His head lowered. Oh, hell, when would she learn not to ask personal questions? "I'm sorry . . ."

He raised his head, meeting her gaze. His eyes sparkled with unshed tears. "They died when I was young—seven. A car wreck." He drew in a shaky breath. "I was raised in an orphanage."

Her heart began to break for the poor little boy. "No one adopted . . ."

He shook his head. "I had a speech problem. I stuttered. I was passed over. No one seemed to want a child who wasn't perfect."

She bit her bottom lip, crying on the inside for the child he used to be.

"It wasn't so bad," he told her. "The woman who ran the place told me there was a higher power who would always love me. To Him I was perfect."

She stood and knelt beside the bed, bringing his

hand to her chest. "I'm so, so sorry." She couldn't help herself, she leaned forward and brushed her lips against his, but immediately felt the heat.

She was momentarily blinded by what she was feeling and forgot that she'd initially set out to offer comfort as she lost herself in a kiss that deepened into more than just a brushing of her lips against his.

The world around her ceased to exist. All she could think about was the way he tasted, the way it felt pressed against him, his arms pulling her closer—no wait, that wasn't quite right. He wasn't pulling her nearer to him, but gently moving her back.

Her stomach began to churn. She'd practically forced herself on him. What did that make her? She didn't even want to think about it.

"I'm so sorry," she said as she stood and rushed from the guesthouse.

She didn't stop until she was inside her home, leaning against the backdoor. Her ragged breathing a testament to the riot he'd caused inside her. What had she done? But then, she knew. She'd thrown herself at a preacher.

Oh great, he was probably a virgin.

Five

The next morning Trey still hadn't shaken the guilt he'd felt last night. He eased to the side of the bed, careful of his sprained ankle.

Shake it off, man. Guilt wasn't part of his vocabulary.

What the hell was he supposed to do when Bailey kissed him? When her lips had touched his, all rational thought fled. He'd gotten lost in the sweet taste of her mouth, and the kiss had quickly turned to heated passion.

And his body had reacted. The last thing he'd wanted was her to see the condition she'd caused and get confused. Hell, she would've been mortified.

Oh, he'd done exactly what he was supposed to do and played the part of Trey Jones, preacher. He knew the role well and exactly what had happened to the character as a child. He'd studied the script—every line. Including the fact that the character had been raised in an orphanage, never chosen for adoption.

Apparently, he'd given her his best performance because Bailey had bought every lie that fell from his lips. He hadn't expected the tears of pity to well in her eyes. For just a second, he might have felt a little remorse, but only for a second. Why should he feel any at all?

It's a role. A character in a movie for Pete's sake.

But he hadn't expected her to kiss him. That had taken him by surprise and he'd responded.

If she knew the truth, that he wasn't a preacher, she'd kill him. He wasn't even a poor orphan—not by a long shot. His acting had given him more money than one man could possibly spend in a lifetime.

He ran a hand through his hair.

His father was still alive and living in California. Orphanage—no. He'd been an only child; his mother had died when he was eight. His stomach knotted. No, he wouldn't feel guilt about that, either. It had been her choice.

He drew in a deep breath, staring out the window. There was a light on in one of the rooms. Bedroom? Was she just getting up? They were from two different worlds. She could never understand his.

Growing up hadn't been easy. His dad had worked hard to scrape by. A hard man who'd taught his son hard lessons, but it made him who he was. So his father had knocked him around a few times. It toughened him up. Made him realize nothing came easy in life. You had to claw your way to the top. Trey had proven it could be done. This role would measure his worth and he wouldn't let it slip through his fingers.

He stretched until he reached his suitcase, then dragged it to where he sat. A shower and clean clothes had never sounded so good. He needed to wash away the past.

He hobbled his way to the closet-size bathroom. As long as he didn't put weight on his foot, he was pretty much pain free . . . and bored. There was no way he would be able to stay holed up in the guesthouse for a week.

Not that he planned to. Interacting with people would give his acting more depth. That and the fact that Bailey intrigued him despite his knowing he was walking in dangerous territory when she was around.

Her brother was another matter. A cop. The sheriff of Two Creeks. He really knew how to pick them. It was a good thing Monty arranged for him to have everything he needed to pass himself off as Trey Jones, preacher. Made him wonder what his agent did before he became an agent. Shady past? He wouldn't doubt it. Everyone had their secrets.

Trey carefully removed the fake scar that ran down the side of his face and laid it to the side. Except for the darker hair, Jeremy Hunter stared back at him. He was surprised that he'd pulled off the transformation with only a couple of changes: fake scar, green contacts, and hair dyed black.

Why wouldn't he succeed? These people were honest. They didn't expect him to be anything less than what he told them. Correction, Bailey didn't. And he was a damn good actor.

He shaved first, then tested the water in the

shower stall before stepping inside, leaving his wrapped foot on the outside of the plastic curtain so that it would stay marginally dry.

He was finished and drying off when he heard a knock. Bailey? Heat swept over him. He couldn't have stopped it even if he'd wanted to . . . and he didn't. He liked the way she made him feel.

"Come in," he called, and then when he heard the door open and close, continued. "I'll only be a few more minutes. I was taking a shower."

"Take your time. I thought you might want some breakfast."

"You shouldn't have gone to any trouble."

Her laughter was a little nervous. Probably because of last night.

"I didn't go to any trouble," she told him. "I hate cooking. If I can't microwave it or use a toaster oven then I don't buy it."

He'd pictured her in a frilly apron cooking up a storm. So, he was wrong on that account.

"For your dining pleasure I have microwaved sausage and biscuits. Name brand. Nothing but the best."

He chuckled as he finished dressing. Before he left the bathroom, he made sure his scar was in place as well as his contacts. He opened the door before adjusting the crutches and stepping out. Maneuvering in the small area was a feat in itself but he managed.

And then he was looking at her. His gaze slowly drifting over her. She'd pulled her hair away from her face and wore a red turtleneck, jeans, and tennis shoes. She was beautiful, sexy, and the very essence of purity. And all she saw was a preacher. A shame.

Bailey could barely swallow. Her throat had gone dry the minute he'd stepped from the bathroom. When she'd gotten up this morning, she'd almost convinced herself that she'd only imagined how great Trey had looked.

Nope, he looked even better today.

"How's your foot?" she finally asked, breaking the silence.

"Still attached." He grinned. Her heart flip-flopped. "I'll live."

"Good. I mean, who wants a dead body in their guesthouse?" Open mouth, insert foot. She was doing that a lot. Maybe she should just change the subject. "Would you like to see some of the town? It's not much but if you want to get out, I'll be happy to chauffeur you around."

When he turned the full power of his gorgeous green eyes on her, it was all her legs could do to hold her up.

"You read my mind."

She only prayed he couldn't read hers. Mind out of gutter, she silently ordered. "You might need your jacket. It's not that bad today but a little chilly. But food first."

"Keep me company," he said, as he eased to the side of the bed.

Not a hardship at all. She sat in a nearby chair and looked pointedly at his bandaged foot. "I hope you didn't have to be somewhere."

He shook his head and bit into the biscuit. "I travel to the people. I like it that way." He raised the biscuit. "The best I've ever tasted. Better than a five-star restaurant."

"Have you eaten in a lot of five-star restaurants?" Her smile wobbled when she saw his startled expression. There went her other foot. Of course he probably hadn't eaten in a five-star restaurant. He'd grown up in an orphanage, and he was a traveling preacher and probably as poor as a church mouse.

"I've never eaten in a five-star restaurant, either, if it makes you feel any better." She laughed. "I'd be scared I wouldn't know which fork to use."

Rather than answer her, he drained the glass of milk and was left with a milk mustache. "Ready."

She laughed and grabbed a paper towel from the roll on the counter. When she went to dab the mustache away, his gaze met hers. She trembled from the heat of that one look. He reached up, his hand encircling hers. She drew in a shaky breath. He gave new meaning to the "got milk" phrase.

"Do I have a milk mustache?" he asked, breaking the spell.

She stepped back trying to think of something clever to say so he wouldn't guess what he did to her. "Yes, you do." Oh, yeah, she'd really outdone herself with that one.

"Ready?"

She nodded as she stood.

He slipped on his coat, then reached for his crutches. At the last minute, he turned and scooped up his bible. "Never leave home without it." He smiled.

He was so godly, and she was such a sinner. And a liar to boot. She'd wanted to be in his company. Who wouldn't? The guy could be a centerfold for *Playgirl*.

And he was an orphan. Poor man. Her heart had nearly broken when he told his story last night. Then she'd thrown herself at him. How pathetic. How could she have kissed him? "About last night . . ."

"I've been meaning to mention that."

Here it comes. He was going to have her do penance or something. Pray for forgiveness. Go without chocolate for a month . . . No, surely he wouldn't go to that extreme. It was just a kiss. A very heated kiss. Her body tingled to awareness.

"I just wanted to say thank you," he said.

Thank you? She'd been told she was a good kisser. Somehow coming from Trey it meant more. Then again, how much experience could he have?

"I listen to a lot of people in my profession," he said, breaking into her thoughts. "It was nice having someone listen to me."

Oh, not the kiss after all. Her ego quickly deflated. So much for getting a compliment about her kissing abilities. She had to keep remembering he was a preacher. If he were embarrassed to talk about it then she wouldn't mention it, either.

At least he'd saved her embarrassment by not bringing up the kiss. She wasn't about to push her luck and hurried out the door, holding it open for him as he slowly made his way down the steps, then a little faster to her car.

She opened the passenger door for him and waited while he eased inside before she shut the door, then hurried to her side and got in. He didn't say anything as she turned the key, then backed out of the driveway, and headed toward town.

The silence was unnerving. She finally broke it.

"The town was established in 1870. It sits between two rivers. The early Indians said that it would never be hit by a tornado because of that."

She glanced at him. He didn't look that enthused with her history lesson.

"And they believed it?" he asked.

She relaxed. Maybe he was a little interested. She continued, "Apparently not since most everyone has a storm cellar." She slowly drove around the square. The Christmas decorations were a little frayed, but festive. Colored lights were strung from each business and there were red bows on the doors. Santa Claus sat in a big white chair handing out candy canes by the old matinee turned community theater.

"It's small," he pointed out the obvious. "Uh . . . quaint."

She chuckled. "I know what you mean. When I graduated from high school all I could think about was getting out of Two Creeks and going to college. Freedom at last."

"Did the city live up to your expectations?"

"Not really. I missed everything I thought I wanted to escape. The people, the places."

"And what places did you go to in Two Creeks?"

She arched an eyebrow. "We have a park. I walked there every day during the summer. It's a very nice park." She drove a couple of blocks and pulled into the parking area. "Isn't this the best playground you've ever seen?"

"The absolute best." He grinned.

He had a very nice smile. She faced front. Much safer to look at the playground equipment. "I used to swing in the middle one." She pointed toward a group of three swings. "My friend Amy was on one side and Maggie on the other." She sighed, remembering as if it were yesterday.

"And where are they now?"

"Amy is a model and Maggie a lawyer. They moved to the big city and stayed, but we get together when they come home. We all meet at the park and catch up with what's going on."

"And you got your teaching degree and came home."

She shrugged. "What can I say, I love Two Creeks. We're down to earth, and we have very little crime." Well, except when John Cavenaugh blew into town and attempted to kill Wade and Fallon. Other than that minor incident, it was fairly quiet. Hardly even worth mentioning. "What more could you ask for?"

"Big city, excitement, restaurants, shows . . . a little variety?"

She studied him. Why would a preacher be interested in material things? He met her gaze and cleared his throat.

"That is, for regular people. I'm perfectly content no matter where I'm at."

Of course. They'd been talking about small town versus big city and nothing specific. For a second there she had begun to question Trey and if he was actually telling the truth about his background. She was getting as paranoid as Wade. She wasn't suspicious by nature and she didn't want to start now. Or maybe it had been wishful thinking on her part.

She started the car. "How do you feel about the theater?"

He choked.

"You okay?"

"Yeah, sure. Uh, exactly what do you mean?" he finally asked after his coughing spell ended.

"My sister-in-law is in charge of the community theater." She grinned. "I have the lead in the Christmas play and rehearsal is in twenty minutes. How would you like to sit in the audience and check us for accuracy?"

"Accuracy?"

"You know, with the bible stuff and all."

He looked a little pale. Odd. But of course, she had to be imagining things again.

Six

Accuracy? Trey glanced down at the worn Bible he'd picked up in a thrift store. The Bible was only a prop. Ah, man, he was screwed. He thought back to the times he'd gone to church, which were sporadic at best. His father didn't believe in much—including God. No, he was in trouble if they asked anything specific.

His past was coming back to haunt him.

"Sure," he told Bailey. "I'd love to be a part of making your play a success." He wondered if they strung people up in Two Creeks.

"Good," she said with excitement, then chewed on her bottom lip. "Uh, Fallon seems a little hard at first but . . ."

"Her bite is worse than her bark?" he finished.

"Yeah. She had a hard life growing up." She glanced across the seat of the car. "Much like you."

"And she runs this theater."

She nodded. "Yeah, well she used to be an undercover CIA agent."

Her brother was the sheriff, her sister-in-law ex-CIA. Man, if they found out he wasn't a preacher he'd be dead meat.

But they wouldn't. He drew in a deep breath, telling himself he'd be getting his Oscar by the time they figured out his real identity. If he could fool them, he could fool an audience.

She parked the car in front of a red brick building and they got out. A sign proclaimed it as Ye Olde Theater.

"Merry Christmas," Santa said in a gruff voice as he sat in the over-sized white chair.

Santa looked an awful lot like the doctor.

"Here," he thrust a candy cane toward them. "I don't know why I have to sit out here freezing my butt off just to make the dentist some money."

Santa sounded an awful lot like the doctor, too.

"You do it because you love it and you know it," Bailey said with laughter in her voice.

" 'Cause no one else will do it," he grumbled, but there was a twinkle in his eyes.

He hobbled inside, Bailey opening the doors. He bet that most kids were afraid to be bad.

"This used to be the old movie house," Bailey said as they walked across frayed red carpet. "Flubber was the last movie shown here. The town is so small that the theater was losing money and had to shut down. Fallon bought the building, and once every couple of months we have a play."

"And the actors?"

"High school students, housewives, some of the older people from the nursing home even join in. We sort of take turns playing the lead. This month is mine."

Great, he'd landed in Mayberry.

They went through double doors, and down to the stage. The seats were in place but the screen was gone. Floor to ceiling deep-red drapes opened to reveal a scarred wooden stage floor. The heavy scent of cedar came from a decorated Christmas tree in the corner.

His father had never put up a tree. They were a waste of time, he'd said. So were presents.

Even now, Trey managed to be out of town during Christmas. Usually, he'd be at his hunting lodge—alone. He liked it better that way.

"You okay? You look . . . sad."

He dragged his gaze from the decorated tree. Sad? Boy, was she way off the mark. "I'll just sit back here," he said.

"Not this far back," she said. "Come down to the front where you'll be able to see."

He reluctantly followed. The front wasn't good.

No, that was Jeremy talking. Trey, the preacher, would be more sociable, more involved.

She pulled over a crate so he could prop up his foot, then stole a pillow from the stage to cushion it.

"Good?" she asked as she knelt by his injured foot and looked up at him. Her hair shimmered in the light and her face fairly glowed.

Good, yeah, she looked better than good. "Great."

Their gazes locked and for just a second he wondered what it would be like to have grown up here, been raised differently. The small town, Christmas, a decorated tree, and presents . . .

A noise from behind brought him back to his senses. What the hell was he doing? Christmas was just another holiday to line the merchants' pockets. Bailey was just as gullible as most people who were taken in by a sentimental attitude.

He turned in his seat and saw the group coming toward him. He almost jumped up and hobbled to the nearest exit. He hated crowds and there was a small one barreling toward him at a high rate of speed.

"You must be the preacher," a tall woman with ebony hair to her shoulders said. She eyed him with more than a touch of suspicion.

The CIA agent. Had to be. He returned her gaze. "The one and only."

She stared, taking his measure as she tried to discover if he were friend or foe. "You don't look like any preacher I've ever seen."

"Actually," a young woman pushed her way to the front. "He looks like that actor—Jeremy what's-his-name."

"Well, he's not," Bailey told them.

"He's a playboy," the young woman said. "A different woman every night. I read all about him in the tabloids. The actor, not you, of course."

Bailey sighed and shook her head. "The one looking at you suspiciously is my sister-in-law, Fallon. The young woman dragging the actor's name through the mud is Callie."

"When I finish college I'm going to Hollywood to be an actress. Fallon said I have talent," she continued.

He wanted to warn the young innocent to stay where she was, marry a rancher and have kids. She'd be a lot better off for it. But he couldn't do that.

"And I'm Audrey," a woman said with a deep southern accent. She wore the biggest reddest hat he'd ever seen. "And he *is* a playboy. The actor, of course, I read the tabloids, too."

"You know what they say, you can't believe everything you read," he told them.

Audrey had a wicked smile on her face. "But honey, that's the fun of reading those sleazy magazines."

Bailey glared at the woman. "He's a preacher," she reminded her.

"We can't practice from down here, either," Fallon said and shooed the whole bunch up on stage.

Trey made himself as comfortable as he could in the seat and prepared himself for a long boring day. The small cast began to assemble on stage. More townspeople trickled in, looked at him with a smile on their face before joining everyone on stage.

"Okay," Fallon said. "We're going to start at the beginning.

The stage cleared. The chatter lowered to a dull roar before going silent. A young man came out pulling a horse on wheels, with Bailey sitting on top.

Now he'd never read the Bible but he was pretty sure Mary was on a mule.

"Joseph, my husband, are thee getting tired?" Bailey asked.

"It does not matter, my wife. We must make Bethlehem by nightfall so you might have a place to rest," Albert told her.

They were so bad that he almost burst out laughing.

Fallon walked to the stage. "No, it's not coming across well. You sound stilted. Just like last time."

"They need to become the character," Trey spoke up before he thought.

Fallon spun on her heel and looked down at him from her lofty position on stage. "That's it!"

"What do you mean?" Bailey asked.

There was no turning back now. He took a deep breath. "Fallon, Bailey said you used to go undercover. So you had to pretend you were someone else, right?"

She nodded.

"It's the same way with acting."

"Of course. I don't know why I didn't see it sooner." Her eyes narrowed. "How come you know so much about acting?"

"I was involved with a teen program when I went through the seminary." He was damn good when the need arose. Still, he didn't breathe easy until Fallon nodded. She'd accepted his lie.

Fallon called on him during the rest of the rehearsal for his opinion. He was okay with that as long as they didn't ask him if the biblical story was accurate.

He'd gotten the gist of what they were doing. Bailey was Mary, and Joseph, he learned, was Albert. And the fact that Bailey couldn't act. Albert was a little better.

But Bailey was sincere. Very sincere and that should count for something.

Callie, on the other hand, had more talent than some big name stars who'd gotten their start because Daddy was in the industry, or they'd kept the director's sofa warm.

The rest of the cast needed a lot of work. Point in fact, a shepherdess that he'd eventually figured out was one of Fallon's twin daughters, and not more than four or five years old, had stolen the baby Jesus. She'd then gone to sit in a shadowed corner of the stage where she preceded to undress the doll.

"Where's baby Jesus?" Fallon asked

Bailey began to look around. The rest of the cast joined in. The little girl scooted farther back into the shadows. Trey laughed. Organized, it wasn't.

"Janey, did you take baby Jesus again?"

"No," came a voice from the folds of the curtain. Then a dark head poked out. "Baby Jesus was wet and I had to make him dry."

Fallon scurried to her daughter and scooped her up. "You have to leave the baby Jesus in the cradle. That's why I let you bring *your* baby."

"I didn't take the baby Jesus, Mommy," the other twin, Julie, piped in. "I'm bein' good."

"For once." But she softened her words with laughter. "Okay, let's call it a day. That's enough practice. Pizza anyone? I hope so because I called it in earlier." She looked at her watch. "And it should be here about . . . now"

Bailey looked at him, he shrugged. What the hell was he supposed to say? No, I'd feel more comfortable back at the guesthouse. That he'd had enough interacting with people for one day.

He clutched the Bible as if it were a lifeline and followed everyone back up front. There was a room off to the side with long tables.

"After Fallon bought the theater and donated

so much back to the community," Bailey told him. "Everyone chipped in and had the addition built. We have a lot of potluck dinners here and it's raised community spirit.

"Potluck?"

"You know, everyone brings a covered dish."

"And you like this bonding?"

"Very much. I want the town to grow. So many little towns fade away to nothing. I had a grandmother who was born in Tokeem, Texas. Ever heard of it?"

He shook his head.

"That's because it no longer exists. I don't want that to happen to our town. First, you make the community strong, then you bring in new business. That way you build on that strength and help it to grow."

He watched the way her eyes danced, and he liked what he saw. This was her passion. Everyone needed to have at least one thing in his life that meant this much.

"Pizza's here!" someone called out.

"Preacher, would you say grace?" Audrey asked in her deep southern drawl.

Oh, God, he had to pray again—no pun intended. Trey made his way to the head of the table. He could do this. After all, how hard was it to pray?

He closed his eyes, bowed his head, and thought back to the last movie he'd watched that was even remotely biblical. Man, he couldn't even think of one.

"Oh, God," he moaned.

Crap, he'd spoken aloud. He swallowed past the

lump in his throat. "Oh, God, please bless this . . . pizza we are about to eat and bless the cast of this . . . this . . . uh . . . wonderful play honoring . . . uh . . . you."

Man, he wasn't this nervous when he faced a hard-nosed director. Okay, he could do this. A quick amen and it would be over.

"Bless all your children." That sounded good. "Amen."

Everyone around the table murmured amen.

That hadn't been so hard. He was getting pretty good . . .

"Could've been worse. If Reverend Benton were saying grace, the pizza would've gotten cold. As it is, it's still warm."

He didn't see who'd whispered the words, but apparently Bailey knew the voice because she sent a quelling look in the direction of one of the teen boys who'd been ogling the teen girls. Bailey offered him an apologetic look. It didn't really bother Trey, though. No, what was bothering him the most was the way he felt every time Bailey looked at him.

Bailey smiled as she drove them back to her house. There was something so infectious and appealing about her that he couldn't help returning her smile.

"You know," she began, "the people who put on the plays at the community theater have very little talent, except maybe Callie. We have so much fun doing it, though. Many of the people are older— retired and on a fixed income. They don't have a

lot of money to go and do things. The theater
gives them a reason to get out of the house and
visit with everyone. It also keeps the younger ones
out of mischief."

"I agree," he spoke solemnly.

She looked at him. "About the fellowship?"

He shook his head, keeping a straight face. "No,
about not having any talent."

She cocked an eyebrow. "You're not supposed
to agree with that part. That was so low. And you
call yourself a preacher." Her affronted air didn't
last and she burst out laughing.

He enjoyed the sound. It wrapped around him,
making him feel . . . hell, he wasn't sure how it
made him feel. He thought he liked it, though.

"I had fun today," he said, and realized just how
much he meant it.

"You sound surprised."

He shrugged. How could he answer her? He
grew up in the city and had always lived in the city.
He'd fought plenty of battles, lived on the edge,
taken risks—but this bonding? It was something
new. It scared him, but it was like an addictive
drug, and he wanted more.

She pulled into the driveway of her house and
came around to his side, but he already had the
door open and was maneuvering out of the vehicle.

"Do you like to watch movies?" she asked.

"Yeah."

"Good. My house. Six sharp. Dinner and a movie."

He watched as she waltzed away. His gaze riv-
eted on the sway of her hips in her tight-fitting
jeans. His grin was slow. Bailey Tanner was flirting

again. He liked when she flirted. It was damned sexy.

Except she was playing with fire. He only hoped she didn't get burned. Or worse, he hoped he didn't.

Seven

"I'm flirting with a preacher," Bailey said into the phone.

"What's your point?" Kathy asked. "They're still men."

She sighed and dropped down onto the sofa. "He's a man of God. I don't want to be married to a preacher."

There was a choking sound on the other end. "He asked you to marry him?"

She frowned. "Of course he didn't. We just met. But if a relationship develops, and I won't deny there's a little bit of chemistry, and we happen to fall in love and he did ask me to marry him then I would be the wife of a preacher."

"You think too much."

"I only want to be prepared."

"But you're the one flirting with him. Don't flirt."

She pulled the pillow under her head as she scrunched farther down on the sofa. "You saw him.

No red—blooded female would be able to resist flirting. He is sooo hot! I need sex. Is it wrong that I want his body? I mean, will I go to hell?"

"Not if you confess."

"I'm not Catholic."

"Does it matter?"

"I'm not sure."

Kathy sighed. "So have a fling, tell me all about it, and move on. That would sort of be a confession. Oh, and ask for forgiveness."

"I don't think they have flings. And you don't even go to church so it wouldn't be the same thing if I confessed to you."

"It might give me a thrill, though. My sex life has been in the crapper since Chad left for his business trip. I really need sex."

"I wouldn't tell you anyway."

"I didn't think you would, but I have to say, if I weren't engaged, I know exactly what I'd do."

"What's that?"

"Seduce him. You can do it."

"And go to hell? I don't think so."

Kathy sighed. "It might be worth it."

They talked a few more minutes before Kathy started getting busy at the burger joint and had to go. When Bailey stood, her gaze automatically went to the guesthouse.

But she wasn't *really* flirting with him when she asked him to dinner—only being neighborly.

An hour later, she had the cheese rigatoni simmering in a pot of water, a chef salad in a glass bowl, garlic bread in the toaster oven ready to toast when Trey arrived, and all the bags and boxes in the trash. A gourmet meal in minutes without a lot of stress and work. And it would taste a heck of a lot better than anything she could make from scratch.

She went to her bedroom and slipped into a pair of beige slacks and a pink sweater. A little lipstick and spritz of perfume and she was ready.

Flirting? She'd thought about it all afternoon and she was almost certain that she wasn't. It had been flirting when she'd winked, but she'd had a good excuse. He'd been leaving her life forever. Straddling his Harley and riding off into the sunset—except the sun hadn't been setting. A little harmless wink wouldn't hurt a thing, she'd told herself.

Okay, so she'd been wrong. Now, she was only trying to make up for causing Trey's accident.

As she went back to the kitchen, there was a knock at the backdoor. Her pulse sped up. Calm down, she told herself. You're just having dinner and watching a movie.

She took a deep breath and opened the door. He stole her breath. Jeans and a black T-shirt had never looked so good, especially the way he filled them out. Nope, he didn't look at all religious. He looked wild, untamable, and sexy.

"Hi," she said.

He thrust some weeds toward her. "I picked some of your flowers," he said. "I didn't want to come empty handed."

Her smile turned into laughter.

He frowned. "They're not flowers, are they?"

She shook her head. "Weeds, actually, but I always thought they were pretty." She opened the door a little wider. "Come in."

He followed her to the kitchen.

"You can sit in the living room if you'd like. I have an ottoman you can prop your injured foot on."

"I'd rather sit at the bar. My foot has been propped up all afternoon."

"Okay." Her house was an open floor plan. The living room wasn't that far away. It made her feel good that he'd want to be even closer.

"You look pretty."

She brushed some strands of hair behind her ear. "Thank you." First flowers, now compliments? Maybe he was flirting with her. She drew in a shaky breath. "I hope you like Italian."

His eyebrows rose. "You actually cooked?"

"Not exactly. Frozen rigatoni, garlic bread, and bagged salad, but I grated the cheese. Do you like to cook?"

"Not even a little." He smiled.

She loved his smile. For a moment, she stood there and stared.

"It smells good." He leaned his elbows on the counter.

Cooking, yes, that's what she was doing. She went to the pantry and asked, "Do you have a preference for sauce? I have white and red."

"Red is fine."

"Ragu it is." She took the jar to the counter, opened it and poured the contents into a bowl. "Can you drink wine?" When she looked at him, he nodded. "I hope it tastes good. It's one I haven't tried and at ten dollars a bottle, it better be really good."

"And you're breaking it out on my account?"

"It's the least I can do."

"I didn't have to look back, you know."

Her hands stilled in the process of removing the

garlic bread from the toaster oven. "I guess I never thought about it like that," she said slowly.

"Not going to kick me out of the guesthouse, are you?"

She put the toast in a basket and set it on the table before meeting his gaze. "No, I think I like having you around."

She got the wine and a corkscrew and handed them to him. "I'm terrible at opening wine."

"Now I know the real reason you offered me a room."

"I'm shameless." She brought down a couple of glasses from the cabinet and wondered how she could feel so comfortable around someone she'd met only recently. Maybe because he made her feel comfortable.

"I'm a stranger and yet, you're not nervous around me. Why?"

For a second she wondered if he could read her mind. God, she hoped not. "You said you were a preacher. I believe you."

"I could be lying. Sometimes it's not smart to take people at face value."

She took the glass of wine he offered and stared down into the deep red color. "Well," she began, "it's like my brother said, you checked out when he ran you through the computer at the sheriff's office."

"I could've stolen Trey Jones' identity."

"You also have a bum foot and I could outrun you."

"It'll heal."

She wondered at his line of questioning, but then just figured he was trying to make her see she needed to be a little more cautious.

"I also have a brown belt in karate."

His eyebrows rose.

Why did people never believe her when she told them? "No, it's true. Wade made me take karate years ago. He said I'd be going to college some day and needed to know how to protect myself in case some guy got fresh. I think he just watched too many thrillers on TV where women were victims." She took a drink of wine, savoring the taste before swallowing. It was good. "Besides, I have two more brothers and if you harmed one hair on my head they would all three come after you, and probably Fallon, too, and castrate you."

She turned and went to the rigatoni and poured it into the strainer before she realized she just told him they'd castrate him if he hurt her. Crap.

"Pretend I didn't say that last part."

"You mean they wouldn't come after me?"

She could hear the laughter in his voice. *Ignore it.* She dumped the rigatoni into a bowl. "No, they'd come after you and do exactly as I said—just pretend I didn't say it. Sometimes it's really easy to forget you're a preacher."

He mumbled something that sounded like he was agreeing with her, but she figured she must be mistaken.

"Dinner is served," she told him as she carried the rigatoni to the table.

Trey couldn't have even said what the food tasted like after the meal was finished. He was too busy beating himself up over his twenty questions. Bailey was wrong. She *was* gullible. Hell, everyone he'd met so far had believed him. Why the hell were people so blasted trusting? Couldn't they see he was taking them for a ride?

"I'm so stuffed I feel like a turkey," Bailey said, breaking into his thoughts. "Why don't we go to the living room?"

Why shouldn't he take advantage of what she had to offer? "Sure." They'd wanted each other from the start. It was time to end the games.

They went into the living room and he made himself comfortable on the sofa while she fiddled with the television. That was okay, he enjoyed the view.

She turned the lights down low and sat next to him. "I didn't ask what kind of movies you like but I thought this one would be a good choice." Her eyes were innocent as she looked up at him so trusting.

His conscience told him to back off and not destroy her beliefs. He could drift out of her life just like he'd drifted into it. No harm, no foul.

He studied her face. Opened his mouth to tell her he was a lie and he wanted to make love to her, but the words didn't come. "What movie is that?" he asked instead.

" 'It's a Wonderful Life.' You've seen it, right? I mean everyone has seen it. It's a classic."

He shook his head.

"Really? I love Jimmy Stewart."

He settled back on the sofa. "If you like it, then I probably will, too." When the hell had he become such a coward?

The movie was in black and white. He preferred thrillers. Something with a little more substance. After the first five minutes, he'd already figured out this was one of those sappy movies meant to inspire people to feel good about giving at Christmas time and thus spend more money.

Midway through the movie, he was still scratching his head. Did anyone really buy into this crap? He glanced at Bailey. Her face was glowing. A few times, he'd even heard her sniff.

He couldn't stand staying quiet any longer. "He has the break he's been praying for and he won't take it. The man is an idiot. He's free."

She stiffened beside him. "But look what he has to give up to have his freedom."

"A worthless brother who cares more about his own life, a house that's falling apart, a marriage that forced him to give more of himself than he was prepared to give. The guy is a sap."

She cocked an eyebrow. "Jimmy Stewart is not a sap. I thought you were supposed to be a preacher. Where's your compassion?"

He could tell her now. This was the perfect opening. He looked into her face, then sighed. "I guess I've been working in the slums too long, seeing the . . . uh . . . poor and sick. After a while it starts to bring me down."

"This movie will help."

No, it wouldn't, but he couldn't tell her that. Too many years of having it drummed into his head by his father about the commercialism of the world had hardened him, and nothing would change how he believed. It was too late. He couldn't be changed. He looked at the world with eyes wide-open. That was the smart thing to do.

"You're right," he told her, and pulled her next to him. He'd play his part so her ideals would stay intact, but he damn well wanted to feel her snuggled next to him. He was almost certain preachers were allowed to snuggle.

He settled back. Clarence was funny. He would

at least admit that to himself. But he knew when worse came to worse no one would help poor George out. Nope, the man was going to prison and so he should for screwing up his business so bad.

He continued to watch, feeling himself getting caught up in the movie. Only because he was an actor and Bailey had been right, Jimmy Stewart was great as well as the others. The plot . . . he still didn't buy it.

"This is the part I love," Bailey spoke softly.

His stomach knotted as he watched the towns-people come to George's rescue and Clarence earn his wings. It was a silly movie. People didn't come to the rescue of other people.

No one had come to his mother's rescue. Not one person, and she'd been good. He could still remember the smell of cookies baking, the warmth of her arms around him.

He drew in a deep breath. No, there'd been no one around when she'd slipped into the bathroom and taken a bottle of pills. Not one person had come to her rescue.

Eight

Bailey surreptitiously watched Trey from behind the stage curtain. This was the third time he'd been to their rehearsal. It was almost as if he forced himself to come with her. Since he'd watched, *It's a Wonderful Life*, he'd been pensive, almost sad.

She couldn't even imagine what his childhood had been like raised in an orphanage. And he probably didn't have much more now. A preacher was usually broke, and Trey didn't have his own church. And no family.

But *she* did.

Her family could be his family, and she'd bet the town would take up an offering for him. That was it. She smiled to herself. Planning ahead was the key to success. Leave nothing to chance.

"Okay, let's take a break," Fallon said, then looked at her watch. "Only five minutes, though. I have to take the girls to the potty."

Bailey hurried off the stage. "What do you think so far?"

"That you need a lot more practice?"

She stuck her tongue out at him. "We're free. What do you expect?" She drew in a deep breath. "I know what your problem has been the last few days."

"Do I have a problem?"

She nodded. "I'm going to start a love offering for you."

He choked. She was going to offer him her body? He quickly glanced around to see if anyone had overheard. Her brother would kill her, and him, if he found out she was offering herself.

What? Did she think he was a God or something? And she was making the ultimate sacrifice?

"Yeah, you know, where the town takes up a monetary donation. We've done it before for missionaries so why not a traveling preacher."

Money, not her body. Disappointment and relief swept through him at the same time. He had a feeling disappointment was the stronger emotion.

"You think I'm broke?" She'd kill him if she knew how much money he had.

"You aren't penniless?"

He shook his head.

"Oh, then it must be the other."

"The other what?"

"Nothing. By the way, we're going to my parents for dinner tonight." She stood before he could tell her he didn't think he liked that idea any better.

Damn, what had he gotten himself into?

He didn't have long to find out. The day flew by. He was more than a little hesitant as he approached the door to Bailey's parents' house. If she hadn't been right beside him, he'd have turned around and hobbled away as fast as he could.

He didn't do parents.

His skin went from hot to cold in the space of a heartbeat. It was all he could do to keep his hands from slipping on the grips of his crutches.

If he said his foot throbbed would she buy it? He was an actor, he could pull it off.

The door opened. "Welcome!" A rotund man with thinning hair and a big smile on his face stood at the door. The woman who stood beside him had light brown hair and a welcoming smile. She was trim in a pair of brown slacks and a white top. Other than her hair being darker, she was an older version of Bailey.

The parents.

He'd never had to deal with them until now. The women he dated wouldn't dream of asking him to meet their parents. Definitely a taboo subject and they knew it.

Trey had no experience with parents. And he was afraid. Being afraid didn't sit well with him. Hell, he'd done some of his own stunts for films and hadn't been this nervous.

"Welcome," the woman's voice was soft and sounded like what he would imagine an angel would sound like. Then to top that off, the warmth of her eyes reached deep down inside of him and squeezed his heart.

Man, he'd been in this town way too long.

"I'm Ginny and this is Waylon," she said.

Trey mumbled something appropriate and they went inside. He could do this. He only needed to act, and that was the one thing in his life he knew he was good at. No problem.

Until he walked inside and saw there were quite a few people in the small house.

"Mike, you're home!" Bailey ran to a man that he assumed was one of the other brothers. With a wide smile, she dragged him over to be introduced. "This is the doctor in the family."

He smiled when he looked down at Bailey, and Trey could see the resemblance.

"Barely." He shook Trey's hand. "I've only been practicing a couple of years. Sometimes I amazed myself that I stayed in school long enough."

His words were friendly but Trey knew Bailey's brother studied him, trying to decide if he was worthy enough to be in his little sister's company. He must've passed the test because his smile warmed a half of a degree.

Trey looked around the living room. Fallon waved, Wade nodded, the twins were eyeing the presents under the tree. Bailey's mother had slipped away to the other room.

"Have a seat," her father said. "I was on crutches once and they were murder."

"For all of us," Wade spoke up with laughter in his voice. "He was like a human tank as he barreled his way through the house."

"Man was not made to walk around on sticks," he said with a frown, but his eyes twinkled.

Trey made his way to the sofa and took a seat. He needed a drink bad.

"I'll get you something to drink," Bailey said, and he wondered if she could read his mind. No, not possible. He was still alive.

Janey, the bolder of the twins, sat beside him on

the sofa. He shifted away. She scooted closer. Trey glanced nervously around the room. Couldn't they see the kid wasn't playing with her doll? Kids made him nervous and she was no exception.

"Santy is gonna come see me and sissy. Is Santy gonna come see you?"

"Uh . . . sure."

"Do you like kids?"

No. They asked too many questions. "Sure," he lied.

She slipped her hand in his. Hers was tiny, warm . . . and really sticky. But when she looked up and smiled, her eyes sparkled and her face glowed with childlike innocence, and he found himself returning it and relaxing just a little.

"What have you been eating?" He raised an eyebrow.

She put a finger over her lips. "Shh, candy cane. We're not 'posed to eat dem off the tree. Want me to get you one?"

He shook his head. Her shoulders drooped. He had a feeling they would've *shared* the candy cane, but with an adult involved there would be less chance of her getting into trouble.

"Miss Janey scoot off the sofa and stop bothering our guest." Bailey handed him a soda, then took Janey by the hand. "Icky, someone has been stealing candy canes off the tree."

"Shh, Auntie Baywee." She glanced toward her mother.

"Then go wash up."

"I think we both need to wash," he said.

Bailey smiled. "She likes to hold hands. Come on and we'll all wash up."

She led the way to the bathroom. It was crowded

as they all squeezed inside. Janey laughed as Bailey held the little girl's hands under the water and together they washed up, lathering the soap until they had bubbles going everywhere. After drying her little hands, Janey scooted out of the tiny enclosure.

"Are you going to wash my hands, too?" He leaned on the crutches, staring into her face.

"Are you flirting with me?"

"Turn about is fair play. You've been flirting with me since I walked into the burger joint."

"I didn't think preachers knew how to flirt."

"Flirt . . . and a whole lot more." He propped his crutch against the wall. She didn't move. He wanted to tell her to run away as fast as she could, but when he looked down into her eyes, she took his words away. Hell, she took his breath away.

Unable to stop himself, he slipped a hand behind her neck and pulled her closer, lowering his head and brushing his lips across hers. His body trembled with need and the force it took not to ravage her mouth.

She moaned, pressing against his. He slipped his hand behind her, skimming her back, slipping lower . . .

Laughter from the other room brought him crashing to earth. He ended the kiss, his breathing ragged.

"I'm sorry," she said.

"I'm the one who kissed you," he told her. "And I'm not sorry."

Her laugh was shaky. "I guess preachers know how to flirt—and kiss."

Yeah, and that was his problem. He could talk

just about any woman into crawling between the covers with him. Bailey was different. Not like the women from his past. He wanted her, but his lie stood between them.

They rejoined the others who were moving into the dining room. Everyone was talking and laughing. Wade and Fallon settled the twins on their booster seats.

Trey glanced around the room. This was what a real family did during the holidays. He could feel the love they had for each other. He was the odd man out. A stranger on the outside who was being allowed to look through the window into their lives. But it wouldn't last.

What the hell was he doing here? He didn't belong. They were only being nice. He was trapped. He felt hot then cold. He couldn't breathe. He . . .

Bailey slipped her hand into his, then smiled up at him. Calmness swept over him.

Her father cleared his throat. Silence reigned at the table. Even the twins quieted as their grandfather stood.

He bowed his head. "Dear Lord, thank you for this food we are about to receive, thank you for bringing this young man into our lives so that he could share this meal with us, and Lord, thank you for my family. Amen."

There was a mumbled amen, and the silence was broken as everyone began to talk at once.

"Trey has a Harley," Wade said.

Trey shifted in his seat as all eyes turned toward him, then questions flew from everyone. Questions from what color to the size of the engine. Suddenly he wasn't on the outside looking in. This was one thing he could safely talk about. He had a passion for the Harley.

The conversation carried through the main course. By dessert they had pretty well exhausted that topic and Mike began to talk about his residency, but all of a sudden, the other twin, Julie, burst out crying, surprising everyone.

"Baby, what's wrong?" Wade jumped from his seat and hurried to his daughter.

"No one wants to hear me," she said between sobs.

He hugged his daughter close and looked at Fallon with pleading eyes.

"Honey, we're so sorry. If you want to talk, go ahead," Fallon said.

Julie dried her eyes with the back of her hands, sniffed loudly, then looked at everyone at the table.

"Don't you have anything to say, sweetie?" Bailey asked.

The little girl drew in a deep breath. "My mommy doesn't wear panties to bed at night."

There was a nervous cough.

"And Auntie Bailey and the preacher were kissin' in the baffroom," she continued since she had everyone's attention. "And Grandpa and Grandma were . . ."

"Okay," Bailey's father quickly spoke up. "Who wants pie with whipped cream?"

"We'd better before all the family secrets are aired," Wade said.

Trey nervously laughed along with everyone else. When he caught Bailey's gaze there was a mischievous twinkle in her eyes. He would've thought she'd want to crawl under the table from embarrassment. She was, after all, a fourth-grade teacher.

He smiled and she winked back. Maybe there was more to this teacher than he'd first thought.

When she picked up her knife and tapped it against her glass, everyone looked her way. Now what was she up, too?

"I have a very special announcement to make," she said. "I spoke with the pastors in town and they all want Trey to be one of the speakers during the Christmas service."

Everyone clapped. Wade stood. "A toast. May all your Christmas wishes come true."

His stomach churned. He couldn't do a Christmas service. What the hell could he say? Oh, God, he was going to throw up. Suddenly, he didn't feel like an actor. No, he felt like a fraud.

Later, in the car, he realized for the first time in his life he felt as though he'd been part of something. At least, until Bailey had made her announcement. When everyone discovered he'd duped them, they would turn against him and despise him for the lies he'd told.

"My family can be a little overwhelming at times," Bailey said. "And that was without my other brother. He'll be here Christmas Eve."

"I like your family. They were nice." His glance moved to the window as the Christmas lights of town flashed and sparkled. There was a tall tree on the courthouse lawn decorated with tinsel and lights. A white angel sat on top.

It reminded him of the movie the other night. He closed his eyes, his fingers curling into fists. This wasn't good. He was starting to wish for something he could never have, something that wasn't real. He wasn't a traveling preacher. No, he was a phony.

"We enjoyed having you," she said.

She pulled into her driveway and turned off the ignition. He couldn't get out of the car fast enough. He mumbled a good-bye. It wasn't so late that he couldn't call Monty and tell him that he'd had all he wanted of small-town life.

So what if he was running away. Nothing new for him. He'd gotten really good at leaving people before they left him.

Once he was inside, he grabbed his cell and speed dialed his agent's number. The phone rang again and again but Monty didn't answer. Trey finally gave up and just left a message asking his agent to send a car.

He was tired of pretending to be something he wasn't.

Nine

The temperature had begun to drop. Bailey knew this because an hour ago she had the television on the weather channel. It was either that or infomercials about an exercise machine that twisted you into a pretzel while claiming you could lose all the weight you wanted in as little as ten minutes a day.

No, thanks.

She'd drunk a glass of wine, and enjoyed it so much that she'd drunk another one, and thought maybe she could fall asleep this time if she went back to bed.

Wrong.

She flung the covers off. It might be cool outside but she was burning up. It was all Trey's fault. He'd flirted, he'd kissed, and now she was restless. Every time she closed her eyes, she thought about him.

They were such good thoughts!

What was the use of staying in bed if she couldn't go to sleep? She scooted out of bed and padded through the house. Her gaze strayed to the guesthouse. A light glowed. He couldn't sleep, either.

Interesting.

Or maybe his foot was hurting him. Maybe his crutches had fallen and he couldn't get to the sink to get a glass of water so he could take a pain pill. Maybe . . .

Yeah. Maybe she should write a book. What she was dreaming up would make great fiction.

She went back to the bedroom and slipped her arms into her robe and her feet into slippers. What she was about to do was so wrong. But it felt so right.

Trey flipped through the pages of the magazine. He'd read an article on cleaning tips, one on the best ways to tan, and a horrible one on waxing. Women didn't really do that, did they? He wanted to write an article titled: JUST NOT WORTH IT.

Men weren't. Men were selfish, out for their own pleasure.

He tossed the magazine to the side. He was bored. He couldn't sleep. And the reason why was just across an expanse of yard—a very short expanse. He could be at Bailey's backdoor in less than five. But that was the worse thing he could do and he knew it.

It didn't stop his heart from beating harder when there was a light tapping at his door. He should pretend to be asleep. Man, this was so low—even for him. If she came inside they would make love. He knew that as sure as he knew he would end up breaking her heart. But for one night he wanted to feel whole and he knew Bailey could give him what was lacking in his life.

"Come in," he said.

The door opened, bringing in the cold air—and Bailey. She was so damned beautiful with her mussed hair, full lips that begged to be kissed, and blue eyes that reflected both of their need.

"I wanted to . . . uh . . ." She bit her lip. "Is it so very much of a sin that I want to make love with you?"

He turned the covers back. Their eyes locked. She slowly untied the robe and slipped it off her shoulders. White satin slid down her naked body and puddled at her feet. Trey drew in a sharp breath as she quickly joined him.

She turned toward him as he pulled the covers over her. His lips met hers and he lost himself in her taste . . . in the heat from her body. Trey trembled. Damn, no woman had ever made him tremble.

When the kiss ended, she pulled back and stared into his eyes. "I want you so badly my body aches. I've never felt like this before. Make love to me, Trey."

He wanted her, too, but he couldn't go any further until she knew the truth. He'd lose her, he knew that, but he couldn't leave a lie between them.

"I'm not the man you think . . ."

She placed two fingers over his lips. "You're the man I want to make love with. That's all that matters right now."

He hesitated. She took his hand and placed it over her breast. He groaned, lost in the warmth of her flesh.

He flicked his thumb over her tight nipple. Her moan caressed him, sending shivers of need over him and all thoughts of trying to be a hero fled. Hell, he'd never been a hero before now so why muddy a clean record.

"Beautiful," he whispered as he fondled her breast before lowering his head and taking her into his mouth. His tongue flicked back and forth across her nipple, then scraped it with his teeth.

"Yes," she cried out, arching toward him.

Her hand snaked downward, stroking his hard length. He closed his eyes, lights exploded behind his lids.

"I want to take you into my mouth. I want to taste all of you," she told him. Before he could do more than groan, she'd slid down in the bed and nudged him to his back.

His brain had stopped functioning a long time ago. He mindlessly obeyed. She took him into her mouth, sucking gently, her tongue swirling around the tip of his erection. Wet heat swirled around him as he rocked his hips until he knew he couldn't hold back a second longer.

He reached down with supreme effort and urged her back up and into his arms.

"I can't take any more," he said, his hand moved down to her curls. Soft as silk he massaged between her legs, tugging on the fleshy part of her sex. He dipped a finger inside her, feeling the wetness, knowing she was more than ready for him, but wanting to build the excitement . . . the need inside her.

"I want to taste you," he told her close to her ear, his breath fanning her neck.

"I can't," she told him, her breathing ragged. "I

can't wait. I need you now." She reached to the side of the bed and grabbed her robe, pulling a condom out of the pocket and ripping it open with her teeth.

He took it from her and rolled it down his length. He didn't need any more encouragement then what she was now giving him.

When he sank inside her tight body, they groaned at the same time. He slowly lowered his body, then came back up. Her legs wrapped around his waist as he sank inside her once again. Just when he thought it couldn't get any better than this, she contracted her inner muscles.

Lights exploded around him. He pumped inside her faster and faster. She cried out, her body tightening. He stiffened as his orgasm washed over him in wave after wave. This was so damn frigging good, he thought, as he rolled to his side taking her with him. He never experienced anything like this. He'd never felt so much a part of someone else as he did right now.

"I think I might be falling in love," she said.

Her whispered confession curled around him, tightening like a noose around his neck. No! Don't lose your heart to me, he wanted to tell her but when he opened his mouth, the words wouldn't come. Instead, he brushed a kiss across the top of her head.

You're a liar, he silently told himself. Your whole life has been one big lie. What would Bailey think about him when she discovered the truth?

She snuggled closer, her hand curling around his. Her breathing deepened and he knew she'd drifted asleep.

"I think I'm falling in love, too," he whispered, but knowing she didn't hear his words. He was playing it safe again. Making no commitment, taking no chances.

Bailey believed his lies. She was living in his fantasy world and thinking he was this perfect man of God. Never realizing he wasn't worth her time or trouble.

He slipped out of her arms, grabbed his clothes, and hobbled to the bathroom. He couldn't even look at his reflection in the mirror. He disgusted himself. Why had he let himself get so involved?

The best thing he could do would be to leave before he could do more damage, cause Bailey even more pain.

When he came out of the bathroom, he was dressed. He took one look at her sleeping form and his stomach twisted into knots. He was only supposed to act a part, get into the role. He wasn't supposed to get involved with these people.

He grabbed his jacket and keys, then gritted his teeth and walked out the front door. He didn't need the worn Bible, he didn't need the suitcase of clothes. His ankle hurt but the physical pain was good. It helped him to forget about the rest.

The night air had a chill in it but he didn't care. He welcomed the cold. Why not, he already felt frozen on the inside.

He climbed on the Harley. His foot throbbed as he roared out of the driveway and Two Creeks, Texas. He never looked back.

Ten

Bailey stretched and yawned feeling very satisfied. When she opened her eyes, she saw that Trey wasn't in bed. She slowly rose on one elbow, pushing her hair out of her eyes. He wasn't in the room and the bathroom door was open.

His Bible was on the bedside table, his suitcase next to the bed. Maybe he'd gone to her house to fix breakfast. A nice warm and fuzzy thought.

Her gaze landed on his crutches. Cold chills ran up and down her spine. Something was wrong.

She jumped out of bed, throwing on her robe and belting it as she flew out the door, not even bothering to put on her slippers.

"Trey," she called.

Silence.

Where was he? She ran through the house, just to be certain, looking into each room. What had happened? Was it something she'd done? Well of course it was—she'd seduced him. What the hell was he going to do when she boldly threw herself at him?

He was a fallen angel now. Completely out of God's grace. And her? She was a jezebel. Her life couldn't get any worse.

She shoved her hair away from her face and hurried to the front door, flinging it open. Her hands began to shake as she stared at the driveway.

The Harley was gone.

He'd left the same way he'd come in, except this time he took her heart with him.

She slowly closed the door, made it as far as the living room and collapsed on the sofa. She hugged the pillow close to her, but it wasn't the same as hugging him. Oh God, he must hate her so much. She'd tarnished him.

Two, three hours passed but time meant nothing.

The doorbell rang. She raised her head, not wanting to move. Then hope flared inside her. Trey? Was he back? Maybe to explain why he'd left without a word.

She ran to the door and flung it open, ready to launch herself into his arms.

A chauffer stood at the door, a limo parked next to the curb. She raised her eyebrows when she looked back at the stoic young man.

"Can I help you?"

"I'm supposed to pick up Jeremy Hunter."

"The actor?"

He nodded.

"Boy, have you got the wrong house. The wrong

town for that matter." She started to close the door when he spoke again.

"His agent told me he might be going by the name Trey Jones."

Her body went from cold to hot then back to cold again. She slowly opened the door a little wider. "What?"

"His agent told the limo service I was to pick up Mr. Hunter at this address and take him to the airport." He dug a piece of paper out of his pocket and glanced at it, then at the numbers on her house. "This is the right address."

Jeremy Hunter and Trey Jones were one in the same. He'd used her, got whatever thrill he'd been looking for, then dumped her.

"Is he here?"

She took a deep breath, barely controlling her murderous thoughts. What little dignity she had left, she pulled around her like a cloak. "He's already left."

His forehead puckered. "Oh. I guess I should call the agent and let him know."

"Yes, you do that. Good-bye."

She closed the door, surprising herself that she didn't slam it—then slam it again . . . and again . . . and again! It wasn't the young man's fault that Jeremy Hunter had gone slumming.

Bailey made it as far as the sofa and sat down with a hard thud. Oh God, he must've laughed his ass off at her seduction attempts. Him, the playboy, the big Hollywood star. Her face burned when she remembered thinking he might even be a virgin.

A virgin! She just wanted to die. Or better yet, she wanted him to die!

The phone rang. She stomped over to it and nearly jerked it off the wall. "What?" she demanded.

"What's the matter?" Wade asked.

She sniffed. Her anger dissolved into a puddle at her feet. Wade would know what to do. But he couldn't make it better. No one could make it better.

"Bailey, you're scaring me."

"He hurt me," she wailed.

"I'll be right there."

She dropped the phone back in its cradle and went to the sofa, falling across it and was still there, crying, when Wade and Fallon rushed in.

"Where is he? I'll haul his ass to jail."

"Can't." She hiccupped as she sat up, shoving her hair out of her face. "He's gone. Didn't even say good-bye."

Wade relaxed. "Well, good riddance. You don't want someone like that in your life."

"Yes, I do."

Fallon hadn't said a word, just watched. "You had sex with him."

Bailey fell against the pillows on the sofa and cried harder.

Wade balled his hands into fists. "He touched you? He's a preacher. I'll have him excommunicated or whatever the hell you do to preachers."

"Trey wasn't Trey." Oh, the shame!

Fallon sat on the sofa, pulling Bailey into her arms. "What do you mean Trey wasn't Trey?"

"He was really Jeremy Hunter, the actor. He used us all."

"Then why the hell did he say he was a preacher?" Wade's countenance was growing darker by the second.

She shrugged. "I don't know. He left before I woke up. He didn't even leave a note to explain." She waved her arm in the air. "Pfttt and he was gone."

"He won't get away with it," Fallon told her.

"There's nothing we can do," Bailey said.

"Nothing we can do?" Fallon's eyebrows rose. "Oh honey, you haven't seen exactly what I *can* do and no one makes my favorite sister-in-law cry."

"I'm your only sister-in-law."

"That's beside the point. Trey or Jeremy—whatever he's calling himself this week will certainly face the music. I'm not ex-CIA for nothing." She tapped her fingernail against her chin. "And you forget my sister is a cop." She frowned. "Except Jody is pregnant. Okay, she's out but we know two bounty hunters who don't play by the rules. Josh and Cody will be glad to help."

Wade looked at his wife. "Heaven help him."

"Sweetheart, he'll need a lot more than God's help." Her smile was wicked.

Bailey stood. "No, I don't want you to do anything. He's not worth it. He lied not only to me but to the whole town. Just forget whatever plan you might be cooking up."

Fallon looked at Wade. He shrugged as if to tell her if that's what little sis wanted . . .

And it was what she wanted. It was. No matter how much it hurt.

"Okay, if you're sure," Fallon said.

"I am." But she didn't think she was as positive

as she sounded. She didn't want to be one of those women who would try to get revenge, but she was tempted to make him suffer!

"What happened in Texas?" Monty asked. "You were supposed to become the character, Trey Jones. Don't tell me you let the preacher persona get to you."

He met his agents probing gaze. "I'm still the same man as when I left."

"No, you've changed. No more wild parties, no more women, and you haven't even been in the tabloids."

"Isn't that what you wanted?"

Monty shook his head. "Not to the extent that you would be dead inside."

"I'm playing the part, aren't I?"

"Oh, yeah, the studio execs are thrilled with your performance. Oscar material and all that. But you're not the same."

He stood. "I'm tired. It's been a long week, then we started filming."

Monty sighed as he came to his feet. "If you need anything . . ."

"I don't," he interrupted. He'd heard it all for the last week and a half.

"Tomorrow is Christmas Eve and you don't go back to work until the new year. Are you sure you won't come over to the house? The wife would love to see you."

He shook his head. "I'm going to the cabin. I'll be back next week."

Monty opened his mouth, then must have

thought better because he didn't say anything. Jeremy saw him to the door. He didn't relax until he closed and locked it behind him. He didn't want to talk, to explain about Bailey.

His gut twisted just thinking about her. God, she probably hated his guts. He should've left a note or something. He'd just thought it would be better to make a clean break. He didn't realize it would hurt this much.

What would happen if he called her? Hell, he already knew the answer. He could return to Two Creeks and grovel. The thought of seeing her again sent his pulse racing. That's exactly what he would do. What else did he have to lose?

He'd run away from Bailey but she'd kept something that belonged to him—his heart.

He turned and walked back to the living room of his apartment. When he saw the man dressed all in black, he froze. A noise alerted him to the one behind him and there was another one off to his left. Ski masks covered their faces.

Fear coursed through him but he tried to stay calm. "My wallet's on the bedside table. It's all the money I have in the house.

"We don't want your money," a feminine voice said just before he was clipped on the back of the head. The room went black as he felt himself falling. Someone caught him, eased him to the floor. That was the last he knew.

Fallon tugged the hot mask off and looked down at Trey—no, not Trey. He was Jeremy Hunter. Damned hard to make the transition from preacher to playboy. Well, not too difficult. He was sexy as hell.

Cody tugged her mask off.

"Bailey is going to be pissed you knocked him out," Fallon told her.

Cody squatted beside Jeremy's still form. "Hell, I didn't kill him."

"Sheesh, bounty hunters," Fallon complained. "You have no boundaries."

"Like undercover CIA does? Yeah, right."

"Are you two going to argue all night or are we going to take him back to Two Creeks and Bailey?" Josh drawled, tugging his mask off.

Fallon noticed the way his eyes strayed to Cody. They exchanged heated looks. Fallon rolled her eyes. All they thought about was sex. Actually, she couldn't blame them. She really missed Wade.

"I guess you two expect me to carry him downstairs," Josh said. When neither one of them said anything, he muttered a curse. "At least get the door. I'm not lowering him over the side of the wall. It was bad enough climbing up it."

He rolled Jeremy to his side, pushed his feet against the unconscious man's feet for leverage, and pulled him up and over his shoulder in one motion. He grunted when he took Jeremy's full weight.

"I don't know why Wade couldn't be involved, too. It's just not right that I have to do all the work."

"Because Wade couldn't get away," Fallon explained—again.

"Bailey damn sure better appreciate what we're doing," he said.

"I'm sure she will." Fallon didn't add—in time. Bailey would probably feel more like killing them.

Yeah, she was pretty sure that would be her reaction when they strolled in with Jeremy Hunter all trussed up like a calf ready to be spitted over an open flame and cooked.

Eleven

Bailey peeled oranges for the fruit salad she was going to take over to the community dinner. Her job was to do the fruit salad. She had a feeling it was because everyone knew it was safe—no cooking. Just cut up the fruit, add whipped cream, chopped nuts, and marshmallows. Even she couldn't screw that up.

But her heart wasn't in it.

She glanced at the clock. It was late. She should go to bed. She should do a lot of things. She should be happy—tomorrow was the play, too. She had the lead.

A sob caught in her throat. He'd said she couldn't act. He would know. She put the fruit salad in the refrigerator and covered it.

But when she crawled between the cold sheets on her bed, sleep eluded her. She finally snuggled the extra pillow close to her. It was a poor substitute for the warmth he'd given her. She missed the heat that he'd started inside her and that had never really gone away.

You're a fool. He's so not worth your tears.

She knew he wasn't worth crying over but it didn't stop the tears that fell.

Not only had he left her but now she had to face everyone tomorrow. The whole town knew he'd shamed her. Shamed all of them.

Jeremy glared at Fallon. His gaze moved to the other woman, Cody. She was a looker: long black hair and even longer legs. But a bounty hunter? It was kind of hard to believe—except she'd been the one to clip him and had offered only a lame apology. He had a feeling she'd enjoyed taking him down.

And her partner was cool as a cucumber. Nothing seemed to faze him. At one point, Jeremy had tried to reason with Josh. The man had only smiled and told him that he had to face the music.

Face the music? Just thinking about seeing Bailey again sent a flash of heat through his body. Just as quickly, it turned cold.

She hated him. Fallon had already told him as much. Man, was she going to kill him, and who the hell would convict her? Small Texas towns—they got away with murder all the time. And with Wade as the sheriff, it wouldn't be hard to do. He only hoped it was a quick death.

Ah, damn, he knew Bailey needed closure. That was the only reason they'd kidnapped him. As soon as Bailey finished telling him off, they'd put him on a bus that would take him home.

They pulled into town. His hands began to sweat.

"Where do you want me to take him?" Josh asked.

A slow smile curved Fallon's lips. "Take him to the theater. He owes the whole town an apology."

He sank farther down in the seat. Ah, man, this wasn't good. Not good at all. The town would crucify him.

Josh pulled into the alley and after they got out, all three ushered him into one of the dressing rooms. Fallon looked at her watch.

"At least you won't have to wait long."

Bailey squirmed in her seat. The reverend had just finished his sermon. All the preachers had taken ten minutes to talk about forgiveness and loving one another in keeping with the Christmas spirit.

Ho, ho, ho.

She didn't feel much like celebrating. At least the night was almost over. She could go home and wallow in her misery before she had to go to her parents' home tomorrow and pretend to celebrate Christmas.

The crowd in the theater began to murmur in hushed whispers. She looked toward the stage and saw Jeremy Hunter walking across it. He stopped at the podium and looked out over the crowd.

"I was invited to speak here tonight by the town's clergy, but that was when they thought I was one of them. I lied when I said I was a preacher."

There was some grumbling but Fallon shushed them.

Damn, she'd told Fallon not to interfere. And was that Cody and Josh peeking from behind the curtain? Oh, Lord.

"I don't regret coming here," Jeremy said. "But

I do regret the lie and I owe everyone an apology. It's with sincerity that I offer my deepest regret for any problems I might have caused. I hope in time you'll be able to forgive me." He started to turn away.

Bailey jumped to her feet. "Is that what I was, Jeremy Hunter. A problem?"

He hesitated, then cleared his throat. "No, you weren't a problem."

"You just thought you could have your fun and then run away. I mean, I'm just a small town girl— a country hick."

"That's not what I thought and you know it."

"And how the hell . . ." She glanced at the pastors. "Uh, sorry." Then faced Jeremy again. "How was I supposed to know what you were thinking when everything you told me was a lie? You probably weren't raised in an orphanage, either."

"Not exactly."

"Jeremy Hunter you can go to . . . to hell!"

She left her seat and made her way up the aisle.

"I'm already there," he said. "I've been there ever since I left."

She stumbled to a stop.

"Let him beg a bit more, sweetie, before you take him back," Audrey whispered in her southern drawl.

"I don't want him back," she said.

"I'll take him," Callie murmured with a deep sigh.

"For the first time in my life," Jeremy began haltingly, "I've felt a sense of belonging."

She turned around. "Then why did you leave?"

"Because I was scared. I was a fool." He left the stage and began to walk toward her. "You turned my world upside down. Made me believe in people again. You made me see what was missing in my life. Before I met you I was cold and lonely and didn't even know it." He stopped in front of her. "Please don't send me away. I love you."

"Do you even know what the word means?"

"I didn't until I met you."

She didn't know what he'd lived through in his lifetime, but there was a wealth of pain reflected in his eyes. It broke her heart.

"Don't leave me again," she warned.

"Never. I promise."

"If it was me, I'd kiss her," Dr. Canton said. "Young people take up too much time talkin'."

Jeremy wasn't about to tell Dr. Canton he was wrong.

He pulled Bailey into his arms and lowered his mouth. She tasted so damn sweet. And as the whole town cheered, he knew life really could be wonderful.

Epilogue

The winner for best actor in a motion picture is Jeremy Hunter for his portrayal of Trey Jones in A Time For Mercy.

Jeremy stood, the applause was deafening. Bailey squeezed his hand and smiled. He dropped a quick kiss on her lips, felt the heat, the essence of her as he hurried on stage.

"I have a very special person to thank tonight," he said when he got to the microphone. "My beautiful wife. She showed me what it meant to live. I thank God every day she granted me the mercy of forgiveness."

He paused.

"And to the town of Two Creeks, Texas. Where everyone knows each others business but they forgive you anyway."

Bailey smiled. This had been a long time coming and Jeremy deserved to win the Oscar. God, she loved this man so much. Her heart swelled with pride.

"And to my sister-in-law Fallon," he continued. "For breaking into my apartment with her friends, kidnapping me, and making me realize just how much I'd be giving up if I didn't confess my sins and tell Bailey I loved her. And now sweet wife, we have no secrets between us."

Fallon, who was sitting right beside her groaned and sank farther down in her seat.

"You kidnapped him!" The room had grown quiet so her words echoed throughout the cavernous room.

"Well, it worked didn't it."

"Just wait until we get back to Two Creeks."

She looked at Jeremy, knowing he'd told her in front of the crowded room so he wouldn't get into too much trouble.

"Don't think you're off the hook, either. And since we're going public with our secrets, then congratulations." She smiled sweetly. "You're going to be a father."

"What?" he croaked, right before he passed out on stage.

"Oops."

"You could've chosen a better time," Wade whispered.

Bailey stood, but before she hurried on stage, she looked at her brother. "Well, at least I didn't tell him we were having twins."

Home For Christmas

Dianne Castell

One

LuLu Cahill looked out from the gazebo to the falling snow, Christmas lights and carolers on the corner, and knew with absolute certainty that she wanted to be anywhere but home for Christmas! Too many couples, smiling faces, families and total happiness, when all she felt was totally pissed off. She grabbed the railing and growled like a poked dog.

"Not exactly the joyous sounds of the season," said a guy who walked up next to her. "Anything I can do to help?" He handed her a travel mug. "I'll share my apple cider."

"You can help wring my cheating ex-boyfriend's neck who maxed my credit cards then left me." She took a sip then handed back the mug. "And you're here alone because you're a stranger in town?"

"That, and I was dumped at the altar, have guests without a Christmas Eve wedding to attend and had to get out of the house and away from their pity party. If your ex shows up I'd be glad to help with the wringing idea. Course then we'd be sharing a jail cell instead of cider."

He was tall with buzzed dark hair, clean shaven, a little lonely, and a whole lot handsome. "Can't believe a good-looking guy like you got dumped."

"Lost out to the drummer from Blue Sticky Notes. Bachelorette parties should be outlawed. Miss your guy?"

"Miss the sex." She slapped her fingers to her lips. "Can't believe I just said that. What's in that cider?"

"Apples." He chuckled then nodded at the crowd. "The natives are leaving, probably to go home to lovers and warm beds." He took a long drink. The carolers finished up their last song, kettle fires got extinguished and the gazebo suddenly went dark, leaving a sliver of moon, the faint glow of street-lights and the quiet of falling snow. She let go of the railing. "Guess this is our cue to go home."

She turned and slipped on ice, stumbling against Handsome, making him lose his balance, too. They both fell onto the wood bench in fits of laughter. LuLu buried her face in his pea coat. "This is the most fun I've had in two months. Gives you a clue how great my life's been lately. Thought twenty-five was going to be the best year ever."

"I was hoping twenty-nine would do it for me." His eyes darkened as he stared down at her and then, slowly, as if giving her time to stop him, he kissed her. It was one of those mutual kisses, the kind that said I really want this and hope you do, too.

And she did, a lot. He tasted of cider and cinnamon, and smelled like fresh snow and one very delicious man. His tongue touched her bottom lip, and her mouth opened as if she'd been waiting for him and this kiss all her life. Amazing what a little cider can do to brain cells. Then their lips mated more than kissed, and her brain cell's sizzled.

"I needed that," he whispered, his breath hot on hers, his voice low, a little rough and a lot sexy. Where'd this guy come from?

"Glad I was here for you." She nodded for emphasis. "I think I'm horny and tired. Good thing I'm leaving tomorrow. If I ever ran into you after saying something like that I'd die of embarrassment."

He grinned, his teeth white against the dark night. "Won't tell a soul, promise. I don't know your name so your secret's safe. I'm out of here tomorrow, too, no reason to hang around."

Then he kissed her again and she ran her hands through his hair and around his strong neck. She sure felt a lot better then she did five minutes ago. He touched her face, his erection pressing into her middle. Been months since she felt one of those and . . . well dang . . . they really did come in sizes.

"What do you want?" Moonlight danced in his eyes. "Tell me and I'll make it happen. It's the code of the dumped. We hang together, gotta be there for each other."

She swallowed. "I think I want what you want but I could be wrong."

He kissed the tip of her nose. "Forget any reference to the word *but* tonight. I've heard it too many times as in, 'I'm in love with you *but* love him more.' Or, 'I'm in love with you *but* you're never there for me.' Or my personal favorite, 'You're a great guy *but* I just want to be friends.' What the hell does that mean?"

His lips claimed hers in a slow seduction this time. What was he doing? What the heck was *she* doing right out here in a gazebo! Then his fingers crept under her jacket and sweater and caressed her nipple, and she suddenly didn't care about making sense. She gasped, his touch exciting, alluring, promising. She really liked the promising part.

"Do you like that?"

"Don't stop."

He grinned—he had a great grin—and kissed the lobe of her left ear. His rough chin on her cold cheek and neck were the sexiest thing she'd ever felt in her life, till he licked a spot behind her ear, stroked her other nipple, and liquefied her insides to that hot stuff that comes out of volcanoes that she couldn't remember what it was called. She swallowed a primal whine and forced herself to breathe. If she fainted and missed the rest of this magic she'd never forgive herself. "How'd you know to do that? Where'd you learn to . . ." She panted again as he took another taste of her.

"Instinct," he said in a heavy voice. "Pure instinct and the right partner."

"Amen to instinct!"

"Amen to the right partner." He laughed, a deep sound that said he didn't take himself too seriously. "I want to make love to you, here and now."

"There's not enough money in the Western Hemisphere to get me to leave."

"I'm pretty good, but with that much money on the line I hope I don't disappoint."

"No buts, remember, and you passed the pretty good mark two kisses ago."

He reached to his back pocket and pulled out his wallet, covered himself then faced her.

"Did you know that Donna W loves Charles M?" She pointed to the gazebo roof.

"Then it must be true. Glow-in-the-dark orange graffiti wouldn't lie." He bunched her skirt to her waist. His brow rose, a laugh on his lips. "Daffy duck undies? I'm a fan." He looked her in the eyes. "Of a lot of things about you."

She felt herself blush hairline to heels and he quickly placed himself over her. "Damn, it's cold tonight."

"It's getting a whole lot warmer." The tip of his erection thrust against her panties and when his fingers pushed aside the strip of cotton and touched her bare flesh she nearly swallowed her tongue. She gulped a lungful of air and her fists tangled into his coat as he did something down there that nearly sent her into an instant orgasm. "Holy—"

He kissed her, swallowing her whimpers, his fingers pushing deeper and massaging as they went, gradually opening her, setting fire to what was already hot and wet.

"Breathe, sweetheart. You got to remember to breathe." He slowly took his fingers from her and she grabbed his coat. "Oh my God. Don't go!"

"It gets better."

She grabbed him tighter. "Handsome, I can't stand better."

He smiled and this time his erection eased into her just a bit, her body adjusting to his size and that she didn't burst into a million pieces was a complete mystery. His eyes bore into hers. "Am I hurting you? You have to let me know. You're so tight."

"You're magnificent."

"You're a flatterer." His lips met hers as he filled her more, stopping, then moving again till he took her completely; making her feel more like a woman and more desirable than . . . what was the name of that guy she almost married?

"Hold on to me, honey." Handsome braced himself over her, dots of perspiration forming over his lip. "I want this to be special for you because it is for me." He entered again, bit by bit. "I want you ready, eager."

She framed his face between her palms. "Any more eager and I . . ." She pulled his face to hers and kissed him as he thrust into her the third time and everyone knows that the third time is . . . "Oh my God!" she gasped into his mouth, a blazing orgasm roaring through her; Drowning out every sound and every sensation, but all-consuming sex and being with this incredible man.

His damp cheek rubbed against hers, his breathing ragged, fast and uncontrolled. "Oh, sweetheart," he panted again. "You are amazing, incredibly amazing." His chest rose and fell against hers, the back of his neck damp, the weight of his body on hers a delicious sensation of them being one. His gaze met hers and he offered a half smile, and a hint of devil in his voice when he said, "Guess we have more in common than getting dumped."

A car slowly circled the town square, snow crunching under the tires, headlights reflecting off the bushes that hid them.

She said, "It's the sheriff. Can we get thrown in jail for sex on the square?"

"If he finds us we'll definitely be the opening act for the a.m. edition of town gossip, and even if we're leaving we have family here who aren't." Handsome took himself from her, making her feel alone and abandoned, even more than when what's-his-name ran off with what's-her-name. Lulu's brain refused to function, a by-product of afterglow?

He zipped then hunkered down beside the bench. She joined him and he took her hands in his, keeping them warm. "You leave first. Just walk naturally," he said. "The sheriff will think you're out for a night stroll."

"What if he or someone else sees you, too? Won't they know something's up?"

A spark of mystery lit his eyes along with a healthy dose of self-confidence. "Sweetheart, no one will ever see me."

"Oh, boy. You're a vampire."

The grin grew. "Better."

She kissed his cheek. "You're great, Handsome."

"Right back at you." His lips grazed over hers. "You're going to be okay. I want you to believe that. You're young and beautiful and have a lot of living to do. Things will get better. Now get the hell out of here."

The hum of breakfast customers at Slim's mixed with *Boogie Woogie Santa Clause* from the green and yellow jukebox in the corner. LuLu straightened her bulky sweater and tied on a waitress apron dotted with snowmen. Yawning she thought of Handsome, since it was the memory of hot sex and tricky fingers that kept her awake all night. Good thing he was leaving, because the next time she laid eyes on the man she'd jump his bones demanding an instant replay.

"You're brooding over that boyfriend again, aren't you?" sister Callie said, taking a sip of coffee while sitting at the bar. "You got to get over him, get out and socialize. Mix it up a little."

If she'd mixed it up any more she'd be in jail for indecent exposure. LuLu hoisted a tray of breakfast coffee cups and full carafes for the customers seated at the tables. "Maybe I should just leave here like I planned on doing." Because every time she glanced at that gazebo across the street she got a severe attack of frustration knowing she'd never experience anything like that night again if she lived to be a hundred.

Callie took a bite of hush puppy. "You're broke, honey, remember? Unless you like walking and camping and trapping food a lot more than I think you do, you're here for the holidays. Slim's needs help and the pay's good. Besides, we haven't been together since my wedding in June."

"You're right. It will be a good Christmas." Sure was off to a bang-up start. But that part was over and it was a pity. "I think I got the men part of my life figured out. The problem is they keep leaving and it's really getting me down. We're good for a while then bam, they up and run off to greener pastures."

"Men?" Callie's left eyebrow rose. "You have *men* in your life?"

"Man . . . just the one man . . . Jerome." She could remember his name now, but last night under the influence of new hunky man and astonishing sex, noway. "Except for Paul when I was in college, who left me for the Peace Corp. And

Eddie who took that accounting job in Columbia and then there's Danny who joined the monastery in Nepal."

"You drove a guy to celibacy?"

"You're not making me feel better here. The point is I end up alone. If any man wants a life of travel and adventure he just needs to hang around me and it'll happen, guaranteed and . . . Oh heavenly days and mother have mercy," she blurted as Handsome ambled through the main door.

She dropped the tray, mugs and coffee falling everywhere. Better than jumping his bones like she'd planned. Her gaze met Handsome's across the room and he stopped dead. Then he grinned. Oh, crap, did he have to grin? What the heck was he doing here?

"Hi," he said in that low rough voice that sent chills all the way to her fingernails.

Callie looked from one to the other. "You two know each other?"

"No," LuLu said as Handsome said, "Yes." Why did he have to say yes? Now there'd be sister questions and those were the worse kind . . . nosey, prying, unforgiving.

Handsome said, "We met last night on the square."

"For a split second," LuLu added. "By the carolers." She said to Handsome, "You should go find a table, have breakfast, are you leaving today? Gee, that's too bad, I'm so sorry. Have a great Christmas. Ta-ta."

Everyone in the bar stared. Guess the ta-ta was a little over the top. "I mean—"

"Let me help you clean up," Handsome offered, till Callie took his arm, ushering him and the older man he'd entered with in the opposite direction. "I'll show you to a table." She threw LuLu a look that suggested she'd clearly lost her mind and that's exactly what happened last night.

When Callie returned she grabbed a mop and helped LuLu and stage whispered, "What the heck was that all about? You're here one day and you already got something going with this guy?"

"No!" she whispered back as the usual chatter in the bar resumed.

"Well drop it, little sister. You're supposed to be rebounding from Jerome.

"What happened to *mix it up?*"

"Not with him. You need some down time from men, least this kind of man, no matter how handsome he is."

LuLu's eyes fogged. "He is dreamy, isn't he and that's not a question."

Callie dumped shards into the trash as LuLu delivered the coffees. When she came back for a tray of breakfast orders, Callie shoved a green and white flyer under her nose. "Here, concentrate on this. A good way to mix things up."

"Live manger scene?" LuLu said. "And why am I interested in that?"

"Think money. Tomorrow's Christmas Eve and then Christmas Day, and the town's desperate for workers. You'll keep busy and keep your panties on."

"How do you know they came off?"

"Been there, done that, know the look." She tapped the paper. "You got the morning shift working here at the bar, the manger is the afternoon shift. You'll be Joseph, the other one eloped to Vegas with the third shepherd." She sighed. "Maybe you shouldn't be Joseph, bad track record."

LuLu dropped off the two breakfast orders, re-filled coffee, stared at Handsome longer than she should then said to Callie, "Do I look like a Joseph? I'll be the shepherd, better clothes and I get to carry that hook thing."

"Shepherd's taken. You're Joseph. You were going to acting school in L.A., act."

"It was for directing."

"Close enough, and there are all kinds of flyers by the door for part-time Christmas employment needed around O'Fallon's Landing, pick up a handful."

LuLu claimed an order of sausage and ribs. Didn't these people ever hear of South Beach, clogged arteries, high blood pressure, triple bypass? She got a whiff of barbecue and drooled. Forget South Beach.

Okay, this was good, thinking about something besides Handsome. Callie was right, if she kept busy she wouldn't have to dwell on her present situation and she'd pay off some bills. Then she glanced at Handsome and she could barely remember her name. The guy had to go!

LuLu made her way to the jukebox next to his table, dropped in a quarter, punched up 4-B for "*My Christmas Man Blues*" then caught Handsome's eye. "Psst."

His brow arched in surprise, and she hitched her head in a gotta-talk-to-you way. Getting the message he joined her. "What's up?"

"Shhhh. Pretend we're studying the song selection. Don't want anyone to put the two of us together in case they saw us last night."

"Uh, you dropped a tray when I walked in here and there was something about ta-ta. Not ordinary conversation. The jig's up, sweetheart."

"When are you leaving? I thought you'd be gone by now, like that two ships passing in the night idea. But you're still here and no passing's going on."

"I thought you were leaving, too."

"I have money issues, I can't afford to leave. I'm sponging off my sister and her new husband right now, and I'm here to tell you that's so not what I want to be doing this Christmas, but for the moment it can't be helped. Now if you can come back in a month I'll be gone and you can have the whole town all to yourself."

"I'm here to finalize some business with Rebecca-the-wedding-planner over there because there's no wedding. She's the gal sitting with me and Uncle Cordell at the table. I should be gone by noon."

"Today?"

He glanced at his watch. "Two hours and fourteen minutes from now."

"Two hours? I can do two hours . . . maybe. Nothing personal but if you're not around, I'll quit thinking about you and last night and us together and . . . You get the picture."

"You think about me?" His eyes brightened with a hint of fire deep inside.

"Maybe. A little," she lied, then glanced at him out of the corner of her eye and felt her knees wobble. Handsome was too handsome and fabulous in bed . . . or park bench. Location wasn't an issue. "I have to refill coffee cups and hand out heart attacks on a plate. Bye. Have a nice life."

Sebastian Moore stood by the fire at Hastings House Bed and Breakfast and hardly noticed

Rebecca-the-wedding planner making everything perfect for the nonrehearsal dinner. Uncle Cordell put his hand on Sebastian's shoulder. "Don't brood, son. You'll find someone else."

He wasn't brooding, more like daydreaming about orgasmic sex in the gazebo with LuLu Cahill that could not happen again. He needed a break from women. Now was not the time to find new ones. He rubbed his forehead, mentally distancing himself from brown curly hair, blue eyes, and nicely rounded curves that fit so well against him.

Uncle Cordell said, "It's going to be fine. Matter of fact, Rebecca and I agreed that going through with the wedding is a first-rate idea."

"Doesn't having a rehearsal dinner when there's nothing to rehearse sound . . . what's the word . . . nuts!"

Uncle Cordell's head furrowed into a unibrow. "With your mom, me and the rest of the family here and everything paid for, why the hell not go through with the arrangements? Maybe it will give you some of that closure stuff I hear about."

"Closure?" Now there's a word he didn't expect to hear from his uncle.

"And, it's Christmas," Cordell hurried on as if needing to get this over with. "You never know what can happen at Christmas time, least that's what I'm told. Now go upstairs and get dressed."

"Okay, what in blazes is going on around here? You are up to something." Sebastian gave his uncle a long steady look hoping for some telltale sign. "You waxing poetic about Christmas or anything else is not your style. Barking orders, now *that* you got down to a science."

Sebastian glanced at his jeans. "And isn't this

good enough? We're just having dinner, right? Unless you've got something brewing that you're not telling me about."

Rebecca-the-wedding-planner in a black sparkly dress and fancy hairdo glided up to Cordell. She hooked her arm through his and smiled sweetly, especially at Cordell. Waving her hand regally over the dining room with white linens, red and white roses at the tables, the harpist doing her harp thing, gleaming crystal and china, she said, "You need to look nice for your family tonight, dear, like your uncle does in his tux." Rebecca patted Cordell's chest then straightened his noncrooked tie. "So very handsome, don't you agree?"

Handsome? Sebastian felt his gut tighten. That's what LuLu called him. His mother walked in and kissed his cheek. "Oh, this is so lovely, nearly perfect in every way."

Sebastian folded his arms. "Nearly?"

"Well, dear, I do want to see you married and happy. Have the love of your life with you like your father and I had each other."

Sebastian sighed, "Okay, that's it. If you've stashed Bevvy somewhere around here and she's telling you she wants to come back to me, I can tell you right now it's not happening. It's over between us for her sake as well as mine and nothing you can say or she can say can—"

"Damnation, boy." Cordell growled in his best military voice, rattling the window panes and making the cat's fur stand on end before he took a dive for cover. "Go change your clothes. The rest of the family will be coming down any minute now and it *is* your party. Hell, we're not asking for a kidney, and I can assure you that Bevvy is no place around here, and this nonwedding is a damn good idea to get your mind off your problems and on to something else."

Sebastian looked from Cordell to Rebecca to his mother. "What have you all done?"

Cordell gave the official colonel stare. "What I did was put on a damn monkey suit for you. It's Christmas time, show some respect for the season and your mother."

Cordell was playing the mother card. This was more serious than Sebastian thought. And he was getting nothing but a bunch of double-talk that went nowhere. But since he'd never win an argument with a retired army colonel or his mother, Sebastian climbed the polished mahogany stairs draped in pine and holly garland in the main hall, to his antique-filled room overlooking the Mississippi River.

Not the kind of accommodations he was used to, though, someone like LuLu would fit in just fine. Frilly lace curtains, lacy towels, girly . . . and LuLu Cahill was definitely all girl, make that voluptuous soft woman who wanted nothing to do with him, and under the circumstances that suited him fine. With luck she'd be busy with Christmas and not even know he was at Hastings House. After the nonwedding dinner tomorrow night on Christmas Eve he'd leave. Even for his family, there was just so much nonwedding he could take.

He dressed, taking care that everything looked correct even though he never felt comfortable in dress attire. Camouflage suited him fine and in one week he'd be back where he belonged, taking cover behind a rock or tree, doing what he was trained to do in some hellhole that needed attention. He wasn't called a snake eater for nothing.

"Can I help you?" Sebastian asked as he trotted down the staircase. A man stood in the entrance hall, his back to Sebastian. A short guy wearing a long brown robe with a hood, donkey probably parked outside. Then the man spun around. "LuLu?"

"Handsome?" Her blue eyes covered half her face. "What the . . . All right, why are you still here? I think I asked that question before." She parked her hands on her hips. "What happened to noon, two hours and fourteen minutes and you getting out of town and us not seeing each other again? That was the plan, right?"

"Why are you dressed like that?"

"And why are *you* dressed like *that?*

Two

LuLu tried to wrap her head around what was going on but didn't get a very good grip. "I'm Joseph and also your friendly neighborhood serving wench better known as juggling two jobs—make that three—because I'm financially challenged." Sounded better than butt-ugly broke. "Rebecca-the-wedding-planner hired me to help with a rehearsal dinner, and I sure didn't suspect it was yours because you're not supposed to be here and you're not getting married and what's with the uniform?"

She swallowed a primal female whine. Handsome had been handsome enough last night in pea coat, jeans and moonlight, but now. Holy moly!

"It's my nonrehearsal dinner and not my idea. I got talked into going through with it because it's paid for and my family's here and for another reason that I wasn't told but getting more obvious by the minute." He shrugged "And as for the uniform . . . Bevvy wanted me to wear it for our wedding. It's the only dress clothes I brought with me and certain people tonight were insistent that I change."

"The boy's Special Forces," beamed an older man as he rounded the corner. He was the same guy who accompanied Handsome to Slim's, and he held out his hand to LuLu and pumped hers hardily. "I'm Cordell, Sebastian's uncle, just retired here to O'Fallon's Landing after thirty years military and I'm crazy about the place. I'm the one who suggested he get hitched here, except it didn't work out between him and Bevvy." Then he grinned like it was working out just fine now.

He pointed at LuLu. "Nice duds. Caught your act in town this afternoon, was that the first time you ever milked a goat? You should take that act on the road."

"I've sworn off feta forever." So his name was Sebastian? She liked Handsome better.

Rebecca-the-wedding-planner swept in carrying a tray of champagne glasses. "Well, my stars, you made it after all. I was getting a mite worried." She grinned, and was that a wink she sent to Cordell? What was with the wink? Guess she caught the goat show, too. "You and Sebastian need to get better acquainted."

"We do?" Except that boat had already sunk, LuLu thought as she claimed the tray. "You hired me to help serve. I should do that, and you all can chat and socialize."

Rebecca grabbed back the tray as another woman in a black silk suit said, "Joseph can't be serving champagne, dear, doesn't seem right somehow. It's lovely to meet you, I'm Sebastian's mother, Isabella." Then she and Rebecca and Cordell left the hall as if exiting from a fire.

"I don't get it," she said to Handsome. "This whole nonrehearsal thing is a little strange. What's going on?"

He let out a long breath and sat on the steps. Resting his forearms on his knees, a little smile formed at the corners of his mouth. The brass buttons of his uniform and his polished shoes glistened under the chandelier light. He was tan, she realized, as if back from a Caribbean vacation. Oh yeah, that's where the army sent all their soldiers these days. "If you planned on us being together like this, I'm going to be totally ticked off."

"Not exactly. Mother and Uncle Cordell have the finesse of a tank. This is a setup job with the help of Rebecca. They're trying to get my mind off my defunct wedding and you're it."

She looked at her robe. "Boy, are they desperate."

"Uncle Cordell and Rebecca saw us together at Slim's. Probably picked up on the vibes."

"We have vibes?"

"Sweetheart,"—his smile broadened and everything in the hall got a little fuzzy—"I'd put us at about eight point five on the Richter."

She considered sitting down beside Handsome because she was tired from adventures with goats, but she was still reeling from seeing him when she just got used to the idea of not ever seeing him again. "None of this would have happened if you'd left when you said you would. What went wrong?"

"A lot of double-talk coupled with the fact that my family drove in for the wedding and it made sense to go through with everything as planned. Least that's the line my dear uncle and his accomplice fed me at Slim's when I wanted to call everything off."

He ran his hand over his fuzz hair. "But now you're here and I'm here and we're alone, and it doesn't take rocket science to figure out what's really going on is family matchmaking and not so much a family reunion."

LuLu leaned against the newel post. "You're a soldier and going away, and I don't mean like off to Cleveland for a shoe convention. You do serious leaving and I've had my quota of men exiting my life. In fact I think I hold some kind of record for that particular kind of guy. I should be the one who leaves right now before this goes any further."

"No, wait." Handsome jumped up and blocked her path to the door. She didn't know a guy could move so fast. "Look, you need the money and I want to spend time with my family. If you leave everyone here will be upset that their great plan didn't work and you'll have to pull double shifts at the stable." He pushed her Joseph hood back, his fingers touching her cheek, making her insides somersault and her heart do the happy dance. "We'll get this nonwedding over with, it's just for tonight and tomorrow. You get paid, I visit and keep my family happy. Then we go our separate ways. And if you're beside me some of the time, they all won't be thinking poor Sebastian. They'll just be looking at you thinking I'm one lucky guy."

From the corner of her eyes she caught sight of Rebecca poking her head around the corner followed by uncle and mother. Like kids peeking at Santa on Christmas morning! They flashed gotcha smiles then retreated. "There is one little flaw, your family's trying to push us together and two days of pushing may be more willpower then I have. Look what happened last night and no one was pushing. You're not the kind of guy I want in my life."

"And I'm not looking for a relationship to leave behind, either. What if we set up diversionary tactics so the meddlesome trio doesn't have time to push so hard."

"Tactics like in blowing up a bridge?"

"Like in turning the tables. Uncle Cordell's been a bachelor all his life and he's taken to Rebecca. We can push them together, then they'll forget about us or at least not concentrate on us so hard."

"What about Isabella? Mothers want to see their kids happy and that translates into they want them married."

A deep male voice with a touch of Tennessee twang sounded from the dining room, "Dinner is served."

Handsome folded his arms and rocked back on his heels. "Not only do we have Rebecca-the-wedding-planner, we have Terrance-the-chef. Mother brought him in from Memphis. All I've heard from mother is Terrance's great soufflé, Terrance's great beef burgundy, and that he could flip her pancakes anytime. I think it's time she had someone special in her life again. She just needs a nudge."

"So, we get the four resident lovebirds together and they'll leave us alone. That might work, worth a try, and right now *I* better get to work." LuLu pulled the robe off over her head and hung it by the door. "Okay, soldier boy, I'm ready to get this show on the road."

Except Handsome didn't move. He just stood

there under the chandelier looking a little thoughtful and a lot yummy. "Damn, you're beautiful. Didn't get a chance to appreciate that fact last night."

She straightened her white overblouse and smoothed out her black pants. "I'm a little thick right now. No compliments needed."

"Sweetheart, I'm looking at great curves and a very fine woman."

She took a deep breath. "What you're looking at is a pregnant woman."

Handsome's eyes rounded.

"That was pretty much my reaction, too. Jerome's reaction was catching the first plane out of LAX with his new cupcake at his side."

"Jerome better say his prayers he doesn't ever cross my path."

"It's a good thing that he's gone. He's not the daddy type, more the which-club-tonight type. No one knows about this besides you. I've been doing the baggy blouse, sweater, jacket over the slacks thing and it's been working okay. Course it's not going to work forever, but I want to get my bills paid off and look responsible when I break the news to my sister. She's worried about me for forever and this once I'd like to take charge. I have skills and I'm a hard worker and not the first single mom to make a go of it."

"And a soldier thousands of miles away is not what you need in your life."

"And you don't need a pregnant woman. We agree, and we'll get along for two days and then go our separate ways no strings attached. But no smoochy-smoochy stuff. My hormones are already a mess, which was proven by the fact that I ravaged you in the gazebo last night."

He laughed a really great happy sound that made her happy too. "Not exactly the way I remember it, but I'll honor the kissing ban."

"Now, I have to help Terrance serve. Save me a place and drink my champagne so I don't have to explain." Before he could stop her, LuLu rushed off for the kitchen. If she stayed another minute she'd say something else stupid. Smoochy smoochy! Dear heaven, where'd that spring from? When it came to Handsome she was out of her flipping mind, but she only had to flip for another day and a half, then he'd be history and she'd have money.

She passed out salad then beef Wellington to Handsome's six aunts, eight uncles, five cousins, three grandparents, one godmother and godfather, his mother and Rebecca, all of them making her feel welcome. She sat next to him and whispered, "You have a great family."

"I have a great date." Then his leg accidentally rubbed against hers and she nearly grabbed him and slid under the table.

Uncle Cordell stood and tapped his glass with his fork. "I'd like to make a toast to all of you for being here and to Sebastian for this great party he decided to have in spite of everything."

Handsome smiled, looking as comfortable as a cat sitting on hot coals. Isabella added, "And to LuLu for filling in as his special guest."

LuLu gave the aw-gee-whiz smile, but deep down inside she liked the special guest comment. Being something special to Handsome mattered more than she wanted it to. She enjoyed his company, his laughter, his bedroom finesse, even when he wasn't in a bedroom, and she liked that he thought Jerome was a pig. Why couldn't Handsome be a farmer? Farmers stayed in one place and didn't get used for target practice.

After she served dessert she reclaimed her place beside Handsome and whispered between bites of ribbon cake, "They're ganging up against us. Your mom just showed me one of your baby pictures she keeps in her purse—you look adorable on a bearskin rug—and Cordell asked when he could meet my folks. We need to launch operation counter-matchmaker right now. I'll take Isabella and Terrance. You handle Rebecca and your uncle."

"Could get complicated."

"It already is."

Rebecca stood and announced, "Brandy and cookies are in the parlor and we'll sing Christmas carols. *Deck the halls with boughs of holly,*" she started as everyone paraded out of the dining room. LuLu said to Handsome, "Think about something romantic to bring the couples together. You know . . . wine, flowers, music."

"What about locking Cordell and Rebecca in the wine cellar?"

"That's it? That's all the romance you have in you? Didn't you ever watch '*Pretty Woman*' or '*Moonstruck*?' "

"You and I didn't need more than a place last night and look what happened. It's the company not the geography. They need alone time."

Actually that idea was pretty romantic all by itself. His eyes darkened and she'd give anything for alone time with Handsome again, like last night, but it was over.

He tweaked the end of her nose and headed for the parlor. She cleared dishes then found a pen in the cherry sideboard and scribbled on a paper napkin: *Meet me at the gazebo in town at midnight.*

She studied her work. Talk about not romantic. She took a little angel ornament from the mantel decorations, added *Isabella, my angel* to the outside of the note and signed it *Your sweet savage chef.* Better!

Another round of fa-la-la-la-la-la sounded from the parlor as LuLu pulled up next to Isabella standing in the back of the little crowd. LuLu whispered, "Found this on the table as I was clearing. Looks important." She slipped the angel onto the sheet music.

Isabella looked from the angel to LuLu who gave a little I-have-no-idea shrug then took off as *God Rest Ye Merry Gentlemen* started. Finding an untapped bottle of champagne LuLu attached the same note but addressed it to *My sweet savage chef* and signed it *Your Christmas angel.* Waiting till Terrance left the kitchen, she set the bottle on the counter then ducked around the corner watching till he found the note. He grinned, blushed, then slid the note in his pocket.

"What are you doing?" Handsome said, his breath on her neck making every inch of her body prickle. She took his hand and led him into the garden room at the back, with wintering plants on white-fern stands and moonlight streaming through big windows. She couldn't think of a better place to be than alone in the dark with Handsome, except that's not why they were together here. This was business. "Terrance and your mom are a go. I'm a natural-born matchmaker. How are things on your end?"

"You're lovely in moonlight."

"That's because you can't see my girth."

"It's because you're lovely in moonlight." He kissed her hair making her feel wonderful and . . . beautiful, just like he said. His arms wound around her, his kisses dropping from her hair to her ear then trailing down her neck. He lifted her right off the floor, her toes dangling, his strong body tight against hers. She slid her arms around him—so as not to fall. That was the reason. "No smoochy smoochy, remember?"

His eyes looked into hers. "I needed to kiss you, needed it all night." His lips were so close to hers she could feel his mouth form the words on her mouth. "Just once more." He kissed her again, a low testosterone-filled growl rumbling in his chest. "Okay, twice more," he said, his mouth still on hers. "But now I'm done."

"Promise?"

"No."

Thank God! Her heart raced, her mouth dry as the cactus sitting in the corner; his erection pressing against her leg driving her insane. He let her body slide down his, feeling his strength under his jacket. Fire licked at her insides and she wanted Handsome to do some licking of his own, on her, naked on one of those bearskin rugs or any place else that happened along.

Then he suddenly stepped away from her. "Damn, woman." He panted "I can't get enough of you. I've walked away from women before but you . . . Why is it so hard with you?"

"And I shouldn't do this or say this, but I got to because I'll never get another chance." She cupped his erection, his eyes snapping wide open, his heat against her palm making her warm and wet deep inside from wanting him. "I really love you hard."

Sebastian felt his brain fry. He'd wanted her all day, and her hand on his dick made the wanting even more intense. "You thought kissing was too intimate? What's this?"

"Temporary insanity brought on by severe frustration. Why didn't you and Bevvy get married in Vegas like everyone else? Really would have simplified things."

"Sebastian?" came Isabella's voice echoing down the hall along with her footsteps on the hardwood floor. "Where are yo— Oh," she said as she flipped on the lights, the two of them parting as if a stick of dynamite exploded between them. Sebastian sidestepped behind a potted fern the bulge below his belt much too obvious.

"My goodness," she stammered. "I should have known you two might be together. I didn't mean to interrupt. I'm just not thinking straight because . . . Well, I'm just not is all."

She looked to Sebastian then started to pace. "I'm going out for a spell, dear. I know it's late but I do so want to see this darling town all snowy and like a winter wonderland. I hear there's a little gazebo and we don't get much of this sort of thing in Florida and . . ." She stopped pacing and sighed. "Oh, what the heck, I'm off to meet a man. There, I said it. I'm an old hussy."

"Dad's been gone five years. You're allowed to have a life." His voice more controlled than he felt at the moment and it wasn't because mother was meeting Terrance, it was because he wanted to take LuLu on that love seat in the corner. "Have fun. I won't wait up."

She giggled then sobered, nibbling her bottom lip. "This is all new for me but it feels right. He's a fine man, Sebastian. I've known it for a while now." She blushed and turned for the hall.

Sebastian took a deep breath. "The plan's working. Mother didn't care what we were up to with a new man in her life. And she deserves this. Works on all fronts."

LuLu headed for the door. "I'll follow your mother and make sure she connects up with Terrance. We don't want her out at night all alone and I feel responsible."

"If this town was any safer it would be in a Disney movie."

She stopped and studied him. "And that's one movie you and I will never star in. When we're alone together it's all sex and steam. We have to stay apart."

"No more meetings in the conservatory?"

"You concentrate on getting Rebecca and Cordell into that wine cellar. I'll check on Isabella and then I'm going home, away from you and convince myself you're just another guy. I'll see you tomorrow for the wedding."

"Non-wedding and I am just a guy."

She let out a little whine then ran off. He headed to the kitchen for cheese and seduction stuff . . . whatever the hell that was. One more day and then he'd be gone, and LuLu and her sexy whine would be part of his past. The thought sat like a lump of coal in his gut. But that was too damn bad. When he put on his uniform years ago he knew there'd be times like this. Trouble was, then it was a noble idea and he hadn't met LuLu.

Yeah, keeping busy was the answer and— "Mother?" Sebastian said as he rounded the corner. "What happened to the walk? The gazebo and the cute town? You're still here."

"Well, you see, the snow is really coming down so we decided to take a walk in the garden out back. It's beautiful under the full moon and—"

"Snow?"

"As in white stuff falling from the sky in buckets. This Bevvy thing has rotted your brain, son."

Oh shit! LuLu was headed into town. She'd freak when she couldn't find Isabella and probably go looking all over the place for her. What if she fell? Got buried in a snowdrift. She was pregnant, dammit!

"Something wrong, dear? You look awful."

"Indigestion. Too much pie. Everything's fine. Enjoy your walk."

"But we had cake for dessert and cookies. I saw LuLu walking down the drive. Does she have far to go?"

He kissed Isabella on the cheek then made for his room. He needed to find LuLu. Why didn't he check the fucking weather? Because he was too obsessed with fucking LuLu.

He took the steps two at a time, changed into jeans and boots, grabbed his coat and was out the door. He headed down the curvy drive and across the two-lane to town. No sign of LuLu except her footprints. She had nice footprints, cute ones. He was getting a hard-on over her footprints . . . He was going insane.

When he got to the gazebo she wasn't there. He

peered through the falling flakes to the blue and red Budweiser sign. He pushed open the door to Slim's and some bluesy tune, and LuLu sitting at a table with . . . Oh damn "Bevvy?"

"Sebastian," Bevvy called across the bar, standing and waving her arms. She grinned and motioned him over. LuLu sat with her back to him, he recognized the brown robe. With luck it was another Joseph in for a visit. She didn't move, didn't look at him, didn't even turn toward him to acknowledge his existence. It was his Joseph all right. Double damn.

Bevvy threw her arms around his neck and kissed him full on the mouth. "Oh, Sebby, you are the best."

LuLu peered up at him, her eyes shooting daggers. "Depends on what best you're referring to. Best soldier, best kisser, best liar."

Bevvy sat and pulled him into the chair beside her. "I met this nice girl dressed up like a shepherd and we got to talking and she knows you."

"Well, look who's here," Isabella said as she strolled up, her arms through Terrance's.

"Mother?" Great. The night was getting better and better. "What happened to the garden walk?"

"We just kept on going because the stars are beautiful and here we are and . . . Well, mercy me, it's Bevvy?" Mother blinked a few times. "When did you get into town, dear? Oh, my stars, you've come back for the wedding!"

"I have?"

"You've reconsidered." Isabella threw her arms around Bevvy. "Welcome to the family. The judge is still scheduled for tomorrow and—"

"*I've* reconsidered?"

Oh damn, for the second time, Sebastian thought.

This was like walking through a land-mine field never knowing what would blow up next.

"Sebastian *is* the best man," his mother went on. "Well, actually he isn't the best man, he's really the groom. A little wedding joke." She laughed. "But now you're here and the wedding will go off without a hitch."

"*I've* reconsidered," Bevvy repeated starting to look royally pissed off with her arms folded over her chest. "What the dickens is going on here, Sebby? Exactly what did you tell everyone about us breaking up?"

LuLu stood. "And let's not leave anything out, Sebby. To be more specific, you said that Bevvy's the one who called off the wedding."

Bevvy's eyes rounded. "Me? But—"

"You didn't end it?" Isabella gasped, staring at Bevvy with her jaw dropping a fraction. "I don't understand. This is all very confusing. Then why in the world did Sebastian say you did?" All eyes zeroed in on Sebastian and enemy fire took on a whole new meaning.

Sebastian stood. "Yes, it was my idea to call off the wedding."

Isabella draped her arm around Bevvy and drew her close. "And here I thought you a little trollop for running off with that drummer person."

"Actually, I did run off with him, but only after Sebby said he and I were through." Bevvy sniffed. "He went and broke my heart, Isabella. He truly did." She brightened. "But I've found true love now and that's why I'm here. I came to thank Sebby for doing what he did. Bruno is the love of my life."

"You lied to us?" Isabella said to Sebastian. Was that steam curling from her ears? "How could you?

We're your family. This entire wedding catastrophe is all your doing?" She tapped her booted foot and shook her head. "I worried about you, fretted something terrible, said novenas, lit candles for your poor old broken spirit and right now I'm thinking about breaking your head."

Sebastian said, "Bevvy got her drummer, the family got to visit. I broke the engagement because I didn't want to leave Bevvy behind to worry about me. I said she called things off because no woman likes to get dumped so I let her do the dumping."

"Wait a minute!" LuLu's eyes grew huge. "You made this decision to not get married all by yourself? You didn't tell Bevvy what was going on in that brain of yours? Shouldn't she have a say?"

"But I did find my Bruno," Bevvy sighed, till LuLu poked her in the chest saying, "You're a grown woman and capable of determining your own life."

Bevvy's eyes got dreamy. "And I want my life to be forever with my drummer boy. He had my name tattooed on his forehead inside a heart. And he has a lock of my hair attached to his earring."

Sebastian said to his mother, "Dad was in the army all those years and I knew you worried when he was gone, and the thought of doing the same thing to Bevvy or anyone else didn't feel right. And she and Bruno had been doing the eye contact thing all night, so I figured letting her go was the best for both of us."

"It was my bachelorette party, eye contact with cute guys is expected," Bevvy said as Isabella stood tall and added, "And I knew full well what I was getting into when I married your father. I do have a brain, you know."

"Well, now," said Terrance as he drew up beside

Sebastian. "I believe I understand what you're doing here. A man's got to take charge in these situations, do the responsible thing for the women in his life. Sebastian here didn't want his new bride to fret so he saved her from that. Right smart thing to do as I see it."

"Save her?" LuLu said. "Like she can't take care of herself? Marriage is a partnership. What century do all you men live in?

"I want to live with my Bruno in any century." Bevvy batted her eyes. "We're going on tour in January, living in one of those big buses and going all over the place with the Blue Sticky Notes."

"See," Terrance said. "Women get so love struck they don't know what they want."

Rebecca and Uncle Cordell strolled into Slim's, and Rebecca said, "Well, my goodness. Looks like the party's moved to here and . . . Bevvy? You're here? How exciting. Does this mean the wedding's back on? Bless my heart!"

"Only if I marry my Bruno," she mewed, then Isabella added, "And there's a new wrinkle. Sebastian's the one who called off the wedding because he didn't want her to worry when he leaves next week, do you believe that?."

"Oh, my," said Rebecca, giving Sebastian the no-good-rotten-scoundrel look.

"But it is the honorable thing to do," chimed in Uncle Cordell standing behind Sebastian, the three men doing the bonding thing. "If he and Bevvy were meant to get hitched, then they could tie the knot when he got back."

Rebecca's eyes lit with fire. "That means marriage is only for the good times. If things get tough, woman should just cut and run, is that it?"

Rebecca, Isabella, LuLu, and Bevvy stood on one side of the table, Sebastian, Uncle Cordell, and Terrance on the other, with customers enjoying the soap opera. Sebastian said, "We're making a scene here. I think it's time for us all to be getting back to the inn."

"I have my Bruno's Hummer," Bevvy said, her lids fluttering. "I'd be happy to give you ladies a lift back to the inn. Bruno said he knew I'd be safe in the Hummer. Wait till you see it. It has a TV." She clasped her hands to her chest. "He is my darling hero."

LuLu sat. "Think I'll hang out here for awhile."

Rebecca added, "A Hummer? Now that's a truck with some major cahonies."

Uncle Cordell's eyes rolled. "What kind of talk is that from a lady?"

"A lady who can make up her own mind, in case there was any doubt."

"I'll wait with LuLu," Sebastian said, making it a statement instead of a question and knowing he'd made a big mistake doing that the minute the words were out. He needed a class in women 102. He flunked 101.

LuLu glared. "There's only one main road through town so I'm not likely to get lost. I can handle it all by myself. And the snow's stopped."

The women, except for LuLu, trooped for the door, the men looking pissed without a nice fat Hummer waiting for them. The customers took up with their food again, sad the new show in town was over.

When Sebastian got outside he stayed on the porch, watching the women load into the Hummer, the men trailing behind. He pulled a cigarette from a pack and lit up, something he rarely did anymore. The porch light caught the "*hazardous to your health*" warning and he considered where he'd be ten days from now. Hazardous was a hell of a lot more than cigarettes and he knew in his gut he did the right thing in calling off the wedding.

He inhaled another drag, turned his collar against the chill and waited for LuLu-the-stubborn to get her very lovely fanny outside so he could walk her home.

Three

LuLu sipped her cider and gazed at the front door of Slim's. Another guy gone right out of her life, but this time like before with Jerome it was a good thing. Not only didn't she need to get involved with another Mr. coming-and-going but this one thought he had all the answers. She didn't need Handsome making decisions for her like he did for Bevvy. What the heck was the man thinking? And why did she have to keep thinking about him? At least she had the night to herself and could work on getting him out of her system.

She headed for the door, stepped outside and straight into Handsome's path. "This is not you going home." And it sure wasn't her getting over him.

"Thought I'd walk you to your place."

"I'm going back to the inn and I can do it on my own."

"Going to the inn because you miss me?"

She did but she'd get over it. "Since you're here

and not likely to leave me alone you can help. We need to get the happy couples happy again. They like each other well enough, some great attraction going on there but your little scheme with Bevvy turned everything upside down and got them doing battle royal instead of making out. We need to fix things, we're responsible since we set them up in the first place."

She was babbling. Being with Handsome in the falling snow on a beautiful starry night was enough to make any woman babble her head off.

"We'll go with the original idea, lure them to the garden room and wine cellar. Cold but isolated and we'll only keep them there for a few hours, which should be enough time to let them work things out."

She resisted the urge to snuggle close to Handsome as they walked to the inn. She needed distance and noninvolvement to get through this night and send him on his way tomorrow without ravaging him. Okay, how'd that last part get in there? She shouldn't even be thinking about ravaging. She was mad at him! No ravaging. She was glad he'd be gone . . . remember!

"I want to get something straight so you don't think I'm a complete jerk. When I went to pick Bevvy up from her bachelorette party she was sitting on Bruno's lap and he wasn't giving her percussion lessons, unless that's done with his tongue halfway down her throat. I figured if she was acting that way with me stateside and our wedding right around the corner, what would she be doing months from now when I was halfway around the world? I didn't want to be worrying about her, and she sure didn't want to be worrying about me. I did her a favor and she knew it. That's why she showed up tonight."

"Dear man, the reason she showed up was to impress everyone with the Hummer." Lights in the bushes led the way up the curvy drive to the warm lights of Hastings House glowing through the windows. "Looks like a Christmas card. Perfect place for a nonwedding."

"And getting the loving couples loving again. With luck there should be so much love in the air by midnight the place will be dripping with it."

"And I can go home and get some sleep." She rested her head against his chest. "What a crock."

"What's a crock?" His arms held her close.

She shouldn't let this happen, she was mad, remember? She really sucked at remembering lately. "As long as you're within a ten mile radius I'll never be able to sleep because I'll be thinking about you." She looked up at him. "Well, more accurately, I'll be thinking about sex with you. Do all pregnant women want to get laid this badly? I don't remember feeling this way when Jerome was around."

"Must be my good looks and great personality."

And it was, but acknowledging that was no way to get over him and she was already doing a really bad job of that. "Mostly it's that you're good— make that great—in the sack. Can't believe I really said all that. Hormones on parade." She wiggled out of his arms and pushed open the door, pulling Handsome inside behind her. She kicked off her boots and hung up her Joseph's coat. "On with the plan."

"I liked our plan outside better."

"We need to stay away from each other. We can

do that. Right now we don't even like each other all that much, except for sex, so it should be a snap. Sex isn't everything."

Sebastian hunted up Uncle Cordell sitting by the fire, sipping brandy. What Sebastian wouldn't give to have LuLu by this fire all to himself, and that her thoughts ran in the same direction only made him think about it all the more. Who knew that horniness was contagious? "Rebecca needs you to help bring up a case of wine from the wine cellar."

"And your arm's broke?"

"Hey, she asked for you and I am not getting between two opposing fronts. Maybe she's looking for an opportunity to apologize, consider that. You really get along and a little difference of opinion over decision making shouldn't get in the way."

"Criminy sakes." Cordell gazed into the fire. "What is it with women? If I live to be a hundred I'll never understand them. You think you're trying to protect them, put yourself out for them and take care of them, and then they get their panties in a twist and get all huffy about taking care of themselves and doing their own thing, and suddenly you're the bad guy."

"You are asking the wrong person about this. I got a bad track record in the female department."

"True enough." Cordell offered up his drink in a salute. "Neither of us is worth a damn when it comes to women. But if Rebecca needs me I'll help her out, and maybe she does want to apologize. She really is all wrong on this protection idea."

"Uh, you might want to soft-pedal that idea a little if you're wanting her back. No woman wants to hear about being wrong."

"Well, she is, dammit. But I'll go see what she wants all the same."

Which was good since Sebastian just told Rebecca that Uncle Cordell wanted her to pick out the right wine for tomorrow's dinner. That was one way of getting them into the cellar at the same time. He sucked at telling lies.

"Can you forget about being right for a little while?" he called after Cordell.

"Hell, no."

This part of the get-them-back-together plan was not going well. "Maybe you should try one of those bottles of wine while you're in the cellar." Or two bottles or three.

"Not much of a wine drinker."

"Now's a good time to start." Following Cordell at a distance Sebastian waited for him to go down into the basement part of the old house.

Cordell called, "Rebecca?"

"In here looking for you." He entered and asked Rebecca what she wanted. Then she asked why he was here. She said she could pick out her own wine, thank you very much, and Cordell said something about a fickle woman and Sebastian slammed the door shut. Least that stopped them arguing for a minute before they both started pounding on the door. Good thing it was in the basement so no one else could hear the commotion.

He sprinted back upstairs to the dining room and LuLu fluffing red tablecloths over tables. He stood in the doorway watching her work, appreciating the way she walked, moved, held her head, the way her hair fell across her shoulders. Getting too close was dangerous for both of them after her "in the sack" confession, and at the moment he couldn't trust himself not to tackle her to the carpet right there in front of the roaring fire.

"Well," he said to break the silence and start thinking of something else besides LuLu. "The two hardheads have cheese, bread, soft lighting, and lots of wine and if they're ever going to make a go of it, it's now. If they find out I locked them in that cellar they'll either thank me or lynch me, and when I left them the lynching theory was winning big time."

"Isabella and Terrance were fighting like rutting rams when I shut them in the garden room and locked the door. Hope they don't break any windows trying to escape from each other. Maybe it'll all work out."

"Maybe pigs fly." Sebastian looked around. "Where is everyone else?"

"Sleeping, or at least in their bedrooms. Even the owners retired for the night. Lots of snow, and big fireplaces in each room brings out the romance in everyone." Her eyes locked with his and he stepped farther into the hall putting more space between himself and so much temptation in the form of one dynamite female, talking romance.

She said, "Why don't you go to bed?"

Did everything have to remind him of the two of them never being together, when he wanted it more than air? He ached. She looked pained too and hurried on with, "I have to set things up here then get going in the kitchen or Terrance will never have breakfast ready on time and any good feelings he has with Isabella could be lost in the chaos of running late. We don't want that."

"You know how to cook?" He put plates on the table doing one side of the room as she did the other. Talking was okay as long as he kept his distance.

"I know how to organize." She set out the glasses. "In school I was the one who got the cameras, people, sets together. Never knew what to do after that but I got things ready to roll." He set the last plate and his back brushed against LuLu's. He stopped, the connection sending little jolts through his body. Slowly, he turned and faced her.

"Thanks for setting dishes." Her cheeks flushed and big blue eyes darkened.

"Glad to help." He hated small talk.

"You . . . smell so good."

Okay, he needed lots of small talk, something to take their minds off each other and being alone. "I think it's the gorgonzola. I put it out in the wine cellar for Cordell and Rebecca. That is some strange cheese."

Her lips softened and she placed the tray of glasses on the table. "I think I have an attraction to gorgonzola. Actually . . ." She sighed. "Actually, I hate cheese so that means it's you." She licked her bottom lip. "All you and neither of us wants it to be, do we, but that's the way it is."

"Oh, boy." Then he snapped her into his arms and kissed her, her sweet body molding against his chest, her hands in his hair—what there was of it— and shooting their nonattraction, stay-away ideas all to hell and back.

"We can't do this."

"We always do this."

"Then we have to face it for what it is."

"Insanity?"

"Sex. Nothing else. No promises, no commitments, no planning for the future. You don't want someone worrying about you when you're gone, and I don't want to have another revolving-door relationship that leaves us with sex." She gave a sassy smile. "And that's not all bad. We can do just sex. I think we're aces at just sex."

"But there's something between us."

She kissed him, flattening him against the wall by the door with a sold thud. "Yeah, really good sex. Focus on that, only that."

"Okay, got it." His tongue fondled hers as he drew her deeper into his arms. "And we can walk away from sex easily enough, is that the idea?"

"Nothing personal, basic carnal involvement, simple stuff like you and me and fitting parts together." She gazed up at him. "It's all the rest of the complications about leaving that makes us nuts. Sex is pretty straight forward. And . . . and I really like it. In fact—" She pulled in a quick breath. "The more I talk about it with you right now, the more I like it and want it."

They dropped to the rug by the hearth, knocking over a stack of napkins. The logs crackled and hissed, Sebastian's insides did the same. Nothing could be more erotic than sex with LuLu in front of a blazing hearth on a cold snowy night. He tore off his shirt.

"You are really one ripped male."

He laughed deep in his chest. "With what I do, it's be in shape or be dead."

Her eyes clouded with concern and she bit her bottom lip, the very thing he intended to avoid, he quickly added, "But I am in good shape."

She touched a thin scar on his shoulder.

"It was nothing and I know what I'm doing and I'll be fine. Don't think about that now. Sex, remember. Nothing but you and me and being here." He kissed her hair.

She let out a deep breath. "Maybe I'll write you."

"You're losing focus here." He pulled off her fluffy sweater and grinned. "Better."

She slid off her bra.

"Much better. You are so gorgeous." Then he took her in his arms giving them bare skin against bare skin, a delicious sensation as his hands stroked her back and her hands stroked across his shoulders making him aware of his physical strength against her graceful form. His hands molded to her sides to the indent of her abdomen, then up to the gentle swells of her breasts. "You have skin like silk." He kissed her shoulder.

His pulse drummed as he kissed her slender throat and gently laid her back. He kissed the furrow of cleavage between her firming breasts and she moaned, her body arching to meet his as his fingers found one dusky hard nub and his tongue worshiped the other.

"Oh, God, Handsome. You're too much." Her fingers pressed into his shoulders while he dropped kisses, to her navel; the rise and fall of her chest quickening. He undid the button on her slacks then unzipped, the sound a promise of sweet things to come. He kissed her slightly swelled belly.

"Pregnancy is good for you." He looked up, catching her gaze. "You are so sexy. Glowing. Completely feminine."

"It's the hormones and I'm fat and going to get a lot fatter."

"You're pregnant and perfect."

"What men don't say to get into a woman's pants." She gave him a half smile.

"Sweetheart, I've already been there and beyond." Then he kissed her stomach again before sitting up. "I need to see you, all of you, every inch in the firelight." He peeled her slacks and panties down over her rounded hips, her eyes smoldering as he uncovered her dark mysterious patch that hid the wonderful secrets that drove him wild. "Just for me."

He slid off her slacks then his own jeans, her eyes wide in watching him, hungry then devouring him. He pulled a condom from his jeans and she sat up and held out her hand. "That's just for me."

His insides clenched at the suggestion, and his arousal hardened to the extent he had to pull in deep breaths to keep himself in control. "I don't know if I can stand your hands on me that way."

She ran her forefinger up his midsection, over his pecs and neck, stopping at his lips. She kissed him with a lot of tongue then grinned. "Let's find out."

"Vixen."

"I'll give it my best shot." Then she tugged him down and straddled his middle, her hot wet sex across his bare thighs. The thought of her open, ready, and wanting him fogging his brain. She tore open the package, his heart rate jumping into overdrive. As she slowly rolled the condom over his dick he pulled in a breath between clenched teeth. "You're killing me, babe."

She stopped and kissed the tip of his erection, the warmth of her lips and tongue penetrating clear through the latex. "You can't do that," he hissed, her mouth taking him a bit more. His control deteriorating to the breaking point as she completed covering him, her mouth following. His blood roared, it was all he could hear. His chest tightened like constricting bands of steel. He framed her face between his palms and brought her head up. "Too much, babe."

"But I want to and I'm on top." She gave a wicked smile. "I think I like being on top a lot. I could get used to this."

In desperation, he captured her shoulders and rolled them over. "Not fair," she protested with a sassy pout, her hair streaming out behind her, her lips full and smiling up at him in the changing light.

"I'll make it up to you, I promise." He kissed her, sucking her tongue deep into his mouth, her hands on his face now, making him feel like a king. Then she pulled him down, all of him, his body covering hers. He planted more kisses down the middle of her naked torso. His hands massaged her firm breasts while wedging himself between her legs, the nest of hair rubbing against his chest an added bonus. He put a soft kiss on the inside of her right thigh and her breath caught.

"What are you doing?"

"Picking up where I left off."

"Enough. I want you in me."

"Hold that thought, but right now it's definitely not enough. I'm enjoying myself, I'm enjoying you." He knew he had to hear that catch in her voice again. He wanted to please her more than anything, make her believe she was sexy and lovely. He licked the inside of her left thigh then kissed the wet spot, her legs trembling. Then he kissed higher and heard that sweet catch, making his erection harder, throbbing this time with anticipation.

"You are an incredible lover."

He pushed her legs apart, wide. "And you're a delicious partner."

"This is a little embarrassing."

"Sweetheart, this is heaven." Then his tongue found her clit and her gasp of pure pleasure made him happier than he thought possible.

"Handsome!" she whispered, her voice ragged. "What are you . . . I can't . . . Oh, dear Lord!"

He suckled the sweet spot, her little cries filling the room. "Just let it happen, sweetheart. Let go, thrill me." His tongue took her again and again, then plunged deep into her damp heat. Her moans raw and real, her body quivering then convulsing in orgasm as his tongue pleased her one more time.

"Handsome," she whimpered. He laid back over her, taking her mouth in a deep satisfying slow kiss. "What you do to me . . . How can you do it over and over again?" She kissed the tip of his chin. "Each time is better. I don't know how it can be, but it is."

"I love making you happy." He'd take this memory of making love to LuLu with him, cherishing their time together by the fire, no problems no entanglements, pure pleasure.

"But you . . . what about you? I want you inside of me, I want you to do me."

His dick pulsed hard and painful against her mound, her legs circling him now, her sex exposed and waiting for him. Her eyes danced with the fire. "Take me. Make love to me. Hard."

He arched his brow in question.

"I want to feel you entering me like . . . like a man who knows what he wants."

"I know, believe me on this."

"But I want to be a woman, all woman just for you. I want to be ravaged by someone who means it and wants this as much as I do. I want the soldier. Is that bad?"

Oh shit! His vision blurred, the suggestion nearly sending him over the edge for the millionth time tonight. That he hadn't lost it already amazed the hell out of him. He swallowed, his mouth too dry to speak as his blood pounded and then he kissed her hard as he entered her in one driving force, careful not to hurt her but giving her all of himself without holding back or stopping or pausing to let her catch her breath. She gasped once then twice as he filled her completely, her sex pressed to his tight and searing and soaked.

"Again," she whimpered, her breaths ragged now, eyes dilated, her legs in an unyielding embrace. "Do it again . . . harder," her whimpers more intense, her head dipping back, hair streaming down, shining like a million strands of brown silk.

Gritting his teeth he withdrew, her eyes liquid as she watched him, her face pink with desperate desire for him. The pressure surrounding his arousal as he moved in her a mixture of torture and bliss; her passion more intense then anything he'd ever experienced before. Her legs held firm as he plunged into her again, her hips lifting in perfect unison to his demanding thrust, his insides erupting into a blinding orgasm. He drove into her one more time, making her his, claiming her body as his own, knowing he'd never forget this moment or LuLu or their lovemaking.

His body stayed molded to hers as his orgasm

subsided, his body spent. He hated that the moment was over. Too powerful, too fast. "Did I hurt you? God, I hope not, but I think I'm ruined for life. Probably broke something important. Damn. Last orgasm I'll ever have." He gazed at her. "And I got to tell you it was worth it."

"If it's any consolation, you've ruined me for anyone else."

"There can't be anyone else," he blurted, but he meant it with his whole being even though it couldn't be true. "But," he forced himself to say, "I know that can't be. How can sex suddenly be so complicated when the whole point of this was that it wouldn't be complicated at all?"

He rested his head beside her, her legs still enfolding him, their bodies united. "I hate this," he whispered in her ear. "I hate loving you, as if you're the only woman on earth, then leaving you and not knowing if I'll ever see you again. Guess that's where the complication part's coming from. I think we slid beyond the just sex part."

"But we can't." She exhaled in resignation that sounded more rehearsed than heartfelt. He slid himself from her needing to break the intimate connection so he could think. He sat up to look at her, the firelight on her breasts and torso primal, the way men have been looking at women, desiring them since they lived in caves. He disposed of the condom in a napkin and dropped it in a trash can by the serving cart. Then he held her close because he needed to have her near one more time.

Maybe the realistic approach would work. "We have to think of this as a great time, a good memory, something we can both move on from and—"

"I don't believe that door slammed shut and

locked us in," came Isabella's voice thundering down the hall. "I'm freezing, I need to sit by a fire and get warm. Why couldn't you pop out a window to inside the house so we didn't have to traipse through the snow outside to get here? My feet are wet, everything's wet. Where is everyone?"

"Sleeping until you wake them up with your infernal blabbering, and I couldn't break out a window to inside the house because the windows are for the outside. Gripe, gripe, gripe that's all you've done since we got locked in the garden room. Get over it."

"And all you've done is be bossy and opinionated and a darn nuisance."

Sebastian's gaze locked with LuLu's. "Oh, damn, operation matchmaker is a bust. They're battling worse than ever."

"And they're headed our way."

A twinge of panic sliced through LuLu as Handsome grabbed his jeans and shirt and shoes. She snatched her slacks and blouse, and they rolled together under the table seconds before Terrance and Isabella stormed into the room. The tablecloth reaching to the floor offered a perfect hiding place, but Handsome's body pressed to her front and the gyrations to get here made her want him again. What! How could that happen so fast?

She needed a distraction to get her mind off Handsome and his nakedness and her nakedness. It would have to be one heck of a diversion. Something like jumping up right now and admitting they were parallel parking by the fire. That would grab some serious attention, kill any sex drive in a flash and as an added bonus it would end the fearsome foursome trying to get them together because they'd obviously already been there and done that.

Too much drama. Instead, she peeked under the cloth at two pair of shoes by the fire and a pink lacy bra on the red carpet . . . her pink lacy bra. Okay, now that was a distraction and a half and from the expression on Handsome's face he thought so, too.

Isabella said, "Did you get us locked in there on purpose? You know, you could just say you're sorry and that you are wrong about Bevvy and Sebastian."

Terrance groused, "I sure as hell didn't do anything to get us trapped in that dang room tonight and I'm not wrong, you are."

"So it's back to Sebastian and Bevvy again, is that it?"

"You started it again."

"Nothing's changed. We have different ideas and different tastes."

Handsome sneaked his hand out, trapped the bra between his thumb and forefinger and eased it under the table as Isabella said something about that taste extending to Terrance's beef burgundy because it needed more burgundy, and his reply of Isabella not knowing a good burgundy if she tripped over it in broad daylight.

Handsome rolled his eyes, LuLu smothered a giggle and then he kissed her, making her oblivious to anything but him and them together. His arousal pulsed against the inside of her thigh and her legs parted. He slid into her again, hard and ready, her body welcoming him and she was instantly overcome by another orgasm. How? Why? Oh my God!

She couldn't get enough of him! No thoughts about him leaving or her being pregnant or them being caught in the act diminishing that craving one bit. See, that's because it was sex, she reassured herself, her heart still slamming her ribs. Nothing but sex could consume her this way. She'd miss it when Handsome left but she'd move on, you could do that with sex because it was replaceable, right?

"I think they've gone," he whispered in her ear.

Gone? They? She did a mental head shake to get her brain on what was going on. Isabella and Terrance . . . she remembered now. LuLu listened, trying to get beyond the gentle sound of Handsome's breaths in her ear and the feel of a man's weight, *this* man's weight, on her.

The fire spit and hissed, but she heard nothing else so she lifted the cloth and peeked out again. Handsome rolled off and peeked, too. He gave her a thumbs-up. They shrugged into their clothes, did one last peek then crawled out.

"I wonder how Cordell and Rebecca are getting along because the other dynamic duo is behaving worse than before." She finger combed her hair so it didn't look too much like, *I've been screwing by the fire.*

"Maybe we should just give up on getting any of them together." Handsome tucked in his shirt.

"Except we're the ones who messed up the budding relationships to the point where they don't have a chance now. I feel terrible that our problems have become theirs. So, we need to fix things or burn in relationship hell when we croak. Not a pretty thought."

Cordell and Rebecca rounded the corner, Cordell saying, "You don't understand what being a soldier is all about. It's dangerous out there."

"And you underestimate women. That weaker sex idea bit the dust a long time ago, Cordell." Rebecca parked her hands on her hips. "Who thought of taking out the pins in the hinges tonight so we could get the door off of that wine cellar and get out of there?"

"And who gave you their coat so you wouldn't get a chill, tell me that. The reason chivalry is dead is because you women killed it deader than Lincoln with all your feminism talk."

His gaze turned to Handsome. "Don't you agree, boy? Of course you do, you went and left Bevvy, didn't you, and you have no intention of pairing up with anyone right now. Women don't understand it at all. It's a man thing."

Rebecca's eyes thinned to slits and she drew up beside LuLu. "The way these men talk you'd think we have no backbone and are just good for being barefoot and pregnant and making dinner."

LuLu looked down at her bare feet and realized Handsome was, too.

She gulped and he grinned. He said, "I like that particular idea a lot, least the first part. I can make my own dinner." He rocked back on his heels, eyeing her as if he could eat her in one bite.

Lulu said, "That is such a chauvinist crack. And isn't it a little clichéd?"

"Yeah, and it suits some people very well." He winked and she ground her teeth. Why didn't he just hang a sign around her neck with *knocked up* on it.

Isabella and Terrance came back into the room

and the four of them made eye contact. Isabella said, "Uh . . . we women want an apology from you men for . . . for talking down to us, that's it."

"No one's talking down to anyone," Terrance said with an added eye roll as if he couldn't believe what he was hearing. "We want to protect what's ours and that means you. Argue, argue, argue that's all we do."

Rebecca looked confused. "This evening is over, we've had enough of you men and your medieval ideas and we're all going to bed now . . . alone, very much alone and we hope you enjoy your solitude."

"And I'll be going home, too," LuLu said.

Rebecca snatched her hand. "Not a good idea. You should spend the night here with us."

Isabella nodded in agreement, "Keeps you right here for . . . for getting things organized in the morning for the wedding. A very busy time with lots to do and you certainly don't want to be late, it wouldn't do for you to be late or delayed."

"Nonwedding," Handsome corrected.

"But I don't live here and I have the morning shift at Slim's, and I've got to find someone to cover for Joseph at the manger and the goat needs milking."

Rebecca pulled her toward the main stairs. "No morning shift. It's Christmas Eve, they don't need you and they already have another Joseph so you're covered there. I did that because I knew I'd be needing you all to myself. You're terrific at organizing."

"None of my things are here. I need my jammies, my toothbrush, this is not a good idea."

"Trust me," Isabella said in a low voice. "It's a

darn terrific idea. The snow's too deep for you to be making your way home now and maybe you won't make it back tomorrow and that really would ruin everything. You can share my room, I have extra stuff you can use. Then tomorrow we'll finally get this wedding over with and everyone can be on their merry way by afternoon and all will be right with the world . . . finally!"

Four

LuLu straightened her day-old clothes then folded the last napkin and set it on the tray. She said to Rebecca, "I'll take these into the drawing room for the continental breakfast. The rest of the family should be coming down any minute now."

Rebecca arranged the croissants. "We'll have a light breakfast, the ceremony, then a full brunch. Sounds perfect, I hope it works that way, too. This is so stressful."

"But you've done hundreds of weddings."

"Some are a lot more stressful than others." She frowned at Cordell across the room as he set the fire. "You're not putting enough wood on, it's going to be a right puny fire in that hearth."

He groused, "Bossy woman." But it didn't sound all that sincere. Hmmm, maybe he was softening. There was still hope in getting them together.

Isabella came into the room. "Look at these Danish pastries. Terrance needs to do better than that. I'll give him a piece of my mind." She scurried off toward the kitchen. Guess not everyone was softening.

LuLu took the napkin tray nearly colliding with Handsome as she turned . . . and he was handsome in jeans and a black sweater. "No dress uniform for your nonwedding?" She shook her head. "Forget I said anything. I'm not talking to you."

"The barefoot and pregnant crack last night? It's only natural for a man to want to care for a woman in that condition and like I said, I like you just the way you are now."

"See, see. That's why we can only do the sex thing," she whispered. "It's the only common ground we have, everything else we argue over."

"You don't like being pregnant?"

"I'm okay with it now." She did a slow smile. "Yeah, I think it's going to be fine. Maybe more than fine."

She swept past him to the tables and Cordell threw another log on the fire. Terrance set out covered silver dishes of quiche and fruit. Rebecca frowned at the tables and tapped her foot. "Where are the flower centerpieces? Aren't they delivered yet? This is an outrage." She turned to Cordell. "Did you hide my flowers just to tick me off?"

"Oh, for heaven's sake, woman," Cordell huffed. "This whole plan of yours is getting out of hand. I can't imagine how it will ever work out."

"What whole plan?" Handsome asked as Isabella came in and announced, "I have good news, everyone."

"We can all go home," Cordell groused.

Isabella made a face and rushed on with, "Bevvy called and she's going to swing by here after the nonwedding and take Rebecca and me into Memphis in the Hummer. Blue Sticky Notes has a gig and—this is the fantastic part—the Four Arachnids are opening for them. What a terrific Christmas Eve!"

"The Arachnids!" Rebecca gasped and her eyes lit. "Oh, my stars, I remember them from my college days. And they're still around! Like the Eagles. They just keep going on and on. What hunks."

"They're old," Cordell said, while Isabella giggled like a school girl then added, "I think we should be groupies for them. Sure get more action than we are around here." She looked from Cordell to Terrance.

"Like hell," bellowed Terrance. "I have plenty of action in me."

Isabella put her hands to her chest in swoon mode. "I wonder if the Four Arachnids have T-shirts? I always wanted one but my mother had a conniption at the thought. Girls didn't wear T-shirts like that back in the day."

Terrance folded his arms and glared at Isabella. "You are not going anywhere near a rock band. You're fifty, for crying out loud. Act it."

Isabella fluffed her hair. "Fifty-six to be exact and it's about time I do what I want, and if that's being a roadie then that's what I'll do."

"Roadie!" Cordell turned red as the Christmas napkins on the table.

"I still have my first miniskirt," Isabella beamed. "Sure wish I had it with me."

"I remember when I burned my bra," Rebecca said. "Now those were the good old days."

Terrance threw his hands in the air and left the room, and Cordell boomed, "You both have gone completely nuts."

"Well that's just the opinion of an old fogie," Rebecca said, then exited with Isabella in tow.

LuLu stared at the commotion. "What's going on? Full moon?"

Handsome blinked a few times. "I think they're on something. I've never seen my mother like . . . this."

"Sign here," Terrance said as he rushed back from the kitchen. Yanking the tray from LuLu's hands, he shoved a clipboard mostly covered with a bouquet of flowers at her. "The florist delivery finally came and I am not signing for something that's part of Rebecca's setup, and right now I'm not talking to either of those two loopy women."

LuLu said to Handsome, "You didn't cancel the flower order?"

"Too late."

"Good grief. This has got to be costing the earth," LuLu scribbled as the rest of Handsome's family wandered in for breakfast. "Hope they enjoy themselves."

"Hope they aren't taking whatever Mother and Rebecca are taking."

Terrance shoved the board at Handsome. "I should have you sign for the flowers too since you paid for them."

Handsome shook his head. "It's flowers, I don't care if they come or not."

Terrance nodded toward the front door. "Man's waiting, boy. He needs your signature. Give him a good tip, too. It is Christmas Eve after all."

Isabella stuck her head around the corner, her hair pulled back in a ponytail, blue eye shadow to her brows. She gave a toothy grin. "Yoo-hoo, everyone. What do you all think of my sixties look?"

Handsome stared dumbfounded, Terrance nudged the board. Handsome wrote his name, added money, and Terrance shoved the flowers at LuLu. "Enjoy."

Isabella pranced into the room. "Rebecca is tying two napkins together to make a miniskirt for our concert outing. Isn't that fun!"

She rolled her own skirt up at the waist till the hemline was inches above her knees. "What do you think?" She did a twirl. "It's 'Flashdance' all over again."

"Next time . . ." Handsome stared wide-eyed. "If there ever is a next time, which I'm doubting more and more every minute, I'm eloping to Vegas. This is a bigger sideshow than that place could ever be."

LuLu inhaled the scent of star daylilies, baby's breath, a scattering of daisies and white roses. "Bevvy has good taste in flowers. You know"—she took another sniff—"maybe we can get one of our project couples to get married today. Wouldn't that be great?"

"Uh, have you been listening to all this? They can't even exchange a civil sentence."

"But it's such a waste of really great flowers."

"I tried half the night to talk some sense into Uncle Cordell and almost had him ready to apologize till Terrance came in the room with a bottle of hundred-year-old Scotch. Said he sure as hell hoped this worked, caught sight of me then spent the next three hours talking about how women made no sense and right now I believe him."

"Hey, I resent that. Your mom and Rebecca just want to have fun. The wedding's a bust so they're improvising. Women wanting to cut loose a little, can't blame them for that."

The doorbell rang and a minute later a strange man in a black suit swaggered into the room or maybe it was more of a stumble and announced, "Judge Jude here." He gave a lopsided grin. "Isn't that a great name?" He hiccupped. "I love my name. I'm here to . . ." He fished inside his coat pocket and pulled out a little black book. "To say a few appropriate words about the deceased. Marla Henderson was a wonderful woman."

He hiccupped, took another sip from the flask he kept in his breast pocket then shook his head. "Nope, wrong day." He flipped some pages. "Ah, yes, here we are. I'm doing a marriage." He grinned at everyone, his eyes not focusing. "Much better to do a marriage on Christmas Eve than a funeral. You all look so nice today. Wonderful day for a wedding. Is there any Scotch handy? I could use a little Christmas cheer for the road and since I have a driver it's all legal-like."

Handsome said, "I'm sorry, but there is no wedding, it's been called off. I apologize that no one contacted you and saved you a trip out here."

"Nonsense," said the judge. He stepped close to Handsome and LuLu. "Says in my book I'm doing a wedding so that's it. Let's get on with it. It's a busy day, lots to do." He cleared his throat, smoothed his hair over his balding spot in the middle and stood tall next to LuLu. "Dearly beloved, we are gathered here to . . ."

LuLu hid her face and Handsome's behind the bouquet. "The man's totally sloshed and not listening to a thing you say. How do we get rid of this guy?"

The judge droned on with the usual marriage ritual stuff and Isabella yanked down the flowers.

LuLu asked, "You sure you don't want to marry Terrance? Everything's in place, I even have the flowers." She shook the bouquet. "And Terrance is a really great guy, wonderful cook. You could have great eats all your life."

"I made peace-sign necklaces for me and Rebecca out of straws I found in the kitchen." She held up the multicolored art work. "What do you think? Very trendy. Do you like them or do you not, Sebastian? Hmmm?"

His eyes crossed. "Uh . . ."

She shoved them in his face and growled, "Well? Do you or don't you? Say it."

"I do, I do. Holy cow, they're fine, perfect for the . . . occasion. But what should we do about this preacher being here?"

"Judge, dear, he's a judge and he's nearly finished and all will be well so don't worry your pretty little head about a thing." Isabella faced LuLu and put the peace sign an inch from her nose. "Okay, so what about you. Do you like them or do you not?"

"They're great."

Her eyes got beady and her bottom lip did a threatening curl. "No, you don't understand. Do you or do you not! Tell me right this minute." She nearly stepped on LuLu's toes she was so close.

"I do, I do I really do for heaven's sake. It's a peace sign, remember. Peace! I think you need a nap."

"Wonderful. We did it," beamed Isabella as Judge Jude said, "I now pronounce you husband and wife!"

He suddenly didn't look so inebriated and Rebecca, Isabella, Terrance, and Cordell broke into huge smiles and everyone in the room clapped and cheered. Cordell said to Handsome, "Well done. Congratulations, boy." He kissed LuLu on the cheek. "Welcome to the family, dear."

Eyes huge, Handsome cut his gaze from one to the other. "What the hell's going on now?"

Judge Jude said, "You may now kiss your bride and I suggest you do it. A lot of people did a lot of planning to get you two married."

LuLu stared at Handsome. "Huh?"

Handsome opened his mouth but nothing came out. Uncle Cordell came over and slapped him on the back. "You're now a married man."

"I don't get it," Handsome stammered.

"Course you do," Isabella chimed in. "You and LuLu are married just the way you should be but were too stubborn to get on with it so we helped. That's all there is to it. We set you up."

She put her arm around Terrance and he draped his arm around her shoulders in a very friendly way that belied all the bickering before. "We decided to get you two together just like you tried to get us together, except we were already together all along and thought we'd return the favor. Does that make any sense?"

Handsome said, "But you've been fighting and carrying on like lunatics."

"For distraction, all for distraction to keep your mind off what was really going on," Cordell laughed. "And it worked. Neither of you knew what hit you."

Everyone clapped again and Handsome said, "But we didn't sign anything except . . ." His gaze fused with Terrance. "Oh, damn, the flowers."

Terrance grinned and Handsome's mother added, "And you did say the obligatory 'I do' for my completely hideous peace signs. I didn't rightly know how I was going to pull that one off, but I did!"

Rebecca kissed Handsome on the cheek then LuLu. "We got our Christmas Eve wedding after all, and it is truly wonderful like I planned, just a different bride is all."

LuLu shook her head to try and clear her thoughts. "I don't believe I really got married in black slacks held together by a safety pin and a wrinkled blouse that I wore yesterday? That is so not wonderful."

"But you have to admit you had really great flowers," Rebecca said.

Handsome said, "But what if we don't want to be married? Ever think of that?"

"Of course you do," Isabella chimed in. "The two of you have been together at every turn and with only knowing each other for such a short time that counts a lot. You two were meant to be."

LuLu said, "Except there's a little glitch. I don't want someone in my life's who's leaving . . . again. I have bad man-leaving karma and that's a big part of who Hand . . . I mean Sebastian is."

Handsome said, "And I broke up with Bevvy because I don't want to have someone here worrying about me. Remember that little scene at Slim's where you all nearly took my head off and it started everyone arguing? Well, it's the truth, I didn't make it up on the spot. I've thought about all of this a lot."

Rebecca took Handsome's hand. "Honey, the real reason you broke up with Bevvy is that you don't love her. You do love LuLu, we can all see that, and Bevvy is wacko over Bruno. I've seen a lot of couples and you and LuLu are made to go the distance."

Judge Jude said, "And that's exactly how she convinced me to do this wedding. Said there was a soldier getting ready to ship out and needed a boost in the right direction to marry the woman of his dreams. Give him someone to come home to." He winked at LuLu. "That would be you."

LuLu said, "But we don't think we need a boost. We don't want to be together."

Isabella pursed her lips and winked. "You two weren't playing tiddledywinks under that table in the dining room last night, I'll bet my miniskirt on that. Today is Christmas Eve and tomorrow Christmas and it'll take a lawyer to undo this marriage. So that gives you two a day and a half to realize you're meant to be."

LuLu growled and sliced her hand through the air to get everyone's attention, "Listen. To. Me. We, as in Sebastian and I, are not meant to be together in spite of what you all think and all your elaborate plans. I'm sorry, but that's the way it is."

"But you were trying to get *us* hooked up as they say," Isabella grinned, taking Terrance's hand.

"That was to get you all from throwing me and Sebastian together. Give you all something to focus on besides us. Then it changed to just getting you together for your own sakes." She rolled her eyes to the top of her head to see if her hair was as fried as it felt. "This has turned into matchmaking hell."

Handsome added, "Look, we know what we're doing."

Cordell said, "Ten years from now you'll be thanking us at your anniversary party."

LuLu faced Handsome. "Talk to them and then think of someway to get us out of this mess."

Isabella huffed, "You think marrying my Sebastian is a mess?"

"Okay, call it borderline insanity."

"Well, I never."

"And I so wish you meant that. I don't want to be married to anyone and I'm sorry I ruined your Christmas Eve plans but this isn't going to work."

LuLu snagged her Joseph's coat from the hall clothes tree, yanked on her boots and was out the door. She stopped on the front porch, the clear blue sky and bright sun refreshing compared to the pandemonium inside. "Holy crap! What have I done?"

"What have *we* done," Handsome said pulling up beside her. "Just so you know, I had nothing to do with this. I don't want to be married."

"I want it less than you do."

"I doubt that."

She gave him an evil look. "Let's not make this personal, okay."

Handsome held up his hands in surrender. "If you were Gwyneth Paltrow I wouldn't want to marry you."

"But you'd consider being married to me if I was Gwyneth Paltrow?"

Handsome shook his head. "One more time . . . No Gwyneth, no you, no anyone. I really meant it when I said I didn't want to leave a wife, and you would be a wife with a kid and that makes it double tough. Way too much to be concerned about for both of us. Now let's go tell your sister before the early edition of the O'Fallon's Landing gossip gazette spills the beans to her before we do. It's not the way you want a family member to find out you're hitched."

"It's noonish on Christmas Eve so I'm guessing Callie's at Slim's doing a little Christmas celebrating with her family, her new other family." She felt a little twinge. For so many years it was her and Callie, but now she has her own life and that is a good thing but . . .

"New? Other?" They started to walk.

"She was just married and her husband has two brothers and a baby sister."

Handsome raised his brows. "They have a baby sister as in . . . baby?"

"A long story about a kidnapping and missing disk and some bad guys and people falling in love. I'll tell you sometime." Because telling him about it now made her feel alone and she didn't want a pity party.

A sprinkle of snow drifted down adding to what was already on the ground. "The Mississippi looks really cold and forbidding from here, and I can relate to the forbidding part. I'm not exactly the little sister Callie hoped I'd be. I think she was hoping for Little-Miss-Perfect; she wanted me to be a lawyer like our dad." LuLu put her hand over her stomach. "I am so far from perfect it's scary. And now I'm not perfect, I'm married, and I'm pregnant by a guy who's a jerk. Some Christmas present for Callie."

They stood in front of Slim's. "I'll go in with you to tell your sister. I can be great moral support. I should come."

"You're all handsome and honorable and patriotic and there's not a darn thing wrong with you. In fact, you're the one who's perfect. Compared to

Jerome, you rate a twelve on the one-to-ten scale. Heck, next to me you rate a twelve on the one-to-ten scale. So here's the thing, Callie will look at you and you'll say something charming and smile and she'll never get why I don't want to be married to you. She raised me after our parents died so she's more mother than sister, especially at this kind of thing. You know, the white picket fence routine, dog in the backyard, minivan in the drive, husband on the arm."

"Meaning she'll want us married."

"Bingo."

"Even if I tell her I don't want to be married, either?"

"She won't hear that because she'll still be charmed by your smile."

"Are you charmed?"

"Of course. I'm pregnant not dead."

His gaze met hers through the flakes of Christmas Eve snow and her heart jumped. She'd always feel that way when she looked at Handsome and it wasn't just because he was handsome. It was because he was all those things her sister would admire about him. "So here's the deal. I'm going to tell Callie all by myself and you go find us an attorney. That way we can get this over with and move on with our lives and get everything back the way it was before we signed for those darn flowers."

Five

LuLu pushed open the door to Slim's and some I've-lost-my-baby-at-Christmas tune whining from the juke box. Callie and Keefe, her new husband, sat at a round paint-chipped table with Ryan, his brother, and new wife Effie, and third brother Quaid and his wife Cynthia. The triple wedding that married all three couples was the best event LuLu had ever been to and that included the Garth Brooks concert she saw on her eighteenth birthday.

"Hey, little sister," Callie said and waved her over. "You missed your morning shift, and should I ask why you didn't come home last night?"

She studied the six pair of eyes focused on her. What the heck. In less than five minutes they'd all hear about it from someone else in town anyway. "Okay, the long version is I wasn't here because I had to set things up over at Hastings House for the wedding—"

"Nonwedding," Callie corrected. "Least that's what I hear."

"Well, that brings us to the short version of this story. There was a wedding after all . . . mine."

Callie stopped her eggnog halfway to her lips and stared at LuLu. "Huh?" Typical family reaction.

"It wasn't my idea or even done with my consent."

"You were drugged into getting married?"

"Tricked and so was the groom and now we're trying to get out of it, and I didn't even have a great dress but I did have incredible flowers, I'll have to show you."

"You didn't ask me, your own sister?"

"I didn't know I was married till the judge said you may kiss the bride. Gave new meaning to the term quickie wedding. And there's more."

Callie whimpered and Keefe splashed her nog with whiskey from the bottle on the table. She gulped. "Okay, I'm ready, give it to me."

"I'm pregnant."

Callie took the bottle and swigged straight from it, her eyes watering as she choked. "If you're having his baby maybe you should stay married. Least give it a chance."

"Except . . ." oh, boy, "it isn't his baby. I know, I'm a slut, least I sound like one but I'm really not, just bad-man karma."

"I had that once," Cynthia chimed in. "Till I met Quaid." She kissed him on the cheek making him blush. "You just have to find your Quaid and all will be well."

Callie closed her eyes and banged her head on the table. "Kids."

"I hate dumping all this on you but I've got it covered."

"Honey, being Joseph at the manger is not a full-time career move with a baby on the way."

"Granted, I'm not too good in the men department. Actually, I suck. But I am good at directing. Rebecca-the-wedding-planner is up to her armpits in weddings and I can get a job with her. That will keep me nearby and I can do a lot of the job with a baby in tow and get a sitter when I need one."

"It won't be that easy, I can promise you that."

Keefe nodded at his brothers. "Wait a minute. It doesn't have to be all that hard either. Hell, we can all sit the babe. God knows we've had practice enough with Bonnie. They can grow up together."

LuLu blinked a few times. "I'm stunned that you would even offer."

Quaid laughed. "Get used to it. They adopted me and now they're adopting you and your baby. It's what the O'Fallons do and they do it really well."

"But I can handle this."

"With help." Ryan grinned. "Everyone needs help once in awhile."

"I . . . he . . . you all blow me away." LuLu felt a lump the size of Tennesee lodge in her throat. Now these were great guys like Handsome. Except there was no place for Handsome in her life.

Quaid chuckled. "Just don't blow too far."

LuLu said to Callie, "You raised me and had a career and I can do the same thing. I'm not taking on any more than you did, I'm just coming at it from a different angle."

LuLu put her arms around Callie and hugged her tight. "Be happy, I am. I wasn't at first but like our mother said, it's always better to be bringing another chair to the family table than taking one away."

"Amen," Keefe said. He stood looking a little less friendly. "Now I want to meet this guy you married. We all do. What kind of man would let you come in here and face this all alone."

"I didn't," came Handsome's voice from behind her. She spun around as he strolled over. "I'm Sebastian Moore." He shook everyone's hands. "My family is responsible for this wedding, not that I don't care for LuLu but I'm shipping overseas in a few days and we agree that marriage is not what we want. My family thought otherwise."

Keefe held up a longneck in salute. "And I thought our dad was interfering. We've met his match. So, you don't love LuLu and she doesn't love you, is that it?"

LuLu swallowed. "Well, that's not the issue. It's more to do with Handsome going and—"

"Handsome?" Ryan grinned. "Interesting name."

LuLu felt herself redden. "I mean Sebastian. The other is sort of a nickname and you all know that love isn't everything. There are other issues you have to consider when getting married and those other issues don't work for us."

The three couples exchanged looks then broke into laughter that really seemed to go on for a while. Ryan finally managed, "Oh boy, am I glad I'm beyond that. I moved back to San Diego and took a new fancy job before I realized all that mattered was loving Effie." He kissed her on the head and then nuzzled her ear before Quaid said, "Hey, not in front of the kids."

Keefe said, "I was so in love with Callie and so confused over what the heck I was doing that I let some thugs steal my baby sister right out of our house. Not the highlight of my life."

Callie said, "Love *is* all that matters." She smiled at Handsome and LuLu. "Trust your big sister on this one."

LuLu shook her head. "Maybe that works for you all, but this is different."

Effie took Ryan's hand. "That's what everyone of us has said and then we've come to our senses. With luck, you will, too."

LuLu wasn't in the mood to argue with people who were obviously so lovesick they didn't have an ounce of reality left in them anywhere. "I'm going to the house and change."

Sebastian said, "Nice meeting you all and I appreciate you helping LuLu out. She's a great gal."

The men all stood and shook Sebastian's hand looking serious again. Ryan said, "We'll take care of things here, you just take care of yourself."

Quaid nodded. "Remember to keep your ass down and your rifle up."

Keefe added, "Keep in touch when you can." He grinned. "We'll send cookies."

Sebastian gave an almost indiscernible nod and LuLu felt her stomach sink to her toes. Handsome wasn't going off to Germany or Italy or some other nice safe army base and they all knew it. He didn't look worried but worry sat in her stomach like the flu.

She felt his hand at her back as she turned for the door. Outside they stood on the wood porch in front of the window with Budweiser blaring in red and blue neon. They stared into space, neither of them really seeing anything. Handsome said, "Nice people. You're going to be okay with them around. I won't be worrying about you as much now."

"As much? Hold on. It's supposed to be 'at all.'

That was the whole point of us not getting involved. We . . . we walk away, no strings and you do not need to be concerned about me one bit."

He gave her a half smile. "I'll try and remember that."

"No trying, just do it."

"Hey, LuLu," came a familiar voice that made her skin prickle and not in a good way. "I finally found you."

"Jerome?"

"Yeah, girl, it's me." He jumped up on the porch beside her. "I remembered we stopped here on our drive out to California when we first went last year so I thought you might come back here. How's my baby doing?"

She put her hand over her stomach. "Your baby? When I told you I was pregnant you ran out of the apartment so fast you left skid marks and jumped on a plane with . . ."

"Libby."

"Right, Libby. I think that pretty much makes this my baby."

"I knew you'd feel that way, was counting on it, actually. You'll make a great mom. A kid couldn't do better than you."

He glanced at Handsome. "Don't you agree?"

LuLu folded her arms. "You didn't come here to praise my parenting skills. What do you want, Jerome? I'm not going to be hitting you up for child support or any support for that matter so you and Libby can live happily ever after."

"I was thinking more like maybe I'd be a great dad and maybe I'd like to be a part of the baby's life. Do that joint custody thing I hear about. You're not married and I'm not married so neither of us can offer a better home life than the other, least that's what the courts say. I checked. I think we should . . . share the baby."

LuLu let out a sigh. "Sharing like we shared the expenses in L.A. with me picking up the rent, food, car payments, and phone bills and you doing nothing?"

"It worked pretty well."

She reached in her pocket and pulled out the money Rebecca had paid her that morning. "How much will it take for you to think that maybe you don't want joint custody after all?"

He reached for the cash. "That's a good start." In a flash he was pinned up against one of the uprights that supported the porch roof. Sebastian's hand around his neck did the pinning and the ice cold look in Sebastian's eyes dropped the temperature on the porch twenty degrees.

"Or not," squeaked Jerome, eyes bulging, feet six inches off the ground.

"Is there a problem?" came Ryan's voice behind her. She looked back to him and Quaid and Keefe, shoulder to shoulder by Sebastian.

Handsome said, "This sleaze is shaking down LuLu for joint custody of our baby."

The six pair of eyes behind her took on that same look and the temperature dropped another twenty degrees. Did she hear growls?

"No," Jerome whispered through a shrinking trachea. "I reconsider. No custody."

Handsome let go and he collapsed into a heap on the floor, then scrambled off the steps and ran down the street. Ryan said, "Well dang, that was easy. Hoping for a little more action, to tell the truth. Welcome to the family."

As she turned around LuLu realized he'd included Handsome in that greeting as well as her.

The O'Fallons trooped back inside and LuLu forced a grin at Handsome. "Now, go find us a lawyer. See, the baby and I are in good hands."

"Except you aren't in my hands and that's not good. Us being married with extended and supportive family is insurance for you keeping the baby." He gave her a long hard look. "We're staying married, LuLu. I love you."

She slapped the palm of her hand against her forehead. "I knew this was coming the minute you turned Jerome into a wall decoration. You just think you love me because you got this macho protective soldier streak a mile high and just as wide."

"I really do love you."

"Look, I am not marrying someone because I'm pregnant and that is final and if you won't find a lawyer I will, there's got to be someone around here that works on Christmas Eve. I'll meet you at the gazebo at five and I'll have papers. That's where all this started and that's where it's going to end tonight."

Sebastian watched the last of the Christmas Eve carolers stroll from the square, and the twinkling white lights blink off leaving the Landing bathed in moonlight except for the marina on the Mississippi. He paced the gazebo for the millionth time then glanced at the illuminated dial of his watch. Ten o'clock. Where the hell could LuLu be? Footsteps came behind him and he spun around to, "Uncle Cordell?"

"Been looking my eyeballs out for you, boy. Where the dickens have you been?"

"Here for a while, then off looking for my wife who doesn't want to be my wife. Have you seen her by any chance?"

"Not a glimpse." He rested his hand on Sebastian's shoulder. "How are you holding up?"

"What do you mean?"

"Hell, boy. I've known you all your life and know what makes you tick probably better than you know yourself or I never would have gotten involved in that wedding fiasco. You love LuLu and you want to keep it that way."

"There's a wrinkle."

"She's pregnant, I know. But that's not the reason you love her."

"I know that and you know that, but LuLu thinks the reason I want to stay married to her is because I want to make sure she and the baby are safe and taken care of." He banged his forehead against a gazebo column. "Damn, if I had told her I loved her and wanted to marry her before I found out about the baby it would have been so much easier, a hell of a lot more convincing, but now . . . now it's all tied up in that and there's no separating the two."

"Try."

"How?"

"You'll figure out a way. I did."

Sebastian gave a slow grin, glad to have his mind off his own problems for minute. "Care to enlarge on that detail?"

Uncle Cordell returned the grin. "I went and married Rebecca and your mom went and married Terrance. Figured we had the judge and the family all together so why the hell not, we sure aren't getting any younger. And it's Christmas. There's always a bit of magic at Christmas, guessing it was working overtime for us."

"And it's one way to keep the ladies from the Four Arachnid concert." He hugged his uncle. "Congratulations. I know you'll be happy. Rebecca will see to that and she'll keep you on your toes."

"I'd offer to wait around with you but this is up to you and LuLu to straighten out."

He watched Uncle Cordell fade into the swirling snow, the quiet of night settling in around him.

"I thought he'd never leave," came LuLu's voice behind him. "Though the thought of the fearsome foursome married is very cool. We did accomplish something."

"Where have you been? You're five hours late."

"Yeah, I know. And I could tell you that I couldn't find a lawyer but that would be a lie, and if you lie to a soldier ready to get shipped overseas you probably go straight to hell."

"I'm not following."

She pulled in a deep breath and took papers from inside her Joseph's coat. "Divorce papers just waiting for your signature."

She handed him a pen and he shook his head and took a step back. "I'm not signing, LuLu. Forget it. I love you, I really do and it's not because of the baby, I knew I loved you when we made love here and it *was* making love and not just sex. It's never just been sex between us and we both know it, no matter how much we say otherwise. I didn't have the guts to tell you that I love you because I knew it would complicate the hell out of our lives even more. Then Jerome touched your hand and I wanted to break every bone in his body for that and threatening you. That's when I knew I couldn't leave without making you mine, and if you signed those papers they're only getting the one signature."

"I did sign them."

"Too bad."

"I signed Mickey Mouse."

He paused then laughed.

"Hey, that's all my fingers would do because I love you, too."

His heart slammed against his chest. "But it took you so long to get here."

"Yeah, that's the other thing, the big thing." She pulled in another deep breath. "How am I going to live without you for a year?" She took his hand and hers was shaking. "How am I going to live with the possibility that you may not ever come ba—"

He put his fingers to her lips then kissed her softly. "We're not going there. We're going here." He swept her into his arms and this time kissed her like a husband kisses his new wife. "God, I love you and you love me and that's what we're going to focus on for the next twelve months."

He kissed her again. "In one year I'll meet you right back here in this very place with our new baby in your arms." He looked deep into her eyes. "I'll be home for Christmas, LuLu. I promise with all my heart."

Epilogue

LuLu held baby Sebastian close as she peered through the swirling snow. Cedar and holly garland decorated the dark gazebo lit only in moonlight. The square was quiet and lonely. "Okay, Handsome," she said into the darkness. "Where the heck are you because I know you're here." *You've got to be here*, she added to herself.

Nothing except the little coos from inside a swaddle of blue blankets, and then a warm breath on the back of her neck melting the fear she's lived with for a year. She grinned into the darkness then turned. "Welcome home, Handsome."

Also available from Brava this month,
HOT NIGHT by Shannon McKenna. . . .

THE PREDATOR

Gold. The most precious of metals. And someone
would kill to get at the dazzling exhibit of priceless
Spanish treasure Abby Maitland just landed for
the museum. Too bad Zan Duncan had to show up
to protect her, but someone's waiting—and watching. She's in the crosshairs and she doesn't have a
clue.

THE PREY

Abby is mesmerized by Zan's untamed strength
and his very sexual vibe. From the long dark hair,
the thick, hard muscles, and the black leather
jacket right on down to the honed fighting skills
and the tattoos, Zan is everything a bad boy oughta
be . . . and everything Abby has sworn to avoid. Yet
he's a master of subtle seduction, pushing her buttons with tantalizing promises of night after hot
night of secret, endless pleassure. Promises that he
keeps, to the letter . . .

But danger stalks them both, for a lethal game
of deception, greed, and murder is underway—a
game more sinister than Abby and Zan ever imagined. And when no one can be trusted and no place
is safe, passion may be the only thing that can save
them . . .

Abby was floating. The sensual heft of Zan's jacket felt wonderful over her shoulders, even though it hung halfway down to her thighs.

They'd reached the end of the boardwalk, where the lights began to fade. Beyond the boardwalk, the warehouse district began. They'd walked the whole boardwalk, talking and laughing, and at some point, their hands had swung together and sort of just . . . stuck. Warmth seeking warmth. Her hand tingled joyfully in his grip.

The worst had happened. Aside from his sex appeal, she simply liked him. She liked the way he laughed, his turn of phrase, his ironic sense of humor. He was smart, honest, earthy, funny. Maybe, just maybe, she could trust herself this time.

Their strolling slowed to a stop at the end of the boardwalk.

"Should we, ah, walk back to your van?" she ventured.

"This is where I live," he told her.

She looked around. "Here? But this isn't a residential district."

"Not yet," he said. "It will be soon. See that building over there? It used to be a factory of some kind, in the twenties, I think. The top floor, with the big arched windows, that's my place."

There was just enough light to make out the silent question in his eyes. She exhaled slowly. "Are you going to invite me up, or what?"

"You know damn well that you're invited," he said. "More than invited. I'll get down on my knees and beg, if you want me to."

The full moon appeared in a window of scudding clouds, then disappeared again. "It wouldn't be smart," she said. "I don't know you."

"I'll teach you," he offered. "Crash course in Zan Duncan. What do you want to know? Hobbies, pet peeves, favorite leisure activities?"

She would put it to the test of her preliminary checklist, and make her decision based on that. "Don't tell me," she said. "Let me guess. You're a martial arts expert, right?"

"Uh, yeah. Aikido is my favorite discipline. I like kung fu, too."

She nodded, stomach clenching. There it was, the first black mark on the no-nos checklist. Though it was hardly fair to disqualify him for that, since he'd saved her butt with those skills the night before.

So that one didn't count. On to the next no-no. "Do you have a motorcycle?"

He looked puzzled. "Several of them. Why? Want to go for a ride?"

Abby's heart sank. "No. One last question. Do you own guns?"

Zan's face stiffened. "Wait. Are these trick questions?"

"You do, don't you?" she persisted.

"My late father was a cop." His voice had gone hard. "I have his service Beretta. And I have a hunting rifle. Why? Are you going to talk yourself out of being with me because of superficial shit like that?"

Abby's laugh felt brittle. "Superficial. That's Abby Maitland."

"No, it is not," he said. "That's not Abby Maitland at all."

"You don't know the first thing about me, Zan."

"Yes, I do." His dimple quivered. "I know first things, second things, third things. You've got piss-poor taste in boyfriends, to start."

Abby was stung. "Those guys were not my boyfriends! I didn't even know them! I've just had a run of bad luck lately!"

"Your luck is about to change, Abby." His voice was low and velvety. "I know a lot about you. I know how to get into your apartment. How to turn your cat into a noodle. The magnets on your fridge, the view from your window. Your perfume. I could find you blindfolded in a room full of strangers." His fingers penetrated the veil of her hair, his forefinger stroking the back of her neck with controlled gentleness. "And I learn fast. Give me ten minutes, and I'd know lots more."

"Oh," she breathed. His hand slid through her hair, settled on her shoulder. The delicious heat burned her, right through his jacket.

"I know you've got at least two of those expensive dresses that drive guys nuts. And I bet you've got more than two. You've got a whole closet full of hot little outfits like that. Right?" He cupped her jaw, turning her head until she was looking into his fathomless eyes.

Her heart hammered. "I've got a . . . a pretty nice wardrobe, yes."

"I'd like to see them." His voice was sensual. "Someday maybe you can model them all for me. In the privacy of your bedroom."

"Zan—"

"I love it when you say my name," he said. "I love your voice. Your accent. Based on your taste in dresses, I'm willing to bet that you like fancy, expensive lingerie, too. Am I right? Tell me I'm right."

"Time out," she said, breathless. "Let's not go there."

"Oh, but we've already arrived." His breath was warm against her throat. "Locksmiths are detail maniacs. Look at the palm of your hand, for instance. Here, let me see." He lifted her hand into the light from the nearest of the streetlamps. "Behold your destiny."

It was silly and irrational, but it made her self-conscious to have him look at the lines on her hand. As if he actually could look right into her mind. Past, future, fears, mistakes, desires, all laid out for anyone smart and sensitive enough to decode it. "Zan. Give me my hand back."

"Not yet. Oh . . . wow. Check this out," he whispered.

"What?" she demanded.

He shook his head with mock gravity and pressed a kiss to her knuckles. "It's too soon to say what I see. I don't want to scare you off."

"Oh, please," she said unsteadily. "You are so full of it."

"And you're so scared. Why? I'm a righteous dude. Good as gold." He stroked her wrist. "Ever try cracking a safe without drilling it? It's a string of numbers that never ends. Hour after hour, detail after detail. That's concentration." He pressed his lips against her knuckles.

"What does concentration have to do with anything?"

"It has everything to do with everything. That's what I want to do to you, Abby. Concentrate, intensely, minutely. Hour after hour, detail after detail. Until I crack all the codes, find all the keys to all your secret places. Until I'm so deep inside you . . ." his lips kissed their way up her wrist, ". . . that we're a single being."

She leaned against him and let him cradle her in his strong arms. His warm lips coaxed her into opening to the gentle, sensual exploration of his tongue. "Come up with me," he whispered. "Please."

More by Best-selling Author
Fern Michaels